BEFORE THEM W[illegible]
THE GHOSTS O[illegible]

Their transparent fa[illegible]ed weapons. The moonlight shone thorugh them, casting horrible shadows.

"Back up," Halberd whispered to Usuthu.

"Flee from a ghost?" Usuthu answered. "How?"

"Spirits of the dead," Halberd said, "we are sorry to have disturbed you. You are dead and cannot be slain. We wish to live a bit longer."

Though Halberd couldn't understand the speech of the ghosts, his young guide was ready to translate. "You two," said the boy, "are thieves, grave robbers, defilers. You must be slain and taught a lesson in the afterlife."

"Let us try leaving," Usuthu suggested.

Halberd nodded and the three mortals backed up slowly. The horde of ghosts moved with them.

The most venerable of the ghosts barked. "Hold, he says," the boy translated.

"Hold, indeed." Halberd could stand it no longer. "Come and fight!" he called. "Fight me and bring your mortal brothers. I'm sick of hiding. . . ."

THE SERPENT MOUND

LLOYD ST. ALCORN

NAL BOOKS ARE AVAILABLE AT QUANTITY DISCOUNTS WHEN USED TO PROMOTE PRODUCTS OR SERVICES. FOR INFORMATION PLEASE WRITE TO PREMIUM MARKETING DIVISION, NEW AMERICAN LIBRARY, 1633 BROADWAY, NEW YORK, NEW YORK 10019.

SIGNET TRADEMARK REG. U.S. PAT. OFF. AND FOREIGN COUNTRIES
REGISTERED TRADEMARK—MARCA REGISTRADA
HECHO EN CHICAGO, U.S.A.

SIGNET, SIGNET CLASSIC, MENTOR, ONYX, PLUME, MERIDIAN and NAL BOOKS are published by NAL PENGUIN INC., 1633 Broadway, New York, New York 10019

First Printing, January, 1989

1 2 3 4 5 6 7 8 9

PRINTED IN THE UNITED STATES OF AMERICA

To
Merry and Stephen
Who came to Boston to see me
&
who understood when deadline
pressure made me miss the
Main Event

Mälar Feels Pain

The huge arrow rattled off the roof of the cave. The stone arrowhead shattered when it smashed into the rock and the shaft dropped to the muddy cave floor with a thump.

Mälar jerked in surprise. First, because he had been alone with no sound but his own voice for three weeks. Second, because he hadn't thought Usuthu would return so soon. Third, because he was amazed that even the giant Mongol could hit the roof of the cave from so far below, and fourth, because the broken arrow had borne through the damp air a haunch of venison, freshly slaughtered.

Mälar made his painful way to the glistening chunk of deermeat. His food had run out three days ago. He remained unconcerned. A freshet of spring water ran abundantly along the back of the cave and Mälar knew that while food nourishes, water sustains life. Mostly he slept. His left arm still flapped from his shoulder, useless. The gashes in his face and chest were healing, though long scabs ran from his thinning hair down across his forehead to the bridge of his nose.

The huge battle had been three weeks ago. In that time Mälar had not heard from Usuthu, nor had Halberd stirred from the trance sleep that protected him from his near-mortal wound. Tucked against one flinty wall of the vast cave, the Viking shaman still slept, while slowly over his unconscious head the sacred stone knife, Hrungnir, and the Jewel of Kyrwyn-Coyne turned in the air, suspended there by spell and casting their golden protective light over the wounded warrior.

Mälar had not bothered with Halberd; he knew Halberd was safely in the Dream World, far from mortal peril. That Halberd's body seemed to be healing even though Halberd's spirit was not there to occupy it shocked Mälar not at all. Before this journey began he would have claimed to be accustomed to magic. Now Mälar simply felt beyond all surprise.

After Mälar had hurled the last Skræling brave over the ledge of the cave and into the boiling waters far below, after he had dealt with the shock of seeing the image of the foul sorceress Grettir appear floating in the thin air outside the cave, after he had understood the hatred and force of her threat, he had simply slept.

When he awoke it was again daylight. He lay in the thickening pool of Skræling blood in which he had fallen. In the hours or days that he had slept the blood had congealed, gluing him to the rocky floor of the cave. Around him hung the stench of the swelling bodies of the Skræling warriors, the Eerhahkwoi braves who had actually gained the entrance to the cave cut high into the face of the endless cliff. Many Mälar had slain as they climbed the cliff wall. As many he had killed hand to hand at the mouth of the cave. It had been the greatest fight of his long and bloodstained life.

Now, as after all battles, Mälar was faced with the cleanup and, if he was lucky, the preservation of all his limbs and faculties. The former, the old war horse thought, was arduous but manageable, the latter was in doubt.

His left arm, bashed with a stone mallet, hung like a piece of meat. It would not respond, nor could he even feel it. His many slight gashes were swollen and bumpy with new scabs. He could not examine himself too well since he lay flat on his back, stuck to the floor by several inches of rock-hard, coppery-smelling blood.

With a ghastly unsticking accompanied by a bizarre tearing sound, Mälar wrenched his right arm free. The blood peeled from the rocks and clung to his arm like a growth. He could not bring his left arm around to pull the giant clot away from his flesh. He braced with his right hand on the slippery red pond and yanked his legs free, first one and then the other. His right legging held in the solid pool and the deerskin tore before the blood broke, leaving him with one raggedly clad leg. The other came completely free.

Mälar had not moved for some time. He was stiff and starving. It was the work of some minutes to turn over onto his knees. Once there he groped beyond the blood pool with his good hand for a short lance locked in the hand of a dead, green, and bloated Skræling. The corpse would not give up his treasure.

"Will I starve to death next to this rotting bag of flesh?" the old man cried aloud. "Or will I find my strength and stand like a man?"

With this shouted word he forced himself to his feet in a great burst of energy. Once there, his head spun, the world grew dark, and he collapsed again onto the floor of the cave, his head resting on the gas-filled belly of the slain Skræling.

How long he lay after his faint he did not know. It was definitely another day, because the sun was in the morning sky and his beard was thicker.

This time, he vowed, I'll rise with more caution.

He lifted his head gingerly from the swollen belly. The Skræling's face was green and purple, and his limbs several times their normal size. The smell, even for a man covered in the thickened blood of others, was overwhelming. If Mälar had had anything in his stomach, it would have been on the cave floor in short order.

Again he rolled to his knees. Again he braced one hand on the slippery floor. This time he sat back onto his haunches. Even that small movement brought bursts of dark and light into his head and made the unending green wall of the Thundering Falls spin around and around. He lifted his head back against his shoulders, like a wolf howling at the moon. He stared up at the roof of the cave until he felt the world steady beneath him.

Now, he thought. Now, but carefully.

He rose to his feet as slowly as he could, his one good hand stuck straight out at his side, like a rope walker with a balance pole in the Bazaar in the Land of Sand on the Inland Sea. As he stood upright the cave moved once more, but the old salt flexed his knees and waited for the surging floor to quiet down. When it did, he made his uncertain way over the ruins of the log wall Usuthu had built to hold off the Skrælings.

Though sturdy enough, it had proved of little use. Mälar had ended up fighting the entire battle in front of it. He passed the inert, enchanted body of Halberd and the fire pit big enough to cook three oxen. When at last he gained the back wall of the endless cavern, his legs were trembling.

The spring ran fresh and bubbling. He knelt beside it as slowly as he could, his right arm stretched out toward the floor. When his knees touched the rock, he lay down on his side with a sigh of gratitude. The cave receded and the day became black.

Mälar awoke at night. The cave was dark and cold. He was grateful for the impenetrable blackness at the back of the cave. When he first peered into the shallow spring, he did not want to see his reflection. In the aftermath of many battles Mälar had learned the hard way. A badly wounded man should never get a good look at his condition.

The sight of torn flesh, ripped limbs, and shattered bones was always upsetting, but when it was one's own bones, flesh, and limbs, the results could be devastating. Mälar had seen brave men who were not mortally wounded, but merely spectacularly injured, lose faith in their recovery when they got a good look at their wounds in a looking glass or calm reflecting stream.

Mälar needed no such shock. He knew he was hurt. He had no desire to have this knowledge confirmed. In a few days, or perhaps a week or two, he would peer into the stream. Not before.

He reached out into the dark and filled his cupped hand with cool fresh water. The taste of it in his mouth was the sweetest he had ever known.

Mälar knew if he drank too deeply on his empty and shrunken stomach he would be sick. He tried to restrain himself. He drank several slow handfuls before he rolled again up to his knees. Crouching over the stream like an animal, the Viking poured the cool water over his wounded head, over the gashes in his side, over the left shoulder which registered no feeling. His dried blood, and the dried blood of the Skrælings, broke into little brittle bits and littered the cave floor. His right arm Mälar laid into the stream and let the water slowly melt the caking of Skræling blood. His left arm would not reach around to scrub.

Still hunched over the stream, Mälar worked his way out of his tattered linen shirt. It was too filthy to be salvaged. He gently bathed his body and his bloody legs.

When he was at last clean, he felt suddenly revitalized. With this new energy came hunger, sharp and burning.

The rations, he thought without pleasure, lay all the way back across the cave. Perhaps in the morning . . .

When the sun rose again and lit the constant falling wall of the Thundering Falls that flowed in front of, and concealed, the cave entrance, Mälar was utterly content. He sat back against the ruined log wall, eating his fill of dried deer meat, surveying the rotting bodies of men who had tried to kill him.

Was there a finer feeling in any Northman's life? Mälar was alive, almost well, full of food, and there, scattered before him, were men whom he had bravely slain.

Brave men they were, too, he thought, enchanted by the demon witch Grettir or not. But brave though they once might have been, now they were merely meat, rotting meat, and they had to be disposed of. He was full, he was as strong as he was going to get for several weeks—and the Skrælings were growing more and more putrid.

He lurched to his feet with an odd monkeylike motion and hobbled over to the body nearest the mouth of the cave. He remembered receiving no wounds on his legs, yet they were stiff and sore. He knelt behind the greenish corpse and pushed hard with his good right hand. The body rolled easily and disappeared over the lip at the mouth of the cave. It was a long fall to the pool at the base of the cliff into which the cave was cut.

Mälar did not wait for a splash he could not hear over the roar of the Thundering Falls.

Where the Skræling had lain was a teeming, squirming mass of maggots and other crunchy bugs that fed on death and disease. Mälar felt no disgust. In the first Battle of Lyndisfarne, when he was not a young man, the maggots had eaten his own flesh as he lay on the shore, near death with his wounds full of pus, as he waited for the rescue he knew would come. That experience had hardened him to many others. The maggots had probably saved his life by purifying his wounds.

The stiffening force of death had contorted the next Skræling into a fantastic posture. His greenish mouth gaped open and white bugs swarmed in and out. His legs were curled under him and his rigid arms reached for the sky. His fingers were twisted into inhuman knots.

Mälar had need of Halberd's fine battle-ax, which remained embedded in this Skræling's foot. Mälar reached between the tangled limbs. He yanked with his right arm and the ax came free. The ease with which it came out sent Mälar reeling backward, his useless left arm whipping around his chest like an empty sleeve. Mälar ignored the flapping limb and the pain that flared in his head.

He laid the ax against the cave wall and picked up the thinnest log that formed the wall near the cave mouth. With this he levered the Skræling free of the cave floor, out of the cave and into the air. This brave fell as had the one before.

Mälar made his way from corpse to corpse, flipping each free of the floor and then shoving over the cliff edge. The dead who still bore usable weapons he stole from—let them go into the afterlife unarmed if they were so weak a witch might enslave them. His pity and respect had vanished with the difficulty and horror of his task.

When the last warrior had been commended to the empty air and boiling pool hundreds of feet below, Mälar took stock. At his feet lay several stone-headed bashing mallets with double-edged blades and decorated handles. He had one short stabbing lance, also with a stone head, his own sword, Halberd's ax, and three stone daggers. There were also long coils of rope, plaited in the Viking manner but woven from Skræling materials—no doubt the witch Grettir had taught them how. What they had intended to do with the rope Mälar could not figure.

Mälar also had three fine shirts made of deerskin and a thick pair of winter leggings made from a skin he did not recognize. He ripped his remaining threadbare legging off and slid on the clothing of the dead men. Again, it was not the first time.

He had one task remaining before sleep. He hobbled over to Halberd's entranced body. The stone knife and the Jewel of Kyrwyn-Coyne rotated slowly over Halberd, bathing him in golden light. Mälar knelt with some clumsiness and examined the long wound on Halberd's back. The edges had already closed and no infection showed, no pus dripped, no bugs crawled near on the wound. It was not swollen.

Such healing could only be the work of sorcery. Apparently the Skræling woman Ishlanawanda protected Halberd while they both resided in the Dream World. Or perhaps the golden light stimulated healing. Mälar had no wound the equal of the battle-ax blow Halberd had suffered and none of his were anywhere near so healed.

Contented, well fed, sure of his companion's safety, and finally free of the stench of corpses and himself, Mälar slept.

And so, like all men regardless of their circumstances or even their intention, Mälar developed a routine. He awoke with the sun and made his slow way to the spring. There, careful to avoid seeing himself in the clear water, he bathed his wounds and drank his fill. Then he carefully inspected Halberd's wound, which continued its unearthly healing. Each morning Mälar would address the body of Halberd, even though he knew its occupying spirit was far away in some unknowable world.

"Good morning, young Viking," the old sailor would boom. "We are sufficiently alive to be bored, at least. I know you cannot hear me, but I am glad to see you heal so well. I trust you will return to me soon."

Then Mälar would go to the edge of the cave mouth and dangle his legs over the cliff edge into space. There, staring at the back side of the endless, churning drop of the Thundering Falls, he would slowly munch his dried venison. The first day he had eaten until he was full. Now he knew better. Mälar ate carefully, rationing what he had, waiting for Usuthu's return.

He knew the giant Mongol would bring food, but he didn't know when. He did not consider that the black giant might not return. Mälar could think of no circumstances that might bring about the Mongol's death.

When his one meal of the day was done, Mälar would stare at the Falls and remember his various adventures and the women who were connected to them. Around midday he would nap. When he awoke he would heft his sword and practice on the vast woodpile until his right arm ached, or his head wounds broke open, or he grew too bored to continue. His left arm made no progress. It flapped as emptily as before, and Mälar taught himself to fight while keeping the useless appendage behind him.

He remembered the style of the yellow-skinned, slit-eyed warriors he had met in the Land of Sand on the Inland Sea. They held their swords above their heads, with the blades pointed forward and down, parallel to their bodies. It was a tricky style to learn for a man with a lifetime of hacking and slashing behind him, but he worked diligently. One old-fashioned slash would leave him spinning like a top with a stone hatchet buried in his back.

His strength came back very slowly, as he knew it would. It was easier to deal with the weight of life as an old man, but far easier to heal the body when one was young. Still, Mälar reminded himself, young men needed strength, while the old required cunning. In that area, Mälar knew he had suffered no injury.

And so three weeks had passed. In those weeks Mälar had gone through all the stages a man goes through after a close brush with death. That he knew he would go through them did not lessen their power.

For a day or two he was glad to be alive.

Then he was glad to have most of his faculties intact.

Then he was glad to have food and water.

Then he was unhappy he had no companionship. Then he was sorry his diet had no variety. Then he felt great frustration because his wounded and useless left arm prevented him from climbing down the cliff wall below the cave and hunting for game.

Then, he was bored.

It took Mälar two days to run through those stages. For three weeks he had been talking to himself and becoming increasingly restless. Now, a broken arrow bearing deer meat signaled the end of his imprisonment and the beginning of a new adventure.

Well, he thought, to cook this meat I must have a fire.

Mälar had built no fires in the previous weeks. He could not strike flint against stone to make sparks with one arm, he did not feel like hauling the huge logs around, and more importantly, the cave would only seem darker and lonelier when the fire went out. It was easier to sleep at dusk and awake at dawn.

Mälar ran his hands over the scabs in his head. Perhaps, he thought, I should investigate my appearance before the Mongol sees me.

He strode to the stream. His legs and right arm were strong once more. His left remained empty of force.

He knelt beside the spring as he did each morning. This time, though, he did not kneel where the bubbling water raced over the clean white stones. This time he knelt next to a small, still pool, about a foot deep, just below those stones, where the spring collected before vanishing into a hole in the rock floor.

Bracing himself for the shock, he swung his head forward and stared into the cool, still water.

Gazing back at him was the foul demon witch, herself, Grettir.

Mälar felt the hair at the back of his neck rise. His bowels turned to ice. His body became as paralyzed as his worthless left arm. His sword was across the room. Slowly, determined to show her no fear, he looked up over his shoulder. The cave was empty. Mälar stared into the pool once more.

She looked back at him, patient and mocking.

So she was not in the cave. He was not seeing her reflection. Somehow she was in the *pool.*

"Well, Witch." He spoke in the voice of command that comes to a helmsman after fifty years at sea. "Speak your piece and begone."

"Yes," the demon purred, her blond hair wafting back and forth as the surface of the pond shimmered, "you alone of your miserable band may address me as witch. You never saw me as a young girl in my village, as did Halberd and Usuthu."

So saying, Grettir changed her appearance. The mad red glint left her eyes, which became blue and soft. Her mouth lost its hard, tight line and became sweet and yielding. Her chest armor opened to reveal her lovely breasts. Without so much as a gesture, she beckoned Mälar into the pool, into her body, into her soul.

As had many mortals before him, Mälar yearned for her. Truly, he thought, men were the stupidest of animals.

"Your power is well known, demon," Mälar said. "You have the power to stiffen men's cocks, as mine is now stiff, and you have the power to make them kill one another, as I have killed many of those you enslaved."

"These are," she replied, reverting to her more frightening image, "formidable powers, are they not?"

"They are all the power you seem to require."

"Tell me," she whispered, "why did it take you so long to gaze into the pool? Did you know I was waiting for you?"

"I am more simple than you imagine. I was afraid to see my wounds too clearly."

"You fought well."

"Only because the Skrælings you enchanted were weaklings. They did not know how to fight."

"I," the Witch said thoughtfully, "think not. I think you defeated them because you are not afraid to die. That is why I have chosen you to suffer my vengeance."

Mälar said nothing. Under the calm mask of his frozen features his heart pounded. He felt greater fear than he could ever remember.

"Halberd is young and strong," Grettir continued, "and he should be my love. Perhaps I will kill him soon, perhaps not. Perhaps I may yet convert him to my side."

"And the Mongol?" Mälar had never heard the demon speak except for the shouting of cursing or the hissing of threats. If he could learn of her intentions, they would gain a great advantage.

"Usuthu has powers, great powers, perhaps the equal to any I could muster. He, like Halberd, does not realize the depth of this strength. I can still defeat him. I may kill him yet. But for now I choose you. You will suffer greatly."

"Why"—the old sailor made his voice strong and clear—"me"?"

"Because you think you are beyond fear. Because you believe you have endured every death a man may endure and yet not die. You have swum for days to keep from drowning, you have pushed floating corpses into the mouths of sharks to keep yourself from becoming a meal, you have dug into the desert sands for a drop of water, you have clung to masts while ships burned beneath you, and you have climbed over mountains of bodies to fight for a crust of bread. You have lived a full warrior's life.

"If I may convince you that terror awaits, if I might break your spirit so that Halberd and Usuthu can see my power, then I can bring them to my side. Your courage is so great, your indifference to death so complete, that to see you grovel in fear will shatter their hearts."

Mälar drew a breath to steady his shaking hand. "What have you in store for me?"

"I will flee to the South—you must chase me. You must take the highways of water which lead to the Mesipi, the Big River. Follow that river to another sea and the currents will bring you to me. I know you will tell this to Halberd, even though it means your horrible death. You cannot neglect your duty.

"South of the end of that huge river, over a small sunlit sea, live a warrior tribe who worship the sun and build great pyramids of stone. They are learning to worship me as well, and I shall feed them a great warrior—you."

Mälar forgot Grettir as he reconsidered their journey: could they have circled around to the back side of the Land of Sand? Only there did people live who worshiped the sun and built pyramids. But that was long, long ago. Now they traded slaves and bragged of the exploits of their ancestors.

Mälar almost asked the question of the Witch. But he had faith in his own navigational powers—he knew half a world lay between them and the Land of Sand.

"You may try, but I will prove hard to kill, as I always have."

"Mälar, you do not grasp what I am saying. There will be no battle. When the time is right, I'll snatch you by a spell and convey you directly into their hands. Your courage will only increase your value in trade. They require stout hearts from outside their own tribes."

The Witch's voice rose as she described the scene.

"The High Priests, armored and covered with feathers, will bear you to the top of a great pyramid on a sunny day when thousands and thousands of peasants gather to watch. The Priests will bind you to a stone altar."

Her shout rose to a screech.

"There they will slash open your chest with a stone knife, tear your beating heart out of your breast, and eat it, fresh and dripping, before your dying eyes!

"And the last sight you see will not be the chunks of your own heart devoured by these horrible Priests—it will be me, standing at their sides, laughing into your face!"

The truth of her curse went through Mälar like a spear. Blood drained from his face. He could see himself clearly, spread-eagled on some pagan altar, his chest ripped open, his heart pumping in the hand of a squat, eagle-faced dark-skinned Priest.

His fear became instant rage.

"Begone, Witch!" he roared. "I banish you from my sight!"

He smote the surface of the pool. Water splashed over him. Her image shattered.

A thin white arm snaked out of the pool. Grettir

grabbed Mälar behind his head. She yanked him into the pool.

This cannot be happening, he thought as he scrunched up his face. The pool was no deeper than the distance from his waist to his elbow. Mälar braced to feel his face dashed against the rocky bottom of the pond.

Grettir pulled his head below the surface. She stood upright, hovering in an apparently bottomless lake. Her hair floated about her like the hair of a drowned corpse. Her eyes were alight with red fire. Though bubbles escaped her mouth when she spoke, Mälar heard her perfectly.

"Old fool!" she spat. "You dare to give orders to me? I will watch you closely over the coming weeks. I will feed on your growing fear and gain strength from it even as you doubt yourself. You will set the timetable for your own capture. I will take you when your fear is the greatest. No heroism awaits you, only death. You owe me much for your disrespect and I shall be repaid in full."

"That you shall, whore," Mälar answered. "My ax will find your neck, my sword your heart, and my fingers will tear out your liver. You cannot make me afraid."

"We shall see."

She flung Mälar as if he weighed no more than a child. He flew backward out of the pool. He sailed across the cave and landed right on the point of the elbow of his useless left arm. Blood spurted out and he grabbed the reinjured limb.

"Pain!" he cried with joy. "I can feel pain!"

The Nokoni and the Snake

"Why does that make you celebrate?"

Mälar whirled around on his back, never relinquishing the hold on his throbbing left arm.

Usuthu stood at the edge of the cave, a huge, gutted deer hanging over his shoulders. The golden shields he wore on his front and back instead of clothing gleamed in the reflected light of the Thundering Falls. His great sword hung at his side, his silver mallet dangled at his wrist, and his huge bow hung, unstrung, from his shield. He bore no arrows.

He showed no signs of recent wounds or hardship. He appeared well fed. His dark face beamed with happiness and his slitted eyes glowed.

"Because"—Mälar spoke through gritted teeth—"since I awoke after the battle, I have been unable to move or feel this limb. Now it aches like a rotten tooth."

Usuthu dropped his load of venison and knelt beside Mälar. He glanced at the darkening pool of blood forming on the rocky floor beneath Mälar's arms.

"Can you move it?"

Mälar carefully straightened his left arm by pulling on his wrist with his right hand. The arm unfolded to its full length. Sweat burst from Mälar's forehead. His breath came in short grunts. His arm hurt as if it was afire. Usuthu carefully took the old man's hand and stretched out each finger, one by one.

Mälar passed out.

When he awoke, his arm was bandaged with a piece of skin cut from his leggings. What had awakened him was the rich smell of broiling deer. His mouth filled with saliva.

Usuthu sat cross-legged by a huge blaze. The dancing fire lit his hard, flat features. He extended a juicy chunk of deer to Mälar. The helmsman tore into it like a dog. Drool ran down his chin, mixed with the fresh blood of the deer. Halberd said nothing. He, too, had lived on jerky for weeks after a battle. He knew the appetite for cooked, fresh meat that grows every day. But for grunts of pleasure, they ate in silence.

When the huge Mongol finished, he rested his hand lightly on the butt of his sword.

"Do you ever pray, Mälar?"

Shocked, Mälar gazed at Usuthu with care. Three weeks in a strange land equaled an eternity elsewhere. Had the black warrior become enchanted?

"I know," said Mälar, "that you, like Halberd, were a shaman in your own land. But I believe in nothing. Nothing but the skill of my right arm, the treachery of man, and the certainty of death."

Usuthu also watched Mälar with care.

"In your sleep," Usuthu said, "you called out to gods of your childhood. This seemed unlike you. Never have I heard you beseech them. I did not think you considered the gods worthy of your words. I may be able to heal your arm, but the method makes me vulnerable to the evil in your soul, if any. If you've been enchanted in my absence, the danger to me would be great."

"Some gods," Mälar replied, "like Thor, Loki the Trickster, Odin, and others, live as they always have. They are not spirits, but simply Immortals, with great powers and greater vanity. Little reward have they granted me in my life. Likewise, little aggravation. Others, like Njord, the God of the Sea, take my tribute and only once have I asked him for anything in return. I believe all other spirits are the invention of man.

"I'm curious to see whose spirits rule this land. Will it be yours, Halberd's, or those of the Skrælings? I want to see if the gods of your land are able to follow us here, along with the gods of Northland."

"What do you know of my gods?"

"Nothing, beyond your worship of Bahaab Dahaabs."

"For centuries," the Mongol began, looking deeply into the fire, but seeing the treeless steppes of his homeland, "my people worshiped everything. They believed all things were alive: rocks, sticks, dirt, clouds. They created many spirits, good and bad, which soon came to be real and occupied our land.

"But my father, battle lieutenant to the great Khan, observed that in the highest mountains of the Khan's territory lived men who prayed in a more systematic way. They lived alone, in high monasteries, they wore robes, and they seemed content. My father had the most holy of these monks summoned to him. My father studied under his tutelage.

"This monk would have my father follow the way of the Rinpoché, as their god is called. My father would not renounce Bahaab-Dahaabs. This Rinpoché was far too peaceful and lacking in blood lust. But my father learned much of their medicine and sorcery, and he took a new name from them.

"He calls himself Tenya Gyotsu—meaning the Strength of Others."

Mälar rested on his back, feeling the deep stupor of a warm, full belly creeping over him.

"Why tell me all this, Usuthu? Must I now share with you tales of my father, though he has been dead since long before you were born?"

"From him," the Mongol replied, "I have learned a great deal of the medicine of the monks, ways to send my spirit far, far away while my body deals with cold or heat, and other, sacred things. None of their teachings interfere with the more magical and demonic things I learned from the Sorcerors of the Court of the Great Khan, things which would get my head chopped off if the Khan knew I knew them." Usuthu replied, "Anyway, with what I have learned I believe I may cure your useless arm."

Mälar looked sheepishly down at the deer meat dripping over his lap. He held it in both hands. He had raised it to his mouth with both hands and held it there while his teeth tore it to bits. He had not noticed that his left arm now worked. He felt no pain.

"Is my arm not healed already?"

"No. I believe that when next you lift something of some weight, or try to swing a sword, you will lose the use of it once more."

"What," asked Mälar, "would you do?"

"I will take your arm in my hands and from it draw the sickness out of your body and into my own."

"Will not," Mälar shouted in aggravation, "your own arm then suffer as mine has suffered? Do not speak in riddles to me!"

"Calm down, old man." Usuthu grinned widely. "I will draw the illness from you into me and through me into the world around us. You will be healed."

"Does my disbelief in your ability hinder the effectiveness of your method?"

"Fortunately for you," said the Mongol as he crossed the cave and took Mälar's arm in a grip of iron, "it does not. But if the witch had possessed your soul while I was gone, I could be easily subdued."

Mälar tore another chunk from his hunk of venison.

"Must I," he asked, "put down my dinner for your magic to work?"

"It is not magic," answered Usuthu with great dignity, "and the answer is no."

"How do you know I am not possessed?"

Usuthu ran his hands up and down the old man's wiry arm.

"You can't not lie to me in a way I cannot detect. I would recognize Grettir's presence. And if you tried to harm me, I would rip this arm right out of your body. Now be quiet."

Usuthu closed his eyes and breathed deeply. His mouth fell open and his body relaxed as if asleep. His grip never loosened.

Mälar could feel pain in his arm, running in a line from his shoulder to the tip of his thumb. The pain seemed to be receding like the ocean pulling back from the shore. As Mälar concentrated on the pain, it diminished even further. Then, like a horseman riding over the horizon, it was gone.

Strength flowed into his arm like water.

He clenched his fist for the first time since he

awoke. His heart sang. The power of all Northmen, living and dead, ran through him like lightning. He could fight two-handed. He could ride. He could steer a ship. Best of all, he could climb down from his miserable cave.

He was whole again.

Mälar moved his arm slightly in Usuthu's grasp. The Mongol opened his eyes with a start. For an instant he looked at Mälar with deep suspicion. Then he relaxed.

"You are healed, old man," he said. "Are you then in my debt?"

"Why are you talking to me so formally? We serve a common quest. There are no debts here because we may never refuse one another anything."

"That is true." Usuthu sounded chastened. "It's only that I have to demand that you tell me something you may well not want to speak aloud."

"Ask."

"What did the witch say to you?"

Mälar looked at the Mongol for a moment before replying.

"Whenever I think I cannot be surprised, I am," he said. "When I think I cannot feel fear, I almost fill my pants. I do not know my own capabilities anymore. How do you know she spoke to me at all?"

"Because you have a curious light in your eyes I have not seen before. Because normally you do not fly backward out of pools in which you are sunk to your chest, though that pool be only elbow deep. Because never have I heard you call on the gods for protection, whether you are sleeping or awake.

"And," Usuthu finished, "because she spoke to me."

Mälar felt no surprise. Oddly, though, dangerously, he felt jealousy. Jealousy over the attentions of a witch!

Her powers, he thought, are nothing compared to the stupidity of her prey.

"And," he said, "what was her message?"

"She told me I was stronger than I knew, that I was destined to be at her side, and that sooner or later I would betray you and Halberd. That was all she had time to say."

"Why is that?"

"I'll tell you in due course. What did she say to you?"

Mälar swiftly related the witch's threat. Usuthu gazed off at the back wall of the Thundering Falls, deep in thought.

"Will you tell Halberd?" he asked.

"I do not know. If I do not tell him, then how can I justify the route I know we must take? If I do tell him, how can he have faith in me?"

"Do you fear her?"

"I believe that I fear little, very little. I feel ready for death."

Usuthu watched the old man carefully.

"Yes," he said at last. "You will not succumb to your fear."

"How do you know?" Mälar shouted. "Grettir scares me. As soon as I show my fear in any way, I am doomed. Being ready for death and welcoming it are two very different things."

"Mälar, my blood beats in the hearts of the bravest men in the world. The Mongols have no equal. Hardship is bred into us. We ride through snowstorms which blow for weeks, we fight with our entrails dangling. It is our way. Yet I would rather ride into battle with you than any of my own tribesman."

"Am I so great a warrior?"

"In fact, when it comes to skill, you are an average warrior. But you are less afraid than other men because you can laugh at your own fear. I cannot do that. When I sense fear in myself, I become angry and that anger makes me charge whatever frightens me. Yet deep inside I know I am still afraid. But you genuinely fear not. That is a rare quality. Grettir thinks that if she can make you afraid she will weaken our souls. She is wrong. Your fear will not harm us. It should not shame you."

Mälar said nothing, but his heart lifted at the spoken respect from this most laconic of men.

"Do not fear this witch," Usuthu said. "We can save you from whatever you are unable to escape on your own. Now, how fares Halberd's body?"

"It heals like none I have ever seen. His Skræling women in the Dream World must have massive powers. He will even use his arm again. I expect his return any day. He must know that his body gains strength. Now tell me, why did the witch run out of time?"

"Will your full belly put you to sleep before my tale is told?"

Mälar made no reply. His mouth was full of deer meat.

Usuthu returned to his place by the huge fire. He lifted a chunk of venison and tore out a huge bite. He shifted his gaze to the roof of the cave and began.

"When she appeared before me, in spirit form, rising from the headless neck of Halberd's treacherous brother, I felt my testicles turn to water. Never have I felt such fear. Never.

"My fear immediately became anger. The method

with which I slew Labrans showed just how much anger I felt. I crushed his head between my palms like a plum. I had not yet wiped his brains off my fingers when the witch appeared.

"Before she had finished speaking I struck at her."

"How?" interrupted Mälar. "She was in spirit form."

"I invoked one of the oldest spells my secret teachers passed on to me. I had only used it once, as a very young and presumptuous man. It nearly killed me then."

"Usuthu, by my standards you are young and presumptuous still."

The grave Mongol ignored the interruption.

"You saw when Labrans attacked Halberd that I almost wasted the power of my silver mallet. I lose my temper when I am afraid. Perhaps this was not the wisest spell to have chosen. It is very taxing."

"Usuthu," Mälar said, his patience wearing thin, "what spell did you invoke?"

"I took the form of a snake. Once I no longer held my own true form I was fighting in her world. She was vulnerable to me. I struck at her once and missed her. The rage and fear on her face gave me even greater strength. We writhed together atop Labrans' headless corpse. She seized me under my mouth, but I wrapped my tail around her and struck her again. This time I smote her arm, and badly. She vanished into smoke.

"At that moment a large party of Eerhahkwoi poured into the clearing, drawn by the noise of our struggle. I slid under the trees and observed them. They wore different markings than those who pursued us on Grettir's behalf. I believe they did not know who we were. They were shocked by Labrans' body, which they examined at great length."

Usuthu paused to drink a long draft from his water bag.

"They did not understand his dress or the color of his skin or his bodily hair. This I could understand through their gestures. Nor could they fathom how it was that he lacked a head. His head had obviously not been severed, as some fragments of it still remained above his neck. I believe that they concluded that some animal had eaten it. When they sighted my weapons and empty shields and leggings, a great cry arose.

"Their curiosity was obvious—they had never seen weapons of this size or type. Their arms were all made of stone. They took up my equipment and Labrans' body and set out through the bush—what choice did I have? I slithered after them.

"I was deeply concerned. The spell is potent and destructive. It saps the strength of whoever invokes it. If I remained in another form too long, I would die of exhaustion. I had not performed any such spell in years and years. It is too dangerous.

"But now I was without my arms and my clothing. I needed them. I followed.

"They trotted south and west of the Thundering Falls for many leagues. They did not speak or fight or hunt. Several times they turned off the trails to avoid contact with other bands. The game animals here are like the sheep in Northland. They have no fear of man. The deer and larger horned beasts moved aside for the Skrælings but otherwise ignored their coming and going. I was curious. I wonder if the Skrælings enchant these beasts or if they really are so docile.

"After the day grew dark we reached a village much like the one we destroyed in our battle. The houses were long and made of sticks bent over a frame. Many families lived in each house and only three houses were needed for an entire village. I wondered how severe the winters could be if families live in such close confinement for many months.

"The warriors rested, as did I, for I knew what was coming. After dusk fell great fires were lighted and the warriors returned from their longhouses painted and bearing all their weapons. Their hair was tied in a thin line running along the tops of their heads. They looked ferocious. They gathered my arms around the huge fire and I knew they would tell the tale of the capture of my bow and the odd body, which they also dumped in the firelight.

"But what shocked me was that men did not lead these counsels. A wizened old grandmother, clearly the matriarch of the tribe, stood by the fire and chose which man would speak and in which turn. She bore a long white antler which she pointed to make her choices known. Her black eyes burned. She had power. All addressed her as Nokoni.

"After each warrior spoke it was not the men who commented on his tale, but the women, who encircled the fire in the front rank. Younger women knelt in the next rank, learning what they could. The men stood behind them, looking on. Never had I seen such a clan. It was doubly odd in that the men were the hunters and their wives and mothers and sisters prepared the food and served the men as warriors deserve.

"But all decisions were made by the women. And the elder the women, the greater the rank. Have you heard of such a tribe?"

Mälar barely heard the Mongol's question, so deep was his torpor. The magic of the tale, the image of

Usuthu as a snake crawling among the Skræling fires, the thought of Labrans' headless body propped up before some Skræling lodge, had transported him far beyond this cave. Usuthu's question brought him back.

"Once," he replied, "I heard of a race of women warriors and sailors and even scholars who lived in the Beautiful Islands in the northeast corner of the Inland Sea, about three weeks' sail from the Land of Sand. But they were to have existed centuries before."

Usuthu continued:

"The old crone who ran this tribe listened to all who spoke. Then she questioned them intently. Through her gestures she described Grettir's hair. She made lewd motions with her hips and, in so doing, became as a young woman again. Whatever she was asking, the tribesmen denied. I believe she wanted to know if Grettir appeared to them as a lover in their dreams.

"Then the sentries ran in from the shadows. They led a delegation from what apparently was another tribe. Their hair hung down in long spikes, weighted with feathers and quills. They were a bit shorter than the Eerhahkwoi, with broader foreheads. They appeared just as savage. But, like the Eerhahkwoi, they seemed more dignified and noble than any savage I've seen.

"What fascinated me was that these tribes shared a language! I assumed different bands would have different tongues but they did not. Perhaps the Eerhahkwoi are dominant and others have had to learn their tongue. This band, as I could judge from the opening speeches, is known as the Alkonkin.

"The welcoming formalities lasted a long time. I knew I could not remain in my snake form for long, but what could I do? Now even more Skrælings kept me from my arms. The visiting band was patriarchal—no women accompanied them. Their elders smoked with the women elders of the Eerhahkwoi. When the smoking was done, the eldest of the Alkonkin described Grettir with his hands. The word he used for her again and again was Manatou. Thus I learned their word for demon. As I lay under a leaf, aching to inch closer yet knowing a lack of caution would get me chopped into bits, I gained understanding of many of their words.

"The warriors of the Alkonkin laid their stone mallets down and peered closely at the body of Labrans. They examined the hair on his arms and hefted my sword. They hefted my silver mallet. They struck at my shields with it. I grew alarmed. They might unleash its power unknowingly, or worse, they might drain it of all its great strength.

"I slithered forward from the shadow of the long house where I lay. The night was half over and the fire leaped into the black sky. I could barely move. If I remained as a snake any longer, I would die. I forced myself to the center of their counsel. The old grandmother saw me first. She jumped backward as if she had stepped on a coal.

"She opened her mouth and called on her gods. She stared into my eyes. She knew me as a man, not a snake. When a young man started forward with a hatchet, she stopped him with one burning word. He hung his head in shame and stepped behind the front rank of women once more. At that spoken word drums began to beat, though I could not see the drummers. The visiting band waited comfortably, their arms at their sides. They felt no fear. The Nokoni watched me, her hands on her hips, her wrinkled face smiling slightly, her black eyes lit by the fire.

"I raised my head to look into her wise face as a snake raises his head to strike. At that moment she gestured behind her and the ranks of Skrælings parted in a V shape. The old crones seated by the fire moved aside and the ones on the other side of the blaze stood in respect. The Skrælings looked into the black woods with apparent awe and fear. All moved closer together. With my snake's sense I could smell their fear. The crackling of leaves and breaking of branches sounded over the fire. A howl rose from the lips of all the assembled Eerhahkwoi. None of the Alkonkin moved. They seemed grown into the ground. Their slitted eyes were round as apples. I believe they were seeing something no Alkonkin had ever seen.

"I said the spell again, this time in the language of the snakes. I regained my human form as sticks broke and the ground began to shake. All the Skrælings raised their hands in alarm except the Nokoni. She nodded her head and smiled at me, as if I were welcome.

"I could barely lift my arms. I felt constricted and snakelike, even still. I knew if Grettir advanced through the trees she would make short work of me. Somehow I remained convinced it was not her. These tribes gathered to learn how to fight the demon, not aid her.

"The Nokoni gestured to me to peer into the blackness which led back to the trees down a long corridor of standing Skrælings, but the flickering firelight prevented me from discerning what approached. When it appeared at the edge of the counsel, I pissed all over my feet. The Nokoni smiled, but I believe no Skræling thought ill of me for showing my fear. As you know, Mälar, I hate snakes. Though I can become one, I cannot bear the sight of one.

"Waiting at the edge of the clearing was a huge horned serpent, as big as the one we killed when first we touched upon this land. It was larger than our Northland dragon ship. It's body was taller than Halberd, only somewhat shorter than me. It was as big around as the longhouses in which the Eerhahkwoi live. It had two short curved horns on its head and shiny green and gold eyes as large as my fist. Its body glistened with golden scales. It slid to the Nokoni and raised its huge head from the ground. It lifted its head to the height of hers and waited, ready to do her bidding. Smoke rose gently from its nostrils, which were the size of my head.

"I raised my arms above my head, the better to feel some strength in them, and the giant snake moved forward slightly. The Nokoni restrained it with a touch. Whether it was real and she called it forth from its den or unreal and created by spell I do not know. I only know the ground at my feet was muddy from my own bladder.

"I moved without haste to my arms. The Nokoni watched me, doing nothing. I knelt beside the smelly body of Labrans and pulled on my leggings. The Alkonkin warriors stood over me, looking down, silent. I slid my shields over my head and put my bow over my back. I lifted my sword and wore my silver mallet on my wrist once more. What did it matter? I was near death from the length of the spell and the Nokoni knew it. How she knew I do not know, but she was one of the Old Old Grandmothers even my Grandmothers spoke of with great respect from time to time. My Grandmothers respected little but the

Mongol way, yet they claimed that around this world lived women older than they, who bore great and destructive wisdom. The Nokoni had such wisdom.

"I straightened to my full height, armed and armored. Every Skræling man who bore a bow now pointed an arrow at me. Every bowstring was taut. Did they believe me a man who could be slain or a demon who could not? The Nokoni had not uttered one word. Why would she call on the snake if her men were to make a pincushion of me?

"I called the word Manatou and gestured with my mallet that I would kill the demon witch Grettir. This surprised the Nokoni. I believe that she considered me one of Grettir's soldiers. I raised up the bloating corpse of Labrans and put my hands around what remained of his neck. I gestured his killing. The Nokoni fearlessly reached for one of my hands and smelled it deeply. Her eyes lit up at the smell of the dead Viking's brains and she dropped my hand.

"Until that moment I do not think she realized it was possible for us to fight among ourselves. I think all Skrælings believed that all of us served Grettir. This revelation shocked the Nokoni. She looked at me now with curiosity and, I am convinced, respect. For the first time I think she considered that I might be human and mortal. Of course, that meant I could easily be killed by her army.

"My breath came in spurts. I wanted only to sleep and that for days. My eyes drooped. The Nokoni spoke at length in a loud, singing voice. After her first words all the bows lowered and the men and women studied me with care. The sky was lightening to the East. In a short while the night would be be over. The Nokoni quickened the cadence of her speech. I felt that her powers, and those of the snake, might lessen as the day appeared. Her speech hypnotized me and increased my desire to slumber.

"At the precise moment of her last word the drums stopped. How could they know when to halt? I could not even see them. Silence fell over the fire. The Alkonkin moved aside, slowly, and I stood alone with only the snake and the Nokoni inside the vast ring of watching Skrælings. The Nokoni waved to me, smiling. I knew she had commended me to the snake. I could hear the Skrælings breathe and the fire crackle. That was all.

"I had no strength. I had not enough strength even for guile. The snake shifted slightly, with less movement than I could detect, and suddenly it was right in front of me. It eyed me carefully. Just as my own intelligence had informed the snake that I became by magic, so this reptile was much more cunning than his vile form suggested.

"I am not proud of what I then did, but I had no choice. I was not strong enough to fight the snake. I reached out with one arm and snatched the Nokoni by her braided gray hair. At her age she weighed no more than a bundle of sticks. I drew her in front of me and snatched the white antler out of her hand. This I touched against her throat. The Skrælings leaped to their feet, shouting and pointing their arrows at me. None would move into the sacred circle. The snake wound its head backward, studying me.

"The Nokoni twisted in my grip, which no mortal has ever loosened, and looked into my eyes. She spoke directly into my soul, without moving her lips, and though I cannot name the language in which she spoke, I understood every word.

" 'O huge black white-man/god,' she said, 'let my snake eat you and thereby keep the power of the flame-haired demon witch away from my people. It is only just. Your spell failed and I knew you for an intruder from the moment you squirmed into my village. Now you fight as no honorable man would. I know now that you intend to kill the other white men/gods in the name of the Manatou.'

" 'Grandmother,' I replied, 'for one who claims to know so much, you understand nothing. I am not a black white man. I am proud to be a black one. My tribe is different from the white men, as Eerhahkwois differ from Alkonkins, though the black and white men in my world live separated by much vaster lands and seas.

" 'I, with two of the white men, journeyed to the sacred land of the Eerhahkwoi only to kill the Manatou. This man, the blood kin of my spirit brother, conspired with the Manatou to kill us. His head I burst like a melon.'

" 'What,' she said to me in her quaking voice, 'is a melon?'

" 'That is not important, Nokoni,' I said. 'We must be allies in this battle against the demon witch, not enemies.'

" 'I cannot trust you, black white-man/god. How is it that you know my title? How it it that you know our word for the demon? Only she knows our tongue and she learned it as you have, by vilest treachery. I believe that you conspire with her. If you are my ally, tell me why you killed so many Eerhahkwoi on your journey from the coast of the Endless Water to my village.'

" 'We killed only those who sought to kill us. We were strangers here and they attacked us. What would you have me do?'

"She did not want to believe me. The whole idea

was too confusing, too complicated. She had made a choice, and like most savages, she would stick to it.

" 'I would have you die, monster,' she screamed, 'for the trickster and false speaker that you are.'

"She raised her hand to the snake. I knew my time was nigh. The scaly beast opened his huge mouth—he had no fangs with which to strike. Instead he bore vast rows of backward-facing teeth. He would wrap me in his coils and crush me, like the tree snakes in the Land Where It Is Always Warm.

"My strength had returned somewhat. I hurled the Nokoni into the snake's vast tooth-lined pit of a mouth and sprang forward while she was still in the air. She landed in his mouth and, to my amazement, he opened his giant trap and gently spit her onto the ground! Truly, he was hers to command.

"But I had gained the seconds I required. I was upon him as he shifted his head to clutch me in his teeth. I gripped him by the horrible loose fold of scaly skin which flapped below his jaw and swung upward. With all my waning strength I slammed the white antler deep into his green-gold eye.

"Yellow pus, like the blood of a dragon, shot from his ruined eye, which fell from his skull on a long cord. The antler still protruded from the bleeding orb. I slashed at the cord and the eye dropped to the ground. The beast lashed about in his great length in pain and fury. His tail tossed Skrælings like kindling. Through the drenching curtain of clinging yellow blood I could see warriors flung high into the air. Those behind the sacred circle fired their arrows into whatever part of the snake thrashed nearest them. They did not aim. They did not think. They sought only to kill it. In their panic their arrows sailed over the beast and struck their brothers.

"I saw one Alkonkin fall, pierced through the neck. I swung below the snake's mouth, which opened and closed like a trap. The Alkonkins believed themselves under attack. They formed a square and fired their arrows into the massed ranks of the Eerhahkwoi, men and women alike. This square worked away from the snake, toward the black woods. The snake rolled completely over onto its back and broke my hold. I sailed into the dawn sky and crashed into the roof of a longhouse. This saved my life. The longhouse was sturdy and accepted my weight. I lay atop the curved roof like a beached sea mammal, breathing deeply and watching the carnage below.

"The snake crushed many in its death rolls and many more were killed by the Alkonkin, who were buried under a mass of mallet- and lance-bearing Eerhahkwoi before they could gain the safety of the woods. As I watched them being dismembered I realized that night was done—I had no cover under which to flee.

"I slid down the roof opposite the fire and found I was too weary to run. I walked to the woods. No one stood on that side of the longhouse. Terrible screams and cries arose from the other side. I stepped into the woods and there before me stood the Nokoni.

"She raised one hand in my face and opened her mouth to curse me. I feared her power and so I clouted her in the head before she could utter a word. She collapsed like a bag of ashes. I felt no pity in my heart. I examined her closely as she lay unconscious. I estimate her age to be no less than several hundreds of years. Perhaps the giant snake was one of her sons from a lifetime centuries before, whom she turned into a reptile so that he might live as long as she. Or perhaps it was just a spell that she drew from the air around her.

"I raised my silver mallet and considered bashing her brains out onto the leafy ground. I don't know exactly why I didn't. She reminded me somewhat of my own Grandmother, whose age no one can tell. Besides, any enemy of Grettir's is a friend of ours. Perhaps we can communicate with her again one day, and this time gain her assistance.

"Also, the carnage in the village of the Eerhahkwoi was terrible and they would need the Nokoni to keep their tribal strength. I wished them no harm and was sick of death. True, the Nokoni had tried to kill me, but I understood her reasons.

"I left her where she lay and made for the woods. I circled the village and found the path which had led me there. I hiked the entire day, and when the sky again grew dark I climbed the nearest tree and slept. I was nearer to death than I have been at any time since we left Vinland. My body and mind were exhausted. Accordingly, I slept for seven days and seven nights. I woke tired and hungry. I slid down my tree, disdaining discovery by the Eerhahkwoi, and slew the first deer which came down the path. I struck his head from his body with one blow of my sword, so great was my hunger, and I tore the liver from his quivering body and ate it raw. I consumed his heart in the same fashion and climbed my tree again. Once more, I slept for seven days and nights.

"When I again awoke, I felt as though my strength was recovered. I do not believe I can risk that spell again. For the first time I thought of you, Mälar. I knew you would not be slain by the Skrælings but I feared you might be wounded. So I set out upon the path to the Thundering Falls. That which the Eerhahkwoi had run in a day and a night, I required a week to travel. I was weak and slept often. I avoided all Skræling parties and there were many. Once more the countryside is alarmed and all search for us, Alkonkin and Eerhahkwoi alike. Our only advantage is that now the Alkonkin and Eerhahkwoi also search for one another. When they find who they are looking for a small battle ensues. I had to dodge many such battles in my travels.

"Because of the need for stealth I have not had time to make more arrows. I have not had time to hunt. We have only this one deer and soon we must leave this cave, find more food, and prepare to follow the Witch south and west by whatever method presents itself to us.

"The sorceress did not show herself to me as I made my way back and I assumed I wounded her when I took the form of a snake. Now, having failed with me, she stalks you."

Usuthu returned to the spring and drank deeply. He prodded the fire and threw on another huge log. Sparks rose and vanished into the black air.

"That," said Mälar, "is some tale. You hoped it would be a bedtime story. But you have awakened me and aroused my curiosity. It will be dark for some time yet. I have many hours in which to sleep. I am not in a hurry. My belly is full and now my head is as well. You spin the story well. I have some questions for you.

"Have you studied these people as you traveled among them in the reptile's form?"

"Yes, old man," Usuthu said, "as I have since we arrived on the shore of this Unknown World."

"Tell me what you have learned."

"My mouth is dry and my stomach is not so full as

yours. You speak first." Usuthu stretched his legs and tore off another chunk of deer.

"Very well," said Mälar, shifting to make himself more comfortable against his backrest of logs. "These Skrælings have no cities, they have no roads, no castles, no gates, no locks, and few weapons of metal of any kind. Because they don't seem to care about accumulating wealth of any kind, I imagine they don't steal from one another, at least not in their own tribe."

"Further," answered the Mongol, "they lack wheels, gold, agriculture, or systems of communication. They are unused to strangers, whereas the Mongols know the customs of a thousand tribes and the slave traders on the Inland Sea know a thousand more. The Skrælings lack hospitality but not bravery. They are fine archers, superb trackers, and their forests are filled with demons and small gods."

"But," Mälar asked, "what do they also lack that we regard as essential to life?"

"Horses."

"Aha!" cried the old helmsman. "There we see the difference between Mongols and Vikings. I was going to say ships, large ships. We saw many bodies of water when we rode on the shoulders of giants, but we saw no ships. The Skrælings do not travel for commerce. They are a primitive people in a primitive land. The game animals stand around, waiting to be killed and the Skrælings make nothing which they might sell or barter.

"These tribes have lived closely together for years yet they still make war—they have met few traders from other lands or tribes, hence travel over large distances must be unknown.

"So, if we intend to make such a journey and to

follow the Witch, then we must do something these Skrælings seldom so—we must ride the rivers of this land over many, many leagues. We will find neither charts nor maps nor scouts nor, in fact, a single occupant of this entire land who knows anything about anywhere except his own village."

"That is not entirely true. I saw that the Alkonkin trade with Eerhahkwoi and somebody spread the message of our arrival from the coast of the Unknown World to this place," said Usuthu.

"My boy," answered Mälar, "it was Grettir who told all of our coming and she did it via witchcraft and possession. The Skrælings never figured it out for themselves. So . . ."

"So," said the Mongol, "lacking as they do horses or messengers, one tribe will not be able to alert another of our approach. In fact, they would not be inclined to do so. Those tribes who neighbor one another fight like children and no tribe seems to know of anything far from its own territory."

"Now that we are convinced that we are superior to these people," Mälar said, "though they be braver and nobler than many I have seen, what are we going to do?"

"All we can do is wonder where our brother is and hope that he returns to claim his body before we die of boredom. Or worse, before the Witch and her Eerhahkwoi slaves return. I do not think your arm is strong enough to bear you to the bottom of this cliff."

"You're right," Mälar said. "But at least I can sleep."

He rolled onto his side, his back to the warming fire and promptly began to snore.

Usuthu walked softly to Halberd's body. He leaned into the cone of golden light that protected the Viking. Over Halberd's unconscious form the Jewel of Kyrwyn-Coyne and the sacred stone knife, Hrungnir, spun silently, weaving the spell that barred the demon witch from attacking Halberd while his spirit rested in the Dream World. Inspecting the wound that healed more rapidly than nature permitted, Usuthu whispered to his absent blood brother,

"Come back soon, shaman, we need your wits and we must travel on. Also, I grow bored. You have a woman in the Dream World, but here I have none. Thoughts of the company of a woman have plagued me since the sorceress showed herself to me. This may be her plan, or it may be my loneliness. Either way, I want a woman, too. Return to your body so that we may travel, and I can find the satisfaction in my waking life that you have gained in the Dream World."

Unable to sleep, the Mongol took up his sword and leaned against the entrance of the cave, watching the moonlight shine through the unending wall of the Thundering Falls.

End of the Idyll

Halberd leans his back against the rough bark of a tree, his legs splayed in front of him. Below him a grassy knoll stretches down to the gentle riverbank. In the cloudless rosy sky overhead several eagles wheel in the currents, searching for bits of carrion for dinner. The evening star shows on the horizon. A sliver of moon gleams beside it. The calm river is as smooth as glass. It is near twilight. No canoes ply the surface of the river. No children splash on its banks. No braves wrap the stone heads of their bashing mallets with wet rawhide. Everyone in this Skræling village in the Dream World rests in their tipis, eating their evening meal.

Everyone except his love, Ishlanawanda. She rises and falls over him with sweet agonizing slowness, drawing Halberd into her and almost allowing him to escape before she drops gently onto the length of him once more. She straddles him with her knees on either side, her lean, brown back facing him, her smooth rump lifting and falling as she slides up and down Halberd with no apparent effort or intent to stop. Her sweet hot insides grip Halberd like a glove.

Soft gasps escape her. Sweat coats her back with perfect, separate beads. With each elevation and descent, Ishlanawanda's long shining black hair swings across her slim shoulders. Halberd reaches around her and fills his hands with her small firm breasts. She raises her face to the twilight sky. Her mouth opens. Her gentle hands run up between Halberd's legs. Ishlanawanda cups him sweetly. She squeezes Halberd gently, urging him to finish, purring his name.

Halberd knows that he and Ishlanawanda are young and strong. But for one brief lustful encounter with the demon witch Grettir before she left Northland forever, Halberd has known no other woman. He knows that Ishlanawanda has had no other man. The love in Halberd's heart may be strong, but the love in his body is stronger. Ishlanawanda calls on him to stop, but he knows he cannot.

"I cannot bear to stop," he gasps.

Ishlanawanda swings around while still impaled on Halberd. She rests with her knees on either side of him. Halberd is deep within her. Her eyes gleam with fire. She leans into him for a long hot kiss, her face drenched with sweat. She pulls her mouth an inch from his.

"Now," she says, and grips him with all the muscles inside her.

Despite his attempt at control, Halberd's back arches and he spends himself. His racking spurts buck him up off the ground. She rests her head on his sweat-slick chest and wraps her loving arms around him, holding tight. Not until he is finished does she raise her head and open her eyes, the better for Halberd to stare deep into her heart. Her own pleasure sweeps through her, causing her breath to come in delicious grunts, her mouth to open, and her skilled tongue to race across her pearl-white teeth. She grips him with her lovely thighs and rides him through her spasms.

Their sweat mingles in the cooling air as they hold each other tightly, resting under the spreading branches of the huge tree. When they walk hand in hand into the river, the night is full black and stars fill the void.

Lying on a thick robe made from the fur of a beast he has never seen, Halberd stares into the crackling fire. He cuts thick dripping chunks from the breast of a fowl that flies only in the Dream World. As he eats, Halberd watches the love of his life. She lies on her side, eating delicately and staring back at him. Her face fills with a mixture of love, longing, and regret. She sighs.

"Soon, my love, you will go," she says. "Your body heals rapidly and you must return to the Waking World within this period of the moon."

"The urge to return to the Waking World has been strong," Halberd says, "for the previous day and night. My body must be healed, but how it could recover in so short a time from so grave a wound I cannot imagine. Even the powers shown to me in this world could not make my body well so quickly."

"How many days," Ishlanawanda asked, "do you believe you have been here?"

"Four days," Halberd answers, "four days and four nights."

"And," says Ishlanawanda, "how many days do you believe have elapsed in the Waking World?"

Her question brings a jolt to his chest. He never considered that there might be a difference. He says nothing, waiting for the knowledge she will share with him.

"Twenty-five of your days and nights have passed in the Waking World," Ishlanawanda says.

"And three weeks are sufficient to heal my wound," says Halberd, "aided by your power and the strength of the jewel and the knife."

Ishlanawanda watches him, waiting for further comprehension to dawn.

"So I was wrong." Halberd says. "Those who live only in the Dream World are not Immortals. You can die, but you age six times more slowly than I. You will outlive me, I fear."

"Not," Ishlanawanda says softly, "if you never left my world."

He looks up in surprise. Halberd feels no anger. Only love.

"As no other man," he says, looking into her lovely brown eyes, "as no other mortal, I am torn. But my life, my skills, and my quest for vengeance all matter only in the Waking World. If I remain, then I am like a child—I must learn everything anew, from you. How could I respect myself if I abandoned the revenge against the murderer of my brothers? How could you respect me if I deserted the great powers which I have learned?"

"Perhaps," Ishlanawanda says, "your gods granted you the knife and the jewel so you could come to me, to live here as my husband."

"The gods," Halberd says gently, "granted me nothing. I stole the jewel from Fallat, who would have slain me in this very world. The knife I pulled from the skeleton of my dead brother. No god shapes my life. I shape it!

"I sacrificed to gain my powers, and I suffered for them, too. And I'll suffer more, I know. What would you have me do? I cannot stay here and I cannot live my life without you. I will remain torn between these worlds."

Tears run down his cheeks. They match the tears on the cheeks of the beautiful Skræling.

"Can we," he asks, "sleep together, or must I return when my meal is finished?"

"My Elders wanted you gone by star rise tonight, but I told them no. They didn't much care for my rebelliousness. I'm no longer a girl, and they will fear me as a woman. Our love has unleashed strengths in me. My Elders understand that soon they will have to reckon with me as an equal. They are anxious to counsel with me. And, in fairness to them, it is important to our village that my knowledge is shared. Therefore, this is our last night together. You will be unable to return for some time."

Halberd waits to ask his next question. Ishlanawanda observes him calmly. Her eyes reflect new depths.

"Why have your elders refused to speak with me?"

"They still do not trust you. Further, all have sons. These sons wanted me as their wife. The Elders think if I married into their family I might teach them what I know. For all their wisdom, they're idiots—my strengths belong to me and to my village as a whole, to my people. One strength I gain by my love for you is the knowledge that I am free to become the Nokoni for my entire people. I will owe my heart to no one of my tribe. That grants me great freedom."

"So they ignore me out of jealousy?"

"That, and fear. If you remain ignorant in the Waking World, then the tribes of that land might slay you. If they do, you won't be back."

"How can they still desire my death after my stay here?"

"Look at yourself, Halberd, my love. We have done nothing for the good of the village. We've spent these days in one another's arms, exploring our bodies. This has been our marriage, our Days of Peace. We won't enjoy another visit like this one. As for you, my Elders care first about the people, not magical outsiders. When you perform for them, and them only, then they will welcome you, so long as you do their bidding."

Halberd studies the emerging strength in her face. It is true—if she was a girl when he first met her, now she is a woman.

"My own journey from boy to man was written in blood, not love," he says. "I didn't know it, but I was still a boy when my brother Valdane was murdered by Grettir. When we met I had already slain enough souls, mortal and immortal, to be a man. In less than a year I have shed my youth."

"I shed mine in four days," she answers. "That is the way it is. Warriors find their manhood in war and women find their wisdom in love. So be it."

Halberd finds himself restless and uneasy. He watches Ishlanawanda carefully. She studies him in turn. She gazes at him not with lust, but with pride. Pride in herself, pride in their love, pride in him.

"So, my darling," he says, "we have much to learn from one another. We will not make love again on this visit."

"No," Ishlanawanda replies, "we will not. There is too much to tell you and not enough time."

"Let us walk then, and show ourselves as lovers, unafraid and unashamed, to your village."

"We can try."

They leave the tipi and, holding one another tightly, stroll to the path that leads to the main fire in the center of the village. As before, when they near the fire, it recedes like a mirage. At the edge of a group of Skræling men sitting around the fire, three of the eldest stand, their arms across their chests, their faces stern.

Halberd holds his hands out to the elders, palms flat, in a gesture of peace.

"Do not fear me!" he calls. "I love this woman of your village and would be your protector."

The Elders glance at one another. One speaks in a deep sonorous voice.

"There is nothing from which we require protection, save the meddlesome intrusion of mortals from the foul Waking World, who would steal our women and pollute our peaceful world with their evil magic and bloodthirsty gods!"

Halberd steps closer. The Elders and their fire recede by the distance of one step. He cannot touch them. They move steadily away.

"What evil magic?" Halberd calls.

They do not answer. The Elders turn back to the fire. The youngest of the village watch curiously, but none leaves the circle and none speak.

"When the shaman Fallat came here," Ishlanawanda explains, "he attempted to seize our foremost Elder. Fallat's god, the Trickster, wished to make an Elder of the Dream World his prisoner."

"Fallat's god? The Trickster?" Halberd says. "You mean Loki?"

Ishlanawanda nods cautiously.

"You mean that Loki could not enter this world himself? He had to send his minion, Fallat, to do his bidding?"

Again, she nods her lovely head, her black hair shimmering in the moonlight.

Halberd shakes his head. He is reeling from the shock of what he has heard.

"Why," he asks, "could the second most powerful god in Aasgaard, second only to Odin himself, not enter this place at his own command?"

"We are well protected," Ishlanawanda replies. "Our magic is strong. This is the Dream World. To enter it, you must dream and dream with care."

"But," Halberd says excitedly, "Loki might enter my poor dreams anytime he wished. As might Fallat, had I not struck his stinking head from his shoulders the one time he tried."

"Fallat knew something even you do not," Ishlanawanda says. "Mark me well, my love. You could not enter my portion of the Dream World until you strode on this continent in the Waking World. Our lives here are in harmony with life on this continent. Our seasons are similar, we pay homage to Woncan Tonka, as do the natives of the Unknown World. And you had to approach its shore to communicate with me.

"Even Loki exists under the same structure. He would have to travel to the Unknown World to even begin a journey here. None of your gods has ever ventured so far from Aasgaard."

"Further," Halberd says after great thought, "Loki likes the small, secret dreams of mortal men. He cares only for momentary power, for tricks. Odin might wish to come here, but for what? He must remain in his palace to protect himself. The plotting against Odin in Aasgaard is constant, and he has his ravens to inform him of the lives of mortal men."

"Ravens?" says Ishlanawanda. "What are ravens?"

"Birds. Never mind, for now. Tell me of Fallat and Loki."

They sit against a log and watch the fire from a distance. Drums beat and the Elders lead the village men in a long chant. All ignore the two lovers.

"Loki wanted power here, why I do not know. Fallat was his servant and Fallat could come and go as he pleased. We could not stop him. One day he erred. He pulled a rock from the riverbed and tried to strike the Elder from behind. His rock passed through the Elder's head without incident and all became ephemeral to Fallat in every forthcoming visit."

"Do not rush this amazing tale, my darling," Halberd says. "Why did the rock not smite your Elder?"

Ishlanawanda laughs in his face.

"Because, my ignorant love, this, to you and your kind, is the Dream World. To you it's but a shadow. Those from the Waking World cannot touch us, or make us flesh in any way."

"But what of you and I . . . how is it that we may . . ." Halberd is at a loss for words.

"I chose to become real for you, and so I now am. I am vulnerable to you and to every mortal who comes from the Waking World. It is the price I have paid for my love."

"This cannot be. When I travel in the Dream World, the things I see and touch are real. When Fallat cast the great She-bear into my dreams, her claws were real. If she had slain me in the Dream World, then I would be dead in that world and my own."

"Halberd, your power in the Dream World is extraordinary. As for comparing your actions here with the rest of the Dream World," Ishlanawanda says, more sharply than she has ever spoken to him before, "my village is a special place."

"Indeed." Halberd gazes at the cluster of tipis, so

close at hand and so ready to flee his approach. "Tell me what I need know."

"You need know little of my world—you need to know much of your own."

"No!" Halberd speaks with more heat than he intends. "I cannot understand how the people of this land can make themselves unreal to me when all else in the Dream World is as palpable as anything I encounter while awake."

"Halberd, when most mortals from the Waking World dream, are their dreams real?"

Halberd shakes his head. Understanding begins to grow.

"Are they in danger from the beasts, or other people in their dreams? If they dream of falling, do they suffer injuries?"

Halberd shakes his head.

"For you the Dream World is a real place, filled with living beings, including yourself. For most mortals it is a pool into which they peer, never able to enter."

"True," replies Halberd. "Most mortals never comprehend the power of their dreams. They are afraid to understand that the Dream World is waiting to be traversed."

"But mortals are equally unaware," says Ishlanawanda, "that just as they create demons in their minds which come to be real in the Waking World, so do they create allies and enemies in the Dream World. An example of the power of this village and the land in which it lies, is that we are able to prevent these monsters from bothering us. Of course, some spirits which the natives of the Waking World create belong in our land, and these we cannot keep out."

"Then where is this village?" Halberd asks. "And is

it part of a larger world which resides over the Unknown World?"

"This village is part of the Dream World. It mirrors the continent you call the Unknown World and is the land which the mortals of the Unknown World visit when they dream. The Dream World greatly resembles the Waking World near it. There are numerous tribes and villages in this part of the Dream World. You may encounter others."

"If your magic is strong enough to keep all mortals out, how is it that Grettir may come and go as she pleases?"

"Is Grettir still mortal? She has become a demon witch—who knows what she is? Her magic is stronger than any we've seen, much stronger than Fallat's. Our magical shields mean nothing to her. Our Elders fear you because they know she might chase you here and exact revenge upon us."

"Your Elders might have a lot more to fear if Loki pays a visit," muses Halberd. "Then the danger would be grave—I assaulted his sister Hel in the underworld, I slew his magician Fallat, and I owe my allegiance to his rival Thor."

"The gods of your land seldom venture here. I know not of Loki or Thor or anyone other god of Aasgaard except from your own lips."

"What powers do the gods of men have in this land?"

"Your question has no meaning and belies your understanding. Think! There are as many gods as there are men. The true Immortals can come to this place, but they content themselves with those parts of the Dream World proximate to the Waking World where their subjects reside. You are the first of your people to come this far west. Why should your gods come if they have no subjects to command? They cannot rule us. Woncan Tonka holds sway here."

"But, Ishlanawanda," Halberd cries, sensing the great power that lies just beyond the answer to his burning question, "if all dreams take place in this world, where is it that Grettir goes when she enters the dreams of others?"

Ishlanawanda watches Halberd carefully.

"You don't know?"

"If I knew, then I think I would be able to gain that great prize myself: to speak to others in their dreams. It is the power I crave above all others. It would make me the equal of Grettir."

"I can guide you in many things. I can teach you the language of the natives of the Waking World, I can help to heal your body, I can be your love, but I cannot reveal to you what you must discover for yourself. The power you seek has to come from your own discovery or it is no power at all."

"But," says Halberd thoughtfully, "Grettir and Fallat are the only mortals I know who possess that power. Both employ it to enslave. Perhaps to pursue this power is to risk corruption. Perhaps I must sacrifice some element of my soul to achieve it."

"Perhaps." Ishlanawanda's eyes fill with tears. "I cannot save you any pain in this quest. You must accept your destiny. If the right to step into another's dream means so much to you, then you will pay the price."

Halberd looks into the fire.

"I have paid the price for all the knowledge I have acquired and all the leagues I have traveled. Why should this be any different?"

"Now we must talk of the natives of the Waking World. And the route you must follow."

Halberd looks up in shock.

"You know my course? You know my future?"

"I know the natives of the Waking World and I know their dreams. Several tribes dream of Grettir. She has moved south and west, she travels to a land far from here, where the customs are fiendish and human hearts are eaten daily. You must follow her there."

"How will I know the way?"

"It will be revealed to you, how I cannot say, but I know that it will."

"I have never asked you to reveal what you cannot. Tell me about the Skrælings we will encounter."

"The Alkonkin live in the land you will go through. They are no friends of the Eerhahkwoi and have no reason to fear you. It would be well if you give them none. They are better fighters than the Eerhahkwoi. South and west of the territory of the Alkonkin live the Arharaks. Beware them. They seem more peaceful but their habits are foul."

"What of the Skræling tongue? Can you help me speak it?"

"No. But I can enchant you in such a way that you will understand it."

Halberd draws a long breath before he asks his next question.

"Ishlanawanda, you are my soul. I have no choice but to love you and with that love comes trust. I believe all that you tell me. I cannot regard you with suspicion. But I know that you conceal something from me. Loki the Trickster wanted power here. If he sought to capture your Elder, then your Elder knew something which Loki could attain in no other way. Either you are able to tell me more of my world, because you have powers you have not shown me, or your Elders could aid me in some way. I demand that you share with me this knowledge."

"My Elders suspect that Loki foresaw your coming to this world. My Elders believe Loki knew that you would steal Hrungnir, injure his sister Hel, and try to thwart Grettir. Loki already knew you as the slayer of Fallat. My Elder thinks Loki wanted to capture him in order to learn the precise day when you would arrive in this world unarmed and unprotected."

"I am not unprotected," Halberd replies. He hesitates as he tries to understand that the Immortal Trickster would be so interested in a mere mortal. Perhaps Fallat was more valuable to Loki than Halberd had believed. "The jewel and the knife guard me here, as they guard my mortal body in the Waking World."

"Those charms work against Grettir, the Witch. Would they stand up to an Immortal? I do not fully understand your gods or the extent of their powers."

"I truly don't know." Halberd's mind works furiously. "I always assumed the gods cared nothing for me and would leave me alone. Perhaps Loki grooms Grettir as the shaman to replace Fallat. Perhaps the Unknown World is the new territory in which Loki wishes to hold sway."

Ishlanawanda jerks her head in surprise. Halberd looks up, alarmed. He reaches for the sword that does not protrude above his shoulder, then for the ax that does not hang from the holster at his waist. His weapons remain in the Waking World. That is the only condition under which he may enter Ishlanawanda's village.

The village Elder stands before them.

"Are you still here, mortal?" he demands in his

rolling, thunderous voice. "The time has come—begone."

Halberd leaps to his feet.

"Order me not, old man. You need something from me. What is it I know not. But I know you would not suffer my presence here if you didn't. I am surprised you gained the strength of nerve to leave your magic fire and confront me. You have nothing to fear from me; I bear no arms."

"Halberd," Ishlanawanda says, pleading, "do not argue. Go."

"Ignore him," Halberd says. "He is old and his magic fades. You are young and gaining in strength. You may say if I stay or go. What bond does this silent coward, who hides beside his fire, hold over you?"

"The bond," she answers calmly, "of fatherhood."

Halberd swallows his words of anger. The blood rushes to his face. He kneels before the village Elder.

"Forgive my harsh words," he says. "My love and impatience have made me rash and impolite. I should appreciate your hospitality in allowing me to stay with your daughter as long as I have. I apologize."

"Do so over your shoulder, as you move down the trail back to the Waking World," her father pronounces sternly. "If we had the power to keep you out, we would. Your love for my daughter is foretold. It remains unseen as to what fruit that love will bear. If you had agreed to stay here, then we would have known that you were indeed our protector. The two of you would have proved unconquerable by any foe, demonic or human, mortal or immortal, dreaming or waking.

"But you chose the petty motives which drive you

in your blood-soaked Waking World. You are not worthy of my daughter or my village."

"My motives are the same as yours!" Halberd shouts, offended to the core. "I wish to protect that which is mine, and to fulfill my responsibilities. You do likewise. Do not challenge me in a world where I am permitted no response. You cannot keep me from Ishlanawanda, and you will not."

"That," Ishlanawanda says in a cold, level voice, "is true, Father. Do not take a stand which you cannot protect. I have defied you on behalf of this mortal before, and I will do it again."

The Elder nods. His craggy brown face shows great fatigue and great anger, nearly concealed. Despite his own rage, Halberd is struck once more at the nobility and dignity of the Skrælings.

"But you know, daughter, that he must leave, and soon. The spell around the village cannot last much longer, and we must protect ourselves."

"From whom?" Halberd demands. "From me?"

Ishlanawanda's father, his name still unsaid, turns away haughtily. He steps back to the counsel fire.

"When one of the village is outside the protective spell, it is weakened," Ishlanawanda says. "I must return to close up the sacred circle."

"No," answers the Viking shaman. "I see what has been before me and I was too blind to observe. You are the Skald of this village. They cannot maintain their magic protection without your aid. Your loyalty to your village is so great that you dare not tell me this, despite your love for me. You must hold back some knowledge as a hedge against treachery. Even my treachery."

He speaks without bitterness. He understands the responsibility of the village Skald.

"What is a Skald?" Ishlanawanda asks.

"The mystic protector and seer who takes on these duties for a village or tribe. Usually a woman. My mother is the Skald in my village. I learned at her knee."

"Here the word is Nokoni. In the Waking World as well."

"Will you enchant me to speak the Skræling tongue before I go?"

"I have not the time. But I will send you a helper, a young boy of the Alkonkin tribe. He has tried to enter this village several times. He may grow to have great power. I can guide him here and teach him your face and your tongue. He will be in your path at some point, never fear."

"What is my path? Where has the Witch gone?" Halberd burns with shame to demand so much help of his love. Yet he has not forgotten his fate back in the Waking World: his body possibly crippled, his friends dead or wounded, and Grettir fled far far away.

"Grettir flees to the Land of the Sun," Ishlanawanda says as they move toward the trail that leads out of the village and into the sun-dappled forest. "It lies to the south and the west. It is more leagues from the Thundering Falls than the Unknown World is from your homeland. You must travel by water to reach it. Two rivers will lead you to the Big River, the Mesipi. The Big River will lead you south."

"And when," Halberd asks, "will I return to your village?"

"Not for some time. My Elders will observe you in the Waking World. They will note your travel in the World of Dreams."

"Will I not see you, then?"

"We may speak, now and again, but we will not touch until you return here."

Halberd takes her in his arms. She rests her head gently on his chest.

"Whether I am here or not, I love you," he says.

"And I you. Go."

Halberd turns to the trail, his eyes burning with uncried tears.

"My love?"

Halberd turns back at the unexpected sound of her voice.

"Think not too much of me, if you can. The lust you feel for me Grettir may turn against you, and use as a tool for your enslavement."

"I will think of you every night, I am certain."

"If that is so, and cannot be helped, then be alert for the Witch. She may return from the Land of the Sun. By dreams or spell she may come after you, drawn by the power of your desire."

Halberd nods.

"If she does, show her no mercy. She gains in strength every day. Kill her quickly. Kill her for your dead brothers, for your bereaved father, for yourself, and for me, but be certain that you destroy her. Be savage, be swift, be without pity."

Halberd nods again.

"I will, my love."

He moves up the path and into the trees. His tears are dry.

Mahvreeds the Cautious

Everything hurt.

Halberd was not in the Dream World anymore.

The Jewel of Kyrwyn-Coyne and the stone knife Hrungnir clattered to the rocky ground beside him. The protective spell and its golden light were ended.

His back ached from his shoulder to his hips. His left arm would not move. His eyes were gummed together. He desired only to sleep and sleep and sleep. Yet he was moving. He turned from his stomach onto his back and then to a sitting position. He felt a damp wall of stone touch his back. A trickle of freezing water ran down the wall onto his bare skin. Someone had moved him from lying on his face to sitting up with his back against a cave wall.

He remembered the cave. He remembered his deceitful brother Labrans. Halberd remembered Labrans driving the razor-sharp blade of his battle-ax into his back and shoulder. He remembered the sweet smell of Ishlanawanda as they made love. Between the ax crashing into him and Ishlanawanda's sweet kisses he remembered nothing. Likewise he remembered nothing between turning to leave her village in the Dream World and waking in this ensnaring web of pain.

Why was he sitting up? Who called his name? Water touched his lips. He opened his mouth but not his eyes. A tiny bit of sweet, sweet water poured into his mouth. He drank.

He forced his eyes to open. The dim light of a growing dawn shot into his skull like ivory sewing needles from his mother's mending kit. He rolled his head to escape it. The water dripped into his mouth once more. Again, he drank greedily.

"Slowly," Usuthu said, "do not make yourself sick, my brother."

Halberd brought the black face of his spirit brother into focus. He tried to smile.

"So," Halberd croaked, "I am not dead?"

"You live." Mälar spoke with unusual joy in his voice. "As do we all."

"Are we," Halberd asked, his voice like a frog, "all wounded?"

"I am unharmed, but tired," Usuthu answered. "The old man lost the use of his arm, but it is returning."

"And my brother Labrans?"

"I," said Usuthu, "crushed the brains from his skull between my palms."

Halberd nodded and looked away, suddenly exhausted.

"It had to be," Mälar said. "Traitors die or they destroy those whom they seek to betray."

"You were right, old man," Halberd gasped, "and you, too, Usuthu. His death was ordained. I let him live too long. Pity fouled my judgment."

"You cannot turn on your own, no matter what the cause. Blood," the Mongol said shortly, "is blood."

"Young shaman," Mälar asked, "do you want to eat?"

"My mouth feels as if a great bear defecated in it. I need more water."

Usuthu tipped a drinking skin to his lips.

Mälar offered a chunk of fresh deer. Halberd shook his head.

"Let me sleep until dark," he said. "Awaken me once more and I shall eat. My body is racked. I will force myself to heal and move about, but grant me a another day of rest."

"Will you return to your woman in the Dream World?" Mälar asked.

"No. I shall not see her for some time."

Halberd's head dropped onto his chest. He was instantly asleep.

Nightfall found Halberd wrapped in the skin of the deer Usuthu carried up to the cave. The fire roared and venison sizzled. Halberd ate slowly, chewing tiny bites over and over. His stomach accepted the food, but barely.

Usuthu and Mälar told the tales of their adventures. Halberd nodded and said nothing. His pride in the skill and power of his companions was undercut by the realization that he had lain unconscious while they fought battles that were his to fight.

Mälar spoke in detail of Grettir's appearance and threat.

"Ishlanawanda also spoke to me of the Mesipi, the Big River. We must pursue Grettir whatever her route. I cannot turn back. I cannot offer you any option, Mälar, though I suspect you wish none."

"No. I must see how much fear lurks in my heart

after all these years. But I have no idea where the Mesipi lies, except to the south and west."

"We have been promised a Skræling guide," Halberd said. "We must leave this cave to allow him to cross our path."

Usuthu studied him carefully.

"Can you climb down?" he asked.

"Not today," Halberd answered, "maybe not tomorrow, but shortly. And you, Mälar, can your arm support you?"

"Not for days and days, I fear."

"We have three coils of rope," Usuthu said. "I can lower the two of you down."

"Pray," said Mälar, "that no Skrælings come upon us in midair."

"I think the Skrælings know this cave as a lair of the Giants," Halberd said.

"And Grettir," added the Mongol.

"So," Halberd continued, "we needn't worry. Another night of rest and we shall travel south."

Halberd drew the deerskin closer around his shoulders. His spirit was low. He had little energy for the journey ahead and less for the leadership he had to provide. His mood affected the others. They moved closer to one another around the fire. Wordlessly they passed deer meat. The flames filled their vision and weird shadows danced on the cave walls.

"Is this band of warriors so weakened," a dry sarcastic voice asked, "that none stands watch at the mouth of the Giant's cave?"

Usuthu sprang backward to his feet. He whipped his long curved sword from its scabbard. When he raised the sword toward the voice, he lowered his arm in shock and surprise. Mälar clumsily rose to his feet. He tangled in his new leggings and pitched facefirst onto the cave floor by the fire. Halberd simply raised his head in wonder and surprise.

"Mahvreeds, my brother, how can you speak?" Halberd said to the pale ghost that hovered before them. "Was not your tongue cut out by the Dwarfs who served Grettir at the battle of the stone great-house Vinland?"

His older brother's ghost smiled, almost happily. He was simply a pale shadow of the man who had once lived. All his old weapons hung in place. The same rueful smile tormented his empty, transparent features. He still wore a wisp of a mustache and a small vertical beard in the center of his chin. His hair, shaved above the ears, matched the chin beard with a straight ridge of thick hair running from the front of his head to the back. Where once that hair had been kinky and black, now it was glowing white and translucent.

"In death as in life," the ghost replied, "I was barely noticed."

Halberd climbed to his feet, his face filled with love and respect. "I worried for you, my brother," Halberd said. "I feared your soul was lost to me forever. I searched after Valdane in Niflheim, but Hel would not release him to me. I saw him, but he could not speak."

"Your visit to the Underworld of the Dead is well known."

Mälar looked up from the floor.

"Greetings, ghost of Mahvreeds," the old navigator said. "I've missed you."

"How could you miss me, sea dog? I haven't seen you since the war against the wild horsemen of the Odra forests."

"That," answered Mälar, "is why I've missed you.

Also, we heard tales from your brother, or should I say from the poor ghost of your brother Valdane, that you fought bravely and well."

"I fought fairly well," Mahvreeds answered, "but my death sprang from treachery, so my effort was wasted. The Dwarf Suttung put his ax so deep into me I almost broke in half. Had he assaulted me from the front and not the rear, perhaps I might still live."

He turned toward Usuthu.

"Mongol," he said, speaking gravely.

Usuthu nodded his respects to the ghost. In truth, they had never been close. By the time Usuthu had come to Halberd's village, Mahvreeds had begun his habit of keeping to himself. He drew and painted, and undertook bizarre solitary quests. Methodical and complaining, Mahvreeds had earned his nickname by his careful approach to life and adventure.

"Does this visit mean you live in Valhalla," Mälar asked, "fighting day and night, as you deserve?"

"No," replied the ghost of Mahvreeds. "I was slain by treachery, and until that treason is repaid or undone I belong to my betrayer. The Witch Grettir sold me in slavery to the Giant Jotunheim. I was traded to him for a favor to be performed for Grettir by Jotunheim's brother, the vicious Urd."

"Do you know what that favor was, ghost?" Mälar asked.

The shadow shook its doomed head.

"That favor was our deliverance to this cave by that same Giant. Urd thought Grettir waited for us here, but we killed him for his betrayal."

"No, navigator," the spirit that had once been the brother of Halberd said. "Halberd has slain Immortals, that is true, but you did not kill Urd. His voice produces thunder. The gods need him. He has power.

You broke his leg, his wrist, blinded him in his one eye, and sent him back to Midgard in humiliation, but he lives on. Revenge against you means more to him than anything."

Halberd, Usuthu, and Mälar looked at one another in surprise. The Giant had seemed as dead as any mortal when he fell backward out of the cave mouth into the boiling pool at the base of the Thundering Falls.

"I have escaped Jotunheim to come and speak with you," Mahvreeds' ghost said. "I have information to give you and a tale to tell. We talked too little when we both lived. I've come to remedy that."

Halberd felt a vague wave of unease and guilt. The brothers had never been great friends. Never enemies, but also never intimate.

"I am in your debt for coming to aid us, brother," Halberd said, "I regret our past distance from one another."

"What could we do?" the ghost replied. "I was an adult when you were born. I had long since gone my own way. I felt no need for a younger brother and Valdane was the only older brother you ever required. Families make bonds but life makes friends."

"True," said Halberd. "Still, I'm glad you bear me no malice."

"Speaking of malice," Mahvreeds said, with the nastiness for which he was renowned as a living man, "how fares our idiot brother, Labrans? Has Grettir enslaved him completely by now? He used to follow her about our village with his tongue hanging out."

"I slew him for the traitor he had become," Usuthu said quietly.

"He disgraced our father's name. He deserved it,"

said the ghost with great disgust. "Don't waste any time mourning him."

"You're a hard man to please, Mahvreeds," Mälar said.

"I am a man no longer and never will be again," said the ghost.

He spread his arms open wide. "Behold."

Hanging in the air from hand to hand was a chart the trio of living mortals could not recognize. Glowing and transparent like the ghost who produced it, it showed vast rivers cutting through endless lands. Despite the flickering firelight and the ghostly nature of the chart, it could be clearly seen.

Maps that Mälar had drawn and read in his lifetime at sea were usually crude affairs, detailing a harbor or passage or some other small area of land or sea. Men who had sailed the world were expected to remember where they had been. This map, however, was rendered with great care and detail.

"The workmanship of this map surpasses any I have ever seen. Even so, I do not know this chart," said Mälar. "Where is the land it represents?"

"You disappoint me, helmsman," said the ghost, with the evident pleasure he always took at the incompetence of others. "Study it closely and its secret will be revealed."

Mälar peered at the chart, moving from one side to the other. Halberd and Usuthu waited. They saved their concentration. Their skills did not include navigation. It was not for them to judge a chart before Mälar had pronounced his opinion.

"Aha!" the old man cried. "Mahvreeds, you have saved us, though of course you must test me first. Seeing you again has driven the fear of death from my breast."

"Why?" said the ghost.

"Because now I know that when I die I'll be unpleasant as I was in life, just as you are."

The ghost tried to smile, but could not. It was fitting. As a living man Mahvreeds the Cautious did not often smile.

"So," he said, "where is this land?"

"This curved spit," Mälar said, pointing carefully, "is where we touched land on the Unknown World. This region of small lakes"—his finger moved westward—"we traversed on the shoulders of the Giant Urd. The northern mouth of this river is the Thundering Falls under which we now hide. So this cave is just about here."

Mälar stabbed triumphantly at the chart. His finger passed through it. His face flushed with shame.

"Forgive me, ghost," he said softly. "I meant no disrespect. I have not seen a chart since this journey began. To see the whole of this land spread before me has brought me joy."

Mahvreeds nodded. He said nothing.

Mälar returned to his study of the map. He scrutinized the western portion.

"This river," he said, tracing a north–south line that ran the length of the chart, "seems to be the largest one in the Unknown World. Is it the Mesipi, the Big River, of which the Witch spoke?"

Again the ghost nodded.

"Hmm, then we have a long way to go."

The ghost remained silent.

"But," Mälar said, growing excited, "these two rivers intersect south of us, and if we may ride the first one to the second, then the second will bear us to the Mesipi. Mahvreeds, do these two rivers flow in the directions we require?"

The ghost nodded. The chart vanished.

"Were you," Halberd asked, "under a bond of oath regarding what you have just shown us?"

"An oath to an oaf," Mahvreeds said. "I am his slave for all eternity, or until the Witch is slain. She showed him this chart and where she thinks you must travel. Jotunheim wants to slay you. More to curry favor with Grettir or avenge the injuries to his stupid brother Urd I do not know.

"As his slave I may not betray him by telling what I have learned in his service. Clearly, I told nothing. I spoke not a word."

Usuthu smiled a grim smile.

"How," he asked, "did you escape the clutches of Jotunheim today?"

"I told the great fool I would seek you out and trick Halberd into returning to Midgard with me."

"Is he truly so dumb," asked the Mongol, "or does he work some treachery on you to discover our location?"

"He and Urd know precisely where you are. Urd fears the Mongol and Jotunheim would not dare the power of the Jewel and the knife combined. Grettir tells them where she will go. They no longer care about her or her influence. She deals with a different and more savage tribe of mortals now. The Giants desire their own revenge."

"How long can you stay with us, brother?" Halberd asked.

"Certainly I must be gone by the dawn. Have you ever seen a ghost when the sun was out?"

All three living men shook their heads.

"Jotunheim may search for me sooner than that. But I came here with a tale to tell and tell it I will.

"Halberd, you have known me only as Mahvreeds

the Cautious, but you do not know why. Mälar knows the history of my name, but not the adventure which created it. No one living knows the true story of that quest, but I've come here tonight to tell it."

Mälar spoke. "Why?"

"Perhaps you require a parable to find your way across this world, perhaps not. I fear that you might. I have come to do my duty as an older brother in death. In life I never took on that role. I was, as you might have guessed, too cautious."

Halberd nodded.

"When I was a young man and you, Halberd, were barely in your teens, I undertook a quest well to the east of the Iron Mountains, in which live the Short Ugly People Who Fornicate with Bears. Though I was young at the time, I was still older than you are now, my brother.

"I rode in the dragon ship of our father's cousin, and they took me to the mouth of the Odra River. There I ventured east and north on my pony for ten days and nights. I brazenly slept by the trail, daring any passing marauder to attack me. I was not, in those days, cautious.

"The country grew wilder as I moved east and north. The Iron Mountains are gray and cold, but the land beyond them is worse. Rocky, barren, and empty, save for gangs of horsemen who belong to no tribe and claim no village. These I avoided as I rode and hid from as I slept."

"Excuse me, ghost," said Usuthu, "but can you tell us the nature of your quest?"

"I had heard, at a council table in a village to the south of our own, of an enchanted inexhaustible mine of diamonds and emeralds dug by Giants, left unprotected but for its isolated location and the bands of killers who surrounded it. The Giants worked the magic mine only on the third day of the third week of each month. Thus the mine could replenish its riches. The wild gangs on horseback, it was said, did not know the mine existed. The Dwarfs knew everything about the mine, save its location. The giants use the riches of the mine to pay the Dwarfs for their magical weapons.

"One of the councilmen in the village I visited had bribed a Dwarf with the promise of his three prize horses for information about the mine. When this councilman reneged on the deal, the Dwarf is said to have gelded the prize horses, and then to have gelded the councilman."

Halberd stared at the ghost of his brother in amazement. The Mahvreeds he had known would never have undertaken such a wild adventure on so flimsy a premise.

"You went alone?" he asked. "On the word of one storyteller in a village you did not know?"

"Yes. I always went alone in those days. I disliked human company and all their worthless words. Besides, I wanted a personal triumph that might impress Valdane."

Halberd nodded. All of the brothers, himself included, had nearly killed themselves at one time or another trying to gain the respect of their eldest brother, whom Grettir had slain.

"I rode and I rode. Sleet moved sideways through a gray sky and cut my cheeks. I had to wrap my pony's eyes with rags to protect her vision. The storm turned into blinding snow and I lost my way. Frozen and drenched, I made a harsh camp under a vast triangular rock which protruded into the sky. The rock was black and absolutely smooth. It reached higher than three great-houses from our village. Below it, there was a large flat stone and shelter from the wind. There was no wood, so I had no fire. I tethered my horse under the rock and bundled up to wait out the storm. I fell asleep.

"When I awoke I lay in an open field, like the steppes. A treeless plain ran from horizon to horizon. The sun was out, but hidden behind flat, featureless clouds. The light was piercing and bright. I shaded my eyes and tried to figure out where I was.

"The rocks had vanished and so had the mountains. Over me towered two enormous pillars of marble, separated by about a half league of ground. The pillars were like a huge gate. I lay exactly between them. I got up and headed down the long slope which dropped away from the pillars. I walked and walked.

"The land was not fruitful or pretty. There was no water. I grew thirsty and confused but I kept on going. I could not stop myself.

"I heard the thumping of great footsteps. The ground shook. I looked around for a place to hide. There was no cover, no shelter, no trees. I drew my sword and stood my ground.

"A Giant appeared, stomping along. He had long red hair tied in two braids and pockmarked skin. He was solid and muscular. He bore himself like a warrior and carried a huge battle-mace of stone and wood. The mace was enchanted and spoke to him often. The mace asked him who I was. I did not answer. The Giant asked me no questions.

"He carried a water skin and a bag of provisions. I thought he would kill me instantly for trespassing near the mine, but he did not mention it. He acted as if he was glad to see me. His name was Agaar. He bade me walk with him. What choice did I have? He was twenty times my size, at least.

"We walked all day, and all day Agaar insulted Northland, Vikings, and my own character, appearance, and weapons. He commented on our lack of bravery in comparison to other mortals, on our puny size, on the stupidity of our Elders, on the uselessness of a dragon-head ship. I could not reply, though I burned with rage inside. Often he would stop and drink from his skin, which never grew empty. Often he ate from his bag of rations. It, too, was enchanted and always produced food. He offered me none.

"We walked league after league. Twenty of my steps equaled one of his. I was exhausted but could not rest. Whenever I tried, Agaar goaded me about the weakness of the Vikings. I swore to myself that I would walk him into the ground. I was young and stupid.

"When finally the sun set, the Giant lay upon the open ground to sleep. As he snored I drew my sword and crept up to steal a drink from his water skin. He clutched it tightly in his clenched fist. Very well, I thought, I'll just hack off his finger and take the bag. I climbed onto his hand and swung with all my might. My sword disappeared into his flesh and buried itself in the ground. Yet his finger did not sever nor bleed. I was astonished. I braced my foot against his finger and worked the sword back and forth, like a gardener driving a spade into the ground. Still the finger did not separate.

"I withdrew the sword and struck again, this time even harder. The sword went so deeply into the ground I could barely get it back out. Agaar never stirred. I tried chopping on the rope which bound the bag to his hand, but I encountered no greater success. Disgusted, thirsty, and hungry, I slept.

"The next morning the Giant made no mention of my attacks. He insulted me all morning long and walked us to a rude hut, made of sod and grass but built to a Giant's proportions. He bade me enter. Inside, the hut seemed to stretch for leagues. It was carved into the earth like a tunnel. The roof was curved and sagging and covered with huge beads of condensed water. The air was dank and cold.

"Around a long table of planks sat an army of Giants. They hooted at me and called me every sort of name. I was berserk with rage. I called to them, 'You are big and I am small. You shall never die and I am mortal. Yet I challenge you—put me to a test, and if I pass it, then all of you shall apologize and sing the praises of Mahvreeds!' "

The ghost saw that Halberd gaped at him in disbelief.

"Yes, little brother," the ghost said, "once I had the temper of a crazy man.

"The Giants began hooting even louder now. 'Well, he is fat,' said Agaar. "Perhaps he thinks he could outeat us.' 'No mortal,' I yelled, 'has a larger stomach or greater appetite than mine. I can eat every one of you under the table.'

"Of course this was completely untrue. As a living man my belly grew full from a few bites. I never really liked food that much. If it was hot and readily available, fine. Certainly I was never an eater of legend, like Mälar.

"Agaar brought me stew in a wooden bowl the size of a cart. I reached into it with my hands and ate and ate and ate. I relieved myself outside the Giant's hut and ate some more. I never came close to emptying the bowl. By the gods, was I full. I vomited a great deal of stew all over Agaar's feet and fell asleep on the dirt floor.

"I awakened to even more insults and again I challenged the Giants. Agaar said to them, 'Let this loudmouth potbellied mortal wrestle us. He talks tough enough.'

" 'Wrestle you,' I said. 'How can I wrestle a being twenty times my size?'

" 'You,' Agaar replied, 'can wrestle my Grandfather. He's a puny runt like yourself, only not quite so fat.'

"I was so insane with rage and frustration that I welcomed the chance to wrestle his damned Grandfather. 'Bring him on,' I cried. 'Bring him on and let me whip him in front of you, if you have so little honor as to force your own Grandfather into combat.' "

Halberd, Usuthu, and Mälar broke into gales of laughter. The ghost looked down wanly.

"Wait," he said. "This old man, as old as the rocks and the steppes and the Iron Mountains themselves, staggered out to meet me. He was my height, a mass of wrinkles, and had arms like little sticks. He had no teeth in his head and his wispy hair was dead white.

"So, I thought, at last a foe I can defeat.

"Putting mercy aside, I leaped at the wizened old boy and tried to snatch him off his feet, the better to throw his creaking bones across the room. To my amazement he resisted my charge and held me, not tightly and not loosely, but so that I could not attack him. No matter what I did I could not escape his grip. I could move my arms and legs but he held me fast. How this could be I cannot say.

"He laid me upon the dirt floor and my humiliation was complete. I lowered my head to my knees and wept like a child. As my first tear hit the floor the cave vanished. I found myself back under my rock, beside my horse in the midst of a howling blizzard. Next to me, hunching under the rock, was Agaar.

" 'Why are you here, Giant?' I said. 'What further torture have you in mind for me?'

" 'No torture, mortal, just talk,' he said, and he did not sound angry or unkind. 'I have a gift for you, a tribute to your prowess.' Agaar held out to me a beautiful glowing emerald, as large as a hen's egg. Between his fingers it was barely a speck of dust, but it rolled in my palm with a heft that promised great wealth.

" 'Why would you give me tribute to me when I abased myself?' I asked.

" 'You did better than you think. Behold.'

He pointed with one huge finger to the east. The snow stopped falling precisely where he pointed. All around the storm raged, but for this tunnel of empty sky. The wind stopped as if it hit a wall. In the distance I could see a deep river, cut hundreds of feet into an otherwise flat plain.

" 'We deceived you by magic,' Agaar said. 'That deep riverbed you cut with your sword when you tried to steal my water bag. Each slice of your sword rent the earth deeply. You tore a new canyon for the river to flow through. I was not sleeping next to you. You were in the midst of a spell.

" 'Likewise when you ate from the bottomless bowl. We filled that bowl with red-hot molten stone from the spewing mountain in the Land of Ice and Fire. The more lava you ate, the more the mountain produced. You ate so much you caused the mountain to create another just like it.

" 'Your wrestling partner was not my grandfather, but Old Age itself. No mortal can defeat Old Age, though we Giants may command it as we please. You worried Old Age. It had to fight strong to subdue you. As you may have gathered, Old Age cannot attack, but neither can it be resisted. So, be not ashamed of your performance. You underestimate your own power.'

" 'Why bother?' I said. 'Why go to all this trouble to transport me from this place by spell, and then to put me to the test?'

" 'You sniff about where you do not belong,' Agaar answered. He reached out a monstrous hand and shifted the flat stone on which we sat. Looking under it, I beheld a bottomless cavern stretching farther than I could see. Its walls glowed with diamonds and emeralds and its dimensions were unearthly. The width of the walls were greater than our father's farm pasture. It was an unimaginable treasure.

" 'Go home now, little man,' Agaar said, 'and take the respect of the Giants as you go. But'—he raised one huge finger—'if you return to this cave, I will pluck off your arm, beat you to death with it, and happily serve you for our supper. Understand?'

" 'Yes, Agaar,' I said.

" 'Be cautious in your journey home. Besides the homicidal mortals in this forest of rocks and stones, there are Dwarfs who never cease to search for the mine. Do not let them take you. They would be harsh with you to make you tell what you have learned. And if you tell, we would be unforgiving. When you wake up, do not tarry. Get going.'

"I nodded my reply while holding my emerald tightly in my palm. Agaar stepped out into the snowstorm, stretched to his full height, drew his huge cloak about him, and vanished.

"When I awoke, the storm was over. Snow lay several feet thick. I climbed onto my pony and we made our painful way back to the Odra. We camped on the rocky beach and waited for my rendezvous with the ship of our father's cousin.

"I stared into the fire, planning the house I would build with the riches from my emerald. I was not on my guard. I thought no Dwarf would bother me so far from the rocky ground and Iron Mountains. I was wrong. A shadow crossed my fire without sound. I looked into the sky, expecting a bird. Instead I saw a Dwarf, about my size, with three eyes in his head and no ears. His long brown hair hung to his waist in tangles and he wore a blacksmith's apron. His hands reached his knees. His arms were knotted with muscles. He smiled down at me with his black and broken teeth.

" 'Give me the emerald and take me to the mine,' he said. 'I am Othar.'

"He said his name as if I should know him and obey. He expected only my instant obedience. There was nothing to say. His ax hung over his back, but he could have killed me with his hands. He stood next to me, brazen and commanding, like the Immortal he was.

"I shook my head in exasperation and defeat. As he wasted his time sneering I drove my broadsword straight through the side of his knee and out the other side of his leg. He squawked like a hen. Black blood, thick and gooey, ran from his wound. I swung to my knees, got a better grip on my sword haft, and twisted as hard as I could. I levered his foot right off the rocky beach. He crashed onto his back.

"I jumped onto his chest and slammed my dagger through his shoulder, the one opposite his knee, deep into the ground. He was pinned fast. I sprang to my feet and twisted the sword again. His foot was now at an impossible angle to his leg. His knee was sideways to his hip. I leaned on my sword and ran it into the rocky earth until the haft struck the side of his leg. The pain forced him to quit squirming. In a ragged voice he told me that I could not keep him there forever, which was true. I would need my sword eventually.

"Othar twisted when I stepped over him. He reached for me with his free arm whenever I neared him. His huge hand gripped the air over and over. I could not approach him while that hand could grip. I untied my lance from my saddle and stabbed him through the palm of that hand. At least three feet of lance I drove into the ground. Othar was quite strong. I was afraid.

"I stole his ax and rode into the forest. There I cut many thick branches, at least ten, maybe more. I rode back to him and sat next to him as darkness fell, sharpening a point onto every branch with the edge of his ax. One by one I pierced him with these small lances and one by one pinned him fast to the ground. His anger was impressive. For a while he told me precisely what he would do to me for his revenge. When I banged a lance into the back of his mouth and out his skull, he stopped talking.

"I dared not sleep. I feared he would enslave me with a spell or call his friends. For three days and nights I watched him. Every few hours I would pound another stake through him, using the flat of his ax as my hammer. I neither ate nor drank nor slept.

"On the gray morning of the fourth day the ship

of our father's cousin crunched over the small rocks and slid onto the shore. Voices called to me. Feet splashed in the calm sea. A water skin was held to my lips. One voice, more insistent than the others, kept asking me why I had done what I did.

" 'I was being cautious,' I replied.

"Now you know the derivation of my name, but not the end or the purpose of my tale."

The ghost paused and looked at the three mortals. Before he could stop himself, Halberd raised his water skin toward the ghost.

"My throat is not dry, brother. And if it was, so what? I do not drink. I do not eat. I do not sleep. I serve my master, only, always, at every moment. Jotunheim does not allow me to speak. I have never been so happy to hear my own voice. I have not spoken once in the months since I was slain and my soul delivered to Jotunheim."

"Leave us not in such suspense," snapped Mälar. "Tell me what you did with the Dwarf."

"Food and drink and the absence of immediate terror brought a return to my senses. Othar lay on the sand, fuming, as quilled as the knitted ball holding needles in our mother's sewing kit. Immortal that he was, he was not badly hurt, though his thick black blood surrounded him.

"Our father, much to my surprise, was aboard his cousin's ship. Danyeel strode up to the humiliated Dwarf and gazed at him for some time. The Dwarf looked back with great hatred.

" 'Dwarf,' said Danyeel, 'your ugly, three-eyed face is in quite a predicament. If you call your friends to help you, they will humiliate you forever. However, if we turn you loose, you might harm my son. Neither option is any good for either of us. Let us, then, strike a bargain. Under such a bargain we will set you free in return for your sacred vow never to harm my son or anyone of mine or his family.'

"Danyeel gestured for me to unpin Othar's head so that his mouth could work. I must have pulled at least six sharpened branches just from his mouth, neck, and jaw. Othar worked his mouth in silence for some time. He spat blood onto the rocks.

"Danyeel said to him, 'What did you want from my son in the first place?'

" 'The emerald given him by the Giant, Agaar, and the location of the Giant's mine,' replied the Dwarf, though his voice was hoarse and gasping.

"Our father looked at me with new respect. The crew gasped as one man. I felt no pride. I only worried that the Dwarf might somehow get free. I longed to drive the branches I had removed from his head back into him. Now that I had eaten and drunk, I saw many spots on his body I had missed. I could easily have put another twenty stakes through the Dwarf.

"Danyeel gestured to me and I handed him the emerald. I began to consider that I might do something else with the rest of my life than pound stakes into Othar. I had not considered that possibility for three days and nights. Danyeel hefted the emerald in his fist and held it in front of the Dwarf's middle eye.

" 'Swear that for this emerald you will never bother, nor cause to be bothered, anyone here or their offspring at any time forever.'

" 'So long as they live,' answered Othar, his voice full of false sincerity.

" 'Am I possessed of such a stupid face?' screamed our father, as only he can. The Dwarf flinched at the sarcasm and contempt in Danyeel's voice. 'Is my countenance so foolish that even Dwarfs take me for an imbecile? You do not deserve freedom, Othar. You can rot on this beach until the birds eat you. We do not fear idiots, Immortal or otherwise. Good day.'

"Danyeel turned to leave. I was too afraid to move. The crew headed for the dragon ship, but slowly. They lifted provisions over the gunwales and those already aboard ran their oars through the holes.

" 'Come, my boy,' said Danyeel, 'that ugly peabrain is too stupid to worry about.'

" 'Forever,' shouted the Dwarf, 'forever to eternity, whether living or dead, I will not harm them or cause them to be harmed or bothered in any way.'

" 'Good,' said Danyeel, 'and after any of us or our offspring or relatives or loved ones are dead?'

" 'No harm of any kind shall come to their souls from my hand or from my direction or influence.'

" 'Perhaps,' said our father. 'you are not so stupid, but only hideously ugly. One so often follows the other. Let him up.'

"I stood over Othar, drawing my sticks from him one after the other. Some were stuck so deep into the ground that I had to prop a foot against his chest or head or leg to pull it out. Three of us were required to yank my sword from his knee. With every pull he grunted and writhed, but he said not a word.

"When he was free he stood and ran his lumpy hands over his wounds. Blood oozed from some and some were already closing. He held out his hand to Danyeel. Our father dropped my emerald into the Dwarf's palm. Othar's palm closed around it. Instantly he became a hawk, with the emerald in his claw. The hawk sat on the sands and beat his wings, glaring at us. He sprang into the air and flew upward in spirals. We lost sight of him in the hazy clouds.

"That," concluded the ghost, "is my tale."

The fire crackled as a cold wind blew in from the cave mouth. Beyond, the Thundering Falls roared on. No one spoke.

"And its purpose?" Mälar finally demanded.

"When I left on that quest, I was fearless. When I returned, I could not trust my own senses. I believed that nothing in the world was what it seemed. I grew cautious. Very cautious."

"Go on," Mälar said.

"Wait," said Usuthu, raising a huge palm.

Mälar and Halberd looked across the cave, where their weapons rested against the damp wall. The sky beyond the Thundering Falls had changed from black to dark blue. Pinkness showed on the southern horizon.

"It's near dawn," cried Halberd. "Are you safe, ghost of Mahvreeds?"

"No, he is not," replied Usuthu. "Something is near."

The ghost turned toward the mouth of the cave. Mahvreeds looked even more resigned to his fate.

"Yoo!" a shrill piercing voice called. "Yoo, Mahvreeds, are you hiding from me in my own cave? Is anyone from your family there, perchance? Here I come!"

"Is that the voice of the Giant Jotunheim?" asked Halberd, smiling despite his fear.

"Yes," said the ghost quietly.

"He prefers the company of other male Giants," Mälar said. "Does he not?"

"He has," replied Mahvreeds' ghost, "a certain feminine quality. His closest friend in Midgard was Ull. That is why he hates you so."

"Why should he hate us?"

"Because Halberd slew Ull."

"I didn't kill Ull," Halberd shouted. "The Giant Urd did. In a stupid quarrel. How could I slay an Immortal?"

"Never mind that now," Usuthu called from the mouth of the cave. "The Giant is halfway up the cliff."

The Mongol ran to the fire. Mahvreeds' ghost shrank back against the wall.

"Can you," Usuthu shouted to Mälar and Halberd, "fight?"

"I am not healed," said Mälar. "We cannot trust our lives to my bad arm."

"Nor mine," said Halberd, "but we need not. Pull out that log."

He pointed to the largest log in the fire. Its tip had burned down to a sharp fire-blackened point. The log was as big around as any Northland pony.

Usuthu knelt under the unburned end of the log and grunted. He rolled the end of the log onto his shoulder and stood. He raised the log without hesitation, but sweat burst from his forehead and the veins in his arms and legs jumped into view.

"Do not blind him!" cried the ghost.

"How can you fear this Giant?" said Mälar. "You are already dead. We are glad to see you, but not so glad as to join you permanently."

"We dead deserve no more pity than you are willing to offer, Mälar. I do not condemn you for your sentiments. You may live an eyeblink more, in terms of days, but I am dead forever. And so the Giant will live forever. If you injure him too severely, my punishment will last longer than you can imagine."

"Mälar, leave the ghost! Stop talking!" Usuthu shouted. "Seize the log and move to the wall of the cave."

Halberd and Mälar slid under the log, which still leaned its point into the fire. They straightened under it, bearing the down-slanting weight on their healthy shoulders. Usuthu stood over them by almost a foot. They staggered under the mass of the log and leaned against the wall.

"He cannot see us here. The glare of the fire protects us," whispered Mälar.

"Do not give him a chance," said Halberd. "When his head appears above the mouth of the cave, we strike."

The living mortals waited, their breath coming in short gasps, their legs wilting under the weight of the log.

"Mahvreeds, yoo! Here I aaam!" cried the piercing voice.

The mortals crouched in readiness. Jotunheim's head did not appear over the mouth of the cave. Instead, his giant hand and arm swept inward across the floor, grabbing and feeling for anything moving, shuffling and creeping from point to point like a hideous unseeing animal. The hand picked up logs and tossed them aside like matches. It fumbled near the fire pit and yanked back just before the flesh singed. Fingers strained to touch the far wall, but could not reach.

Halberd, Usuthu, and Mälar watched the tips of the giant fingers move nearer and nearer. Their hearts pounded. Mälar's legs began a twitching he could not control. The fingers came within feet of the trio, then withdrew.

"So!" said the voice triumphantly. "It's just as I told the Witch. Only the poor old ghost of Mahvreeds hides here. The mortals have long since fled in pursuit of Grettir."

Another giant arm reached over the lip of the cave. With a grunt, the huge head appeared.

Halberd spat out the whispered command. "Now!"

As befit the slowest, Mälar was in front. He shuffled his exhausted legs, fighting to reach running speed. Behind him Halberd and Usuthu matched stride for stride with great care. In ten steps they were running full bore. The long black tip of the log glowed bright red as the rushing air reignited the smoldering wood.

The tip burst into flame as their feet pounded on the cave floor. The Giant turned toward the sound, his mouth gaping in surprise.

Halberd had time to glimpse two clear blue eyes, a blond beard, and one long up-curving horn in the middle of the Giant's forehead. Jotunheim slapped one hand at them ineffectually. He screamed like a startled young girl. As he turned his head away from their attack one huge ear appeared in line with the onrushing mortals.

"Our target," yelled Halberd.

Three more racing steps and the log flamed from its tip to just in front of Mälar's hands. Mälar gritted his teeth. Two more steps and the sound of the Giant's scream filled the cave.

One more step and—

"Strike!" Usuthu screamed.

The flaming log rammed deep into the Giant's ear. Blood burst out like a wave, washing the three mortals back and tossing them onto the rocky floor. Jotunheim clasped a huge hand onto his punctured ear and dropped out of sight. His high cry sounded until it was drowned out by a splash.

"Halberd, hear me!" called the ghost of Mavhreeds.

A wind roared out of the pool below the cave and sucked at the ghost. His pale, translucent form elongated against the force of the wind. He tried to stand his ground, but his legs were already being yanked out of the cave.

Halberd pushed himself out of the brackish blood of the Giant and stumbled to the cave wall. His weeks of enchanted sleep had robbed his body of strength and speed. He grabbed the Jewel of Kyrwyn-Coyne and the stone knife Hrungnir and made his staggering way to the rapidly disappearing form of his brother's ghost.

Only Mahvreeds' outstretched arms and head remained visible. The rest of him tailed off down the cave mouth like a vanishing wisp of smoke.

Halberd drew a circle in the air around the ghost's head with the stone knife and held the jewel in the middle of the circle.

"This ghost will stand," Halberd said loudly, "until he has said his piece to me."

Halberd released the jewel and it hung in midair, caught in the middle of the circle Halberd had described. It glowed brightly. A fierce yellow light shot out of the jewel and bathed the ghost of Mavreeds.

For a flickering instant the ghost appeared in his full human form. His arms were muscled. His hair was dark black and his white teeth shone. Then the light flickered again and Mahvreeds became a pale shadow.

"I tug against the force of Jotunheim," Halberd said. "I pray you, speak to me quickly."

As the Giant's spell attempted to draw Mahvreeds down into Midgard, the Land of the Giants, Mahvreeds assumed his ghostly emptiness. As the jewel fought his spell Mahvreeds changed back into the shape of a living human. He wafted back and forth between the two worlds for several moments.

The power of the jewel took hold.

Mahvreeds stood before them as he had in life.

"I grew cautious," he said. "I came here to tell you, my brother, not to do the same. You will see things you cannot believe. Life may not be what it seems. Places and events and people are all subject to the magic of the worlds which lie around us and the power of the beings who inhabit them. If things seem strange—ignore it! Fight the enemies which appear before you. Fight them as they are. Worry not if they might be something else.

"Do not give in to fear! Trust yourself to be strong!"

"Is this," asked Halberd, "a prophecy? Do you foresee great magic in opposition to me?"

The form of Mahvreeds threw back its head and laughed.

"Great magic has opposed you at every moment of your quest. It may get worse. I know not. I am only a doomed ghost, here at a peril the living cannot comprehend. I cannot see your future, only my own.

"I urge you, my brother, do not hesitate. Do not think too much. Do not doubt yourself. Be strong! Avenge your brothers! Be strong for all of us! Kill the Witch and set us free!"

The roaring wind grew louder. Mahvreeds flickered between his ghostly form and his human appearance as rapidly as flames wave in a breeze. His face showed great fear. Then it became ghostly and showed no emotion at all.

"My master draws me down. Farewell, my brother."

He tried to lift a hand. He had no time left among the mortals.

The wind from Midgard seized Mahvreeds. The ghost returned to his pale form. The howling wind ghost whirled him over and over. His head contorted and lost all shape. He became as wind, as smoke.

The roar of the wind drowned all thought, let alone words. The living mortals covered their heads with their hands as logs flew around the cave and bounced off the stone walls.

Mahvreeds was now only smoke. His shape could not be recognized. His arms had disappeared. His head was a long pale string. Smoke with a screaming mouth. Smoke in unimaginable torment. The white smoke whirled around and around, forming a spiral in the air of the cave.

Mahvreeds was a white spiral. The spiral whirled crazily, bouncing off the floor, the ceiling, the damp rocky walls. The spiral coursed through the cave, howling like a hurricane. It flashed out into the night air. It hurtled back to Midgard, down, down, down.

The cave was silent. Deafened, the mortals raised their heads.

There was no more wind. There was no more Mahvreeds.

The Jewel of Kyrwyn-Coyne fell to the floor.

Etowah

"The Giants will be upon us," Halberd said, "We must go."

They looked around the cave. For the three weeks that Mälar had lived in the cave its appearance had never changed. Now, it was destroyed.

The enormous woodpile that had lined the far wall was scattered into chaos. Mammoth logs lay everywhere, toppled onto one another and broken like twigs. The jumbled forest reached to the distant ceiling, now invisible.

The fire had been tossed all over the cave. Here and there smoldering logs lit the predawn darkness. Over the mortals' heads a entangled tumble of logs threatened to collapse at any moment. Only the sloping wet wall of the cave held the tumble in place.

Halberd climbed carefully over, under, and through the maze of logs to retrieve the Jewel of Kyrwyn-Coyne. It flickered on the floor. He sat under a canopy of huge beams and worked the jewel back into its silver web at the butt of his broadsword. Halberd used the point of his three-sided stabbing dirk to twist the web closed.

Mälar picked his way through the tumbled forest and gathered his sword. He fastened the sheath belt around his waist. The sword slid into its scabbard. He felt like a whole man once more.

Mälar hefted the weapons he had stolen from the dead Skrælings. He rejected most. The short stabbing lance he no longer needed. His sword would serve that purpose. One stone-headed bashing mallet he tucked into the waistband of his Skræling leggings. A stone hatchet he hung from his neck by a thong. A brown dampness caught Mälar's eye. He shoved aside the huge end of a fallen log. Squashed beneath lay the coiled ropes the Eerhahkwoi had carried into the cave.

"Usuthu," he called, "I believe we have length enough here for you to lower us."

Usuthu nodded. He moved along the wall to the mouth of the cave. Overhead the precarious pile of logs creaked ominously. As Usuthu slid along, Mälar worked the rope free. Just as carefully, Mälar made his way to the Mongol.

They sat on the edge and dangled their legs over the lip of the cave. Hundreds of feet below, the Thundering Falls ended in a boiling pool of white foam and green water. In front of them the massive green wall fell and fell.

Mälar dropped each of the coils in turn and shook them to draw out tangles. The helmsman could not see how far down they reached. He drew them up in smooth, even pulls, flipping them into coils. As each rope was cleared and coiled, he bound one to the other.

Halberd neared them. He stopped under a leaning log. Mälar called to him.

"Find the most stable and largest log and loop this around it."

He threw the end of the rope to Halberd. The rope was as big around as Halberd's wrist, rough and damp. Yet the old man had tossed it like an apple. A tough bird, Halberd thought, strong and proud.

The Northman found a sturdy-looking V of logs. The open ends of the V were trapped under an endless mess of splintered timber. The V would hold.

Halberd slipped the end through them. He carried the rope back to Mälar. The sailor tied an immovable knot. He nodded. The three leaned on the rope gingerly. It resisted their pull. They yanked on it with all their combined strength. The V shifted slightly forward and then fell on itself. The rope held firm, buried under a formidable mountain of wood.

"I am the lightest, also the oldest," said Mälar, "and certainly the most cunning. I'll go first." He wrapped several coils of the thick rough hemp around his chest. He tied off the ends.

"Old man," Usuthu asked, "don't you wonder if the rope is long enough?"

"Also," Mälar said by way of reply to the question, "no doubt I am the most tired of the inside of this cave. So, no, I do not care."

The wet coils glistened in the coming dawn. Usuthu sat down and braced his feet against the side wall of the cave. He grabbed the rope in both hands. Mälar slipped off the cave edge without a word.

Usuthu let the rope out hand over hand. Mälar dangled over the Falls, dropping past the sheer wall he had not seen since the Giant Urd had raised him over it many weeks before.

Usuthu showed no effort from his labors. His hands moved easily. The first knot came through his fists. After a while, so did the second. Mälar had not called to them. If he had, they could not have heard him over the roar of the Falls.

"What happens when we are back on the ground?" Usuthu asked.

"We must make for the river which leads to the Mesipi," replied Halberd. "We need a boat, but there is no need to construct one until we reach the water. Though I have little wind or strength, I suppose we should move as quickly as we can to the river's head."

"What of our Skræling guide?"

"If Ishlanawanda's prophecy is true, he will find us."

The rope went slack in Usuthu's hands. Halberd leaned out over the cliff wall.

"I see nothing but more cliff," he said. "Take my feet."

The slack rope flopped at the cliff edge. Usuthu lay on his belly, his head in space. Halberd lay next to him and wormed his way outward. When half his body folded over the cliff, Usuthu took him by the feet.

Hanging free of the overhanging mouth of the cave, Halberd could see the old man far, far below, standing on a black rock beside the roiling pool, waving and smiling. Halberd, upside down, waved back.

"Pull me in, brother, the old man is safe."

Usuthu drew the wet rope back up the cliff. His brow was furrowed with worry.

"Did you see," he asked, "how determined Mälar was to go first, to show that he does not lack courage?"

"He fears," Halberd said, "that we fear that he has lost his nerve. He seeks to show us otherwise."

"Do you fear it?"

"Not from him. He has been too tough for too long."

"He has never," the Mongol said thoughtfully, "had to think about being brave. He simply is. The Witch, cleverly, has made him think about himself. For some men this is a good thing. For Mälar, I believe it is not."

Halberd stood and pulled his leather armor over his head. His broadsword went into the scabbard along his back. The thick haft stuck up over his head. He snugged it down with a thong. The three-sided stabbing dirk slid into the horizontal holster just above his hips, the stone knife into one just above. His perfectly balanced and razor-sharp battle-ax dropped into the loop on his left side. He felt ready for battle.

"We will keep him brave then," Halberd said, wrapping the thick wet coils around his chest.

"Take care," Usuthu answered, twisting the coils into a knot, "that we do not allow him to get killed proving how tough he still is. If the Witch wants him, she will take him, whether he fears her or not."

"Is she that strong?"

"Yes."

The Mongol jerked his head toward the cliff. Halberd dropped over the edge.

The rope played smoothly over the edge. Halberd hung in space, twirling slowly. Above him the Falls pounded down. Below, the splashing spray leaped up the cliff wall. The descent was breathtaking. The red dawn lit the Falls and the blowing spray soaked Halberd. He felt a bit humiliated. He had been raised to this cave on the palm on a Giant and now he was lowered from it like a baby. As he had lain in the Dream World, Usuthu had climbed down this formidable wall and back up again.

As the boiling pool grew nearer Halberd saw Mälar emerge from the woods, sword in hand. He grinned from ear to ear.

Mälar clambered out onto the huge black rock in the middle of the mad churning pool. He reached up for Halberd's feet and guided him onto the rock. Halberd stood. No more than five feet of slack piled at his feet.

"The Witch planned well," Mälar shouted over the deafening roar of the Falls. "Did she not?"

"She had the Skrælings make no more rope than was needed to lower us from the cave," Halberd bellowed back. "She intended to paralyze us by spell and bind us as captives."

Mälar tugged at the spray-soaked knots.

"So anxious am I," he called, "to get on the trail of the Witch I cannot make my fingers behave. Give me your dagger."

Halberd passed it over and the old man slashed at the rope with no apparent concentration. Halberd flinched backward at the careless stroke, but he was unharmed. The coils dropped, cleaved in two perfect halves.

Halberd was shocked. Mälar had been at sea his entire life. No wet rope had foiled him in the past. Halberd had never seen him use a knife on a knot. Ever. The Witch's words must be rattling around in the helmsman's skull. He was not himself. Halberd said nothing.

The slack rope washed back and forth in the wind from the thrashing Falls. Mälar left the rock. He vanished down the narrow chute by which they had climbed around behind the Thundering Falls. Halberd waited, balancing against the driving spray, craning his neck. A speck appeared on the black wet cliff. The speck became Usuthu, climbing down the rope hand over hand, slowly and steadily.

As Usuthu worked his way down, Halberd's heart filled with admiration. Lost in the middle of nowhere, his companions remained strong and purposeful. No mortal Halberd knew, including himself, could travel hand over hand down five hundred feet of rope. Usuthu began to swing wildly in midair as he neared the boiling pool. Halberd braced himself and held the rope steady. He could feel the wind sing through it. Between the pulling wind and the blowing spray he was reminded of the sea. Halberd longed for the broad deck of a dragon ship under his feet, the oars surging smoothly and a human enemy waiting to fight like men, not demons.

Usuthu's enormous feet swung over Halberd's head. Halberd guided him down carefully. He knew that Usuthu would feel uncomfortable on the rock in the midst of the pool. The Mongol could not swim.

Halberd took him by the elbow and they slid down the rock, jumped a small churning pool, and worked around the curtain of the Thundering Falls. Suddenly they were in front of the endless wall, staring at its massive whiteness from the security of the woods.

Halberd, free of the gloom and dampness at last, felt no sentiment for the cave or the Falls. There his ill-fated brother had tried to murder him. There Mälar had killed at least twenty enchanted Skrælings. Halberd did not consider those men his enemies.

Seduced by Grettir, they had attacked. Those Skrælings were victims, not warriors.

Halberd did not look back at the Falls. He trotted down the muddy path. Mälar stood ready and waiting, sword in hand.

"Can you find the first river?"

Mälar nodded. His face mirrored fierce excitement.

"I need the stars to guide me perfectly, but I can set a course."

"We have to use the existing paths," Usuthu said.

"Yes," said Mälar, "but that poses no problem. The Skrælings need the river, too. There must be a path which leads to it. I can wind our way there."

"We have a full day of light," Halberd said. "Let us trot at our best pace and not stop until nightfall."

"Can you two," asked the Mongol, "keep up a pace all day?"

The two Northmen nodded.

"We must," he continued, "avoid any battles, any party of Skrælings, be they Eerhahkwoi or Alkonkin. Our quest calls us south."

"I cannot bear to kill more of these brave men simply because they stand in our way," said Halberd. "If they invaded Northland, we would fight them. Their behavior is only natural."

"Aye," said Usuthu as Mälar nodded in assent. "Remember, though, I've no more arrows. If we see game, we must kill, butcher, and eat it on the run. No fires for a while, and no time to dry meat, much less to stalk it."

There was nothing more to be said. Mälar, the slowest, took the lead. In a few steps he moved at the graceful warrior's trot. Usuthu and Halberd fell in step behind him. They reached a speed slightly faster than a walk and slightly slower than a run.

Their weapons did not bounce. Their lungs did not burn. They could hold the pace all day. And so they would.

Mälar led them down the muddy trail, moving south and west.

That night Halberd lay cradled in the thick branches of an overhanging tree. Mälar calculated that they had come almost half the distance to the northernmost of the two rivers. He and the Mongol slept in nearby branches. They had avoided several Skræling hunting parties and they felt no fear of discovery. The Eerhahkwoi did not like to venture forth at night.

Halberd gripped his ax in his hand and fell asleep.

Halberd moves down a trail overgrown with green bushes. No sunlight penetrates. Nearby a rushing river is heard. Halberd emerges from the trail to a tiny village. One Eerhahkwoi longhouse stands by a fire pit. The skin flap over the opening hole is thrown aside and a young Skræling man emerges.

Halberd stares at him. The boy is sixteen or maybe eighteen. It is hard to tell with savages. The boy carries a small stone-headed mace. He smiles at Halberd and beckons the Viking forward.

"I am Etowah," he says, speaking not in the Viking tongue, but in Eerhahkwoi. Halberd understands perfectly.

"Where is this place?" Halberd asks, in the language of the Vikings.

"This is the village of my dreams."

"I am in your dreams?"

"Yes," Etowah replies. "It is as Ishlanawanda foretold. Many months ago she prepared me for this night. She told me a white man/god would seek me out and that I would guide him to the land of the flesh-eaters."

"How is it that I am here? I long to travel to another's dreams, but now I have done it without knowing how."

"It is ordained," Etowah says. "I am to aid you and the black white-man/god."

"We are not gods, but merely men," Halberd says with some annoyance. "Mortal and easy to kill. Why do you call my companion a black white man?"

"You are a white man/god, are you not? And your giant friend, who can destroy villages alone and who slew the great snake of the Eastern Nokoni, he is of your tribe, only his skin has been turned black, so he is a black white-man/god."

My black friend, who is called Usuthu, is not of my tribe," answers Halberd. "His people are as different from mine as it is possible for two tribes to differ. He is not a black white man. He is a black man. As I am white and you are brown."

"Is he human?"

"Yes."

"And mortal?"

"Look me in the eye, Etowah, and swear to me that you do not serve Grettir."

Halberd yanks the stone knife from his leather armor and holds it to the boy's heart.

"If you swear falsely, then this knife shall find your heart. I need not put force behind its blade. Your lie will draw the beating organ onto the sacred blade."

"I serve Ishlanawanda, you and the animals from which I sprang."

"Then I will admit to you that Usuthu is mortal and may be slain. Woe betide whoever tries it, however. What do you mean 'animals'?"

"I was raised not by man but by several animals. The wolf, the bear, the mole, and the eagle. I have many skills which I learned from all of them and many other skills which I gained by spying upon man. Many times I have taken the form of the mole and ventured to the village of the Eerhahkwoi and Alkonkins."

"You become a mole?"

"No. I cast my spirit out into the world to perceive as a mole perceives."

"Then," Halberd says with a faint, disbelieving smile, "you must be a powerful young man."

"Not yet," Etowah replies.

"You are neither Alkonkin nor Eerhahkwoi?"

"I am of no tribe. I am of the woods, the animals, and Woncan Tonka."

"Why would you serve Ishlanawanda?"

"She found me in the World of Dreams. She guided me and taught me much. She has promised me that you will show me great adventure."

"But we are in the Dream World. How can you help me? Are you to be my guide in this world now that I can no longer return to her village?"

"You have been to Ishlanawanda's village?" the boy gasps. "None are allowed there but those of her tribe. No outsider ever ventures past the magic screen."

Halberd says nothing. He awaits an answer to his question.

Etowah seems distracted as he looks around the forest surrounding his camp.

"A powerful enemy comes," he says.

"Do you," barks Halberd, in the voice of command, "exist only in this Dream World?"

Etowah looks at Halberd in shock. He smiles as he comprehends Halberd's confusion.

"No," he says proudly, "I am a living, mortal shaman, as you are. I have sought you in this dream so that you will know me when I appear to you in the Waking World."

He looks around fearfully.

"I may not tarry here. I brought no weapon with me, the better to appear peaceful to you when we met. This mace is symbolic. It cannot be used for violence. You may fight the oncoming demon if you wish, but not here. This is my home. If I awake, then none can find it. Leave me."

"What does a man of your powers care if he doesn't have a weapon?" Halberd asks mockingly. "Why don't you turn into an eagle and fly away?"

"My powers are for the world of animals and that is the Waking World. Animals in that world do not dream. Here I have no power."

Shame courses through Halberd. Dangling from a rope, sleeping while others fought his fight; his helplessness has made him unobservant, cruel, even stupid. Why should he mock this boy, whom Ishlanawanda has sent to help him?

"I have little patience for others today, Etowah," Halberd says quietly. "My disrespect shames me, not you. I do not think you a coward. If you must, go."

"Go I shall, shaman. We will meet in the Waking World. Tomorrow."

Down the trail a large tree falls over with a ground-shaking crash. Etowah is clearly scared. His feet long to fly, but his heart holds him until the conversation is done.

"If I survive," Halberd says, "whatever comes down the trail."

"You will," Etowah replies nervously. "But if I stay, I won't. So, good-bye. For now."

Halberd nods, impressed by the young boy's dignity.

Etowah races down the trail to his small encampment. When he reaches the round door opening of his longhouse, the encampment vanishes.

Halberd moves back into the woods. He runs down the trail, clutching his ax in one hand and Hrungnir in the other. Ahead, branches break and trees fall over. Something big, something monstrous, rushes through the forest, ignoring the trail, throwing trees and stones aside as it smashes along.

Halberd takes a combat stance in the midst of the trail. His ax balances like an extension of his arm. Another sapling falls across the trail.

"Come ahead, whatever you are," Halberd calls. "I am in the mood to fight. Come and kill me, if you can."

An enormous brown bear, three times the size of Usuthu, stands erect at the trail head, his paws hanging limply at his side. It is obviously a creature of enchantment. No real bear would waste energy tossing trees about. Its exertions have tired it.

Froth gathers at the corner of his mouth. Yellow fangs glisten. The bear's matted fur glows. His chest is unmarked by battle scars. His eyes are too aware.

"Great bear," says Halberd, "you are not what you seem. Who or what occupies your form in this Dream World?"

The bear looks over Halberd's head. He searches, obviously, for Etowah's village. He does not speak. His breath comes in rasping grunts.

"Come, come," barks Halberd. "I do not really

care. I am filled with frustration at my long inactivity. I need to fight my own battles for once. If you challenge me, I will slay you no matter what you are. So speak freely."

The bear lowers his gaze and scrutinizes Halberd from his head to his toes.

"Who are you, little tough-talking mortal?" it says, "Where is Etowah?"

Blood lust rings in Halberd's heart. His fingers clench the ax handle so tightly his knuckles crack. But Halberd has not lived so long without cunning. The bear's calm tone and distinct pronunciation of the boy's name fill Halberd with caution. And, more dangerously, curiosity.

The bear speaks with a growling grunt, but his language is that of the Northmen. Giants, Halberd knows, do not travel to the Dream World. Nor do Dwarfs. They might be born there, and live there forever, but they cannot travel from one world to the next. This bear learned the Northland tongue at the foot of Grettir.

Or, for all I know of this world, Halberd thinks, it may well be inhabited by bears who speak. Halberd thinks of the only true test; if this bear serves Grettir, then doubtless it should know his name.

"I am Halberd," he replies, no fear in his voice, "and I will cleave you from the nave to the chops if you do not turn tail this instant."

The bear turns his great mouth to the sky and growls long and loud. Loops of spittle run from his mouth. He raises his claws to the sky and stamps one great paw. Halberd fights for balance as the trail shakes from the force.

"Well, Dream Warrior," the bears growls slowly and deliberately, "my mistress will be well pleased with me. Or perhaps not. Perhaps she would rather I brought you to her alive. Alas, this I cannot do. Too much pleasure will I derive from stretching your neck until your head pops off."

Halberd has only the briefest instant to regret his own strong words. In truth, he has never wielded a weapon against a being who dwelled in the Dream World. If his ax proves useless, the fight will be very short.

The bear humps his huge back and brings his paws together in front of him, banging his claws with an unearthly click.

This, thinks Halberd, is not a bear. He revels too much in the strength he has, in his claws, in his size. He is not accustomed to fighting in the form of a bear. That is my sole advantage.

Halberd feints to his left, moving forward. The bear slams one huge paw down where Halberd would have been. Dust flies upward. Halberd jumps back to his right. The bear sweeps a paw sideways. Halberd falls flat to the trail and the paw crashes into a tree, knocking it to the ground.

The tree falls onto the bear, who pushes it aside impatiently. Halberd leaps in between the bear's braced and wide-spread feet. Swinging the ax up and behind his head, as if splitting a huge log for the fireplace, Halberd drives the ax dead center into the bear's matted, furry chest. He powers the blow with all his force.

The bear's chest muscles are hard and springy, like an interwoven armor made of flesh. The ax hesitates, but Halberd leans on the handle and the blade goes deep. The bear shrieks in pain. Blood gouts from the wound, shooting over Halberd's head in a long stream.

Halberd releases the ax and whips his broadsword from the scabbard behind his head. He jumps over the bear's huge paw and circles behind the enraged beast. The bear responds not with the instant anger and complete disregard for pain of his species, but with the shock, hesitation, and dismay of a human.

He no longer roars at the sky. He touches the ax gingerly, pushing at the handle with a great paw. Halberd knows that a real bear would have not even noticed the pain of the ax. The ax barely occupies a third of his huge chest.

The bear seems to have forgotten the fight. Halberd braces his feet like a woodcutter and takes a roundhouse swing. All the frustration of the past weeks drives his sword.

His sword takes the bear in the back of his left knee joint. The blade bites into the joint and sticks, like an ax in a tree. The bear topples over backward, trapping the sword in his folding leg. He crashes into the ground. A cloud of dust rises at the impact.

Halberd pushes through the clinging dust. He shoves Hrungnir into the bear's ear hard enough to bring blood.

"Demon," Halberd cries, "by the power of this knife I command your true form to be revealed."

The bear alters shape so quickly that Halberd is tossed to the dusty ground. His vision is obscured. Halberd waves his hand in the dry air, trying to clear the dust. A whistling sound warns him and he leans back at the waist. The point of his own sword slices through the air, missing him by inches.

Halberd scuttles backward, out of the dust cloud.

He holds Hrungnir in his left hand and his three-sided stabbing dagger in his right. The handle of his ax is the first thing he sees emerge from the dust. It is still embedded in the chest of whatever was the bear. Though still horizontal, the handle is only a couple of feet off the ground.

A Skræling such as Halberd has never seen before steps forward. His blood seeps out around the ax blade. He drags his left leg behind him. He holds Halberd's sword in a limp hand. The blade is half his height. He is no more than four feet tall. He smiles at Halberd and blood bubbles up out of his mouth. Halberd's ax fills him from the top of his leggings to the bottom of his neck. The blade is deep within.

Yet he still holds Halberd's sword and he still comes forward.

"Speak, fiend," says Halberd, backing up. "What are you?"

"Arrhak," the midget Skræling says. His words are drowned by the blood dribbling from his mouth.

"Serve you Grettir?"

The lurching warrior nods. He feebly chops at the air with Halberd's sword.

"Do you belong in this world?"

The Skræling shakes his head. He beckons Halberd nearer with a feeble gesture.

Halberd holsters his dagger and steps forward.

The horrible little man hurls the broadsword like a spear into Halberd's face.

Halberd deflects the feeble toss with one arm, knocking his sword aside. Reaching out, he snatches the ax from the Skræling's chest. With a reverse of that motion he shoves the small dying horror backward. The Skræling collapses into his own blood. His head droops.

Halberd touches the man with the point of Hrungnir.

"You are enchanted still. Therefore I may control

you with this knife. You may not die until you tell me what I need to know. Why are you here?"

"Grettir," the Skræling whispers, "caught me in the Dream World. I am but an apprentice shaman. I used a spell I did not understand. When I fell asleep and dreamed, she was waiting for me. She enslaved me and bade me kill young Etowah. I knew how to assume the form of animals in this world and so I became a bear."

"What," Halberd demands, "is Arrhak?"

"My tribe." Blood gushes from his nostrils.

"You are free to die." Halberd returns the stone knife to its holster.

The little warrior sags to ground.

Halberd awakes.

Mälar and Usuthu listened closely to the tale of his dream. Listening did not slow them in their trot and they made certain that speaking did not slow Halberd.

"If she sees all that is to come in the future," said Mälar, "then we cannot hope to defeat her."

"She cannot see all," countered Usuthu. "She did not expect Halberd to be in the Dream World. She did not expect Etowah to have revealed himself to Halberd. She hoped to slay the youngster before he aided us."

"Trapping the unwary in the Dream World has worked for her before," Halberd said, jumping over a large rock in the middle of the trail.

"I suspect treachery," Mälar said.

Halberd and Usuthu said nothing. Sixty years of shipboard politics had given the old man an instinct for betrayal. They ran another league in silence as Mälar worked it out in his mind.

"The village Elders in the Dream World hate you.

I fear one of them counsels with Grettir and tells her all that transpires in the village."

Halberd stayed silent. The idea had merit. The Elders thought they had nothing to gain by being kind to him. Perhaps they hoped Grettir would be more controllable than he. Or perhaps one of them betrayed his own village out of jealousy. Grettir was an enemy they could not defeat, but how would they know that? She could disguise her intentions.

"Perhaps," said Usuthu, "it is not that simple. Perhaps Etowah is enslaved by Grettir. The Witch might have sacrificed the small Skræling in order to guarantee Etowah's credibility."

Halberd and Mälar nodded. It was possible.

"Once I start to doubt everyone, then any treachery is possible," Halberd said. "I'll take the advice of my brother's ghost and deal with the world as I find it."

"Then you trust Etowah?"

"We will see if he can help us, Mälar," Halberd answered. "And we will watch him as we watched Labrans."

The trail wound south and west. They trotted all day. There was nothing to be said. When they heard voices or sounds of a hunting party, they moved off the trail into the thick forest or up a tree. Skrælings of both tribes moved by without noticing them all day.

When the sun fell and the stars emerged, Mälar waved them to a halt. They squatted by a stream and drank handfuls of cool, clear water.

"I know precisely where we are. The first of the rivers lies less than a league from us."

"Why don't we hear the rushing water?" Usuthu demanded.

"Because this river must be very slow. Halberd, have you considered what sort of craft we will travel this river in? We cannot build a seagoing skin canoe such as we sailed from Vinland to the Beach of Blood. I have seen no water-bound mammals whose hides would serve for the walls."

"In Ishlanawanda's village they traveled the waters in even smaller canoes made of bark over a wood frame. I can draw them, and the trees which provide the bark are plentiful. The shape is similar to our previous native craft, but the bottom is not so flat and the boat remains open. We do not sit in holes cut in skin, but rather kneel on the bark floor of the boat."

"All right. That sounds easy," Mälar said. "How is the bark secured to the wooden frame?"

Halberd gaped at his companions. He lowered his face as it burned red.

"By the gods! I have no idea." Halberd could not remember being so embarrassed as a grown man.

"By sewing together the bark and sealing the joints with sap!"

The unknown voice echoed from a cluster of thick, short evergreens.

"He spoke in the Skræling tongue," Usuthu whispered. "How is it that we understand him?" He crouched by the stream, his sword up, scanning the trees.

Mälar had not moved. He had not drawn his sword. In one hand he lazily held the stone bashing mallet of the dead Eerhahkwoi.

"I understand you," he said, "and you speak in Mongol while I converse in the civilized language of the North. We understand him because we are meant to. That voice could only belong to Halberd's young guide."

"Are you truly so calm?" Halberd asked.

"If I am not, you nor Usuthu nor anyone else will ever figure it out. Including Grettir. Call your friend."

"And if it is not Etowah, but some demon sent by Grettir?"

"Then we shall slay it or it us. Let it happen, whatever it is. Call him."

"Etowah! Come forward in peace."

The trees shifted and the young Skræling emerged. He was dressed for a ceremony. His deerskin leggings were soft and embroidered with porcupine quills. His vest hung with charms and twists of animal hair. He carried a short lance and a long stone knife, the haft wrapped in dried leather. Tied in the black line of his hair, which stood straight up and ran from his forehead to his neck, was an eagle feather. His face was marked with three short red horizontal lines, running from his eyes to his ears.

He raised one hand toward them, palm facing them, fingers pointing up.

Only Usuthu returned the gesture.

"Come, Etowah," the Mongol said, "sit by us and give us your counsel."

"I understand the black white-man/god," the boy said. "How can this be?"

"I am a man, not a god, and I am black, not white. Call me only by my name and not by some title of your invention. My name is Usuthu."

"And mine," said the helmsman, standing, "is Mälar."

Etowah nodded at the group.

"Forgive my curiosity," he said, "but if you are not

a god, then surely you come from a tribe of the largest men this world knows."

Usuthu only shook his head.

Halberd interrupted. "How did you locate us?"

"I sent myself forth as an eagle. I have flown over you, keeping watch, this entire day."

"How near are we," asked Mälar, "to the river?"

"No more than one hour's run, if you maintain your pace."

The old man grinned from ear to ear.

"You are a admirable young savage," he said, chortling with pride. "And you recognize great navigation when you encounter it. Doubtless we will get along just fine."

"What," said the Skræling, "is navigation?"

"Etowah," said Usuthu with grave dignity, "you bear a long knife. Is there some ceremony which you expect of us?"

Etowah answered by drawing the knife along the inside of his left palm. Blood bled brightly along the path it traced. He extended the knife to Usuthu.

The Mongol slit his own hand and offered it to the boy. They grasped hands and so mingled their blood. Halberd took the knife from his friend. The ceremony was repeated. Mälar did not move.

The three waited for him to take the knife.

"I hope you will take no offense, young Skræling, but my life is now in peril and I must beware of all beings, even well-meaning would-be shamans." The old man spoke with kindness.

"I do not distrust you now," he continued, "and I do not anticipate distrusting you in the near future. But if the time comes when I must kill you to save myself, I do not wish the bond of brotherhood to come between me and that necessity. I will die before I will allow harm to befall Halberd or Usuthu. Their lives are all the responsibility I can endure. I will not be responsible for you as well.

"If you are old enough to be a man, then perhaps you can understand. If not, then I am sorry, but that is my way and my way is set."

Etowah looked away, his face burning in shame.

"I do not understand," he spoke quietly, "but I do not challenge your judgment. But I consider you my blood brother and would give my life for yours, if need be."

"So be it," said Mälar. "Life is not fair and neither is your situation or your vow. However, you chose both. If you need to hold yourself to this foolish oath, then you will. If you do not, then I will bear you no malice."

Halberd shrugged at Usuthu. The old man had always been blunt and careful about his choice of friends. His statement had opened their eyes to the new reality; before, they had been three who thought as one. Now a fourth joined them. He joined to serve, but that did not mean he would think as they thought or react as they reacted. He could slow them down, imperil them, get them killed.

Halberd and Usuthu had sworn fealty to this brave savage. He was, they felt, a budding shaman. They owed him brotherhood for that, if nothing more. Each knew the other had not taken the oath lightly.

"Let us," said Halberd, clearing his throat after this blunt exchange, "make for the river."

The three set off at their determined trot. Etowah, young and eager, ran ahead, pulling branches aside and pointing the way. The evergreen forest ran right to the bank.

The river lapped at the shallow bank. The water

was wide, flat, sluggish, and brown. It moved slowly, with no rapids in sight. Small turbulent whirlpools popped up, swirled downstream for a yard or two, and disappeared. The opposite bank showed no sign of life. Trees crowded the water and birds soared overhead.

They leaned out of the trees and scanned down the river. As far as they could see, it ran in a thick tunnel of trees. No other canoe or human was visible.

"If only I had arrows," said Usuthu, "I would feel much safer. On this river we will be completely exposed, with no way to return fire."

"Where," Mälar said to Etowah, "is your bow, my son?"

"I carry no bow," the boy said, searching the far bank for something he did not name.

"Why not?"

"A bow is a weapon of attack. I attack no one. My weapons are for defense only."

"How then," asked Halberd, "do you hunt?"

"I stalk my fellow creatures in the form of a beast. When I have found them, I take myself to them and slay them face-to-face."

"Have you gone hungry for many days?"

"With all respect due my elder, Usuthu, no mortal may track or stalk as I. I have lived among the animals my entire life. No human taint mars my smell or judgment."

"If this be true," said Mälar, "then you will earn your place as my blood brother."

Etowah nodded to the old helmsman, as if bowing to his will.

"On the far bank," he said, "behind that clump of evergreens, lies a copse of the white-bark saplings you require for your canoe."

"Are there none on this side?" Usuthu asked. "I cannot swim."

"This bank is all evergreen, as far as I have seen for some leagues."

"We will tow you," said Halberd, locking down each of his weapons with a piece of thong.

Halberd and Mälar slid into the murky water, which was deep all the way to the bank. The gentle pull of the current had no effect on them at all.

Usuthu put his legs into the water.

"Ah!" he cried. "It's warm."

"Spring is here," said Mälar. "Now shut up and get into the river."

Usuthu turned onto his back. His golden shield shone in the sun. Mälar and Halberd took him by the shoulders and frog-kicked out into the water. Etowah dived in and swam to the middle of the river in a few powerful strokes.

"I am the scout," he shouted. "I will secure the bank."

He swam ahead.

"Many exposed crossings have I made," said Mälar, "but none to equal this."

"If this boy scouts as he claims, then we will not be surprised."

Mälar snorted.

The river seemed wider from the middle than it had at the banks. They paused in its midst, treading the brown water, and stared westward. The river wound through the woods in huge sweeping bends. No settlement marred its banks.

"This current is too slow for our comfort," said Mälar.

"Why?" Usuthu spoke from flat on his back, his arms spread.

"Because it will not carry us at any great speed, as ocean currents do. We will have to paddle for every league we make."

They reached the bank without incident. After shaking off the water, they called for Etowah. They followed the sound of his voice but could not find him.

"Farther," he called.

In a tiny clearing, cut off from view by thick thorn bushes, Etowah sat by a smokeless fire, roasting three rabbits on sticks. Halberd had not tasted freshly cooked meat in three days and nights. The three dropped to the ground and ate without a word. Etowah munched on a fourth rabbit, cooked days before, which hung from a tree.

"How long has this site been prepared?" asked Halberd.

"For two weeks. I knew this is where we would cross. Cut saplings and peeled bark await you, just outside this clearing."

"You are a good boy," said Mälar, tossing his bones into the fire. "I hope you sleep well." He curled onto his side and began to snore.

"I will take the first watch," said Halberd. "Usuthu, you sleep through the night. We will need your strength tomorrow. Etowah, I'll wake you when the moon appears. You will guard us for the rest of the night. You are young. You don't need sleep."

The camp was soon silent. Embers glowed in the cookfire and Halberd stared up at the stars. I cannot pretend, he thought, that my living brothers and parents in Northland see the same night sky. I am too far west for that to be true. Besides, Northland is no longer my home. I must carry it in my heart, with my love for Ishlanawanda.

"And your lust for me?" The whisper cut through to his bones. The fire flared once and died again. An evil twisting wind announced that Grettir had come and gone.

"I fear you not. I lust for you less."

She did not hear his reply. It was a new tactic, this hit and run. She spoke only to rattle him, to show Halberd that she knew where he was. Fine, he thought, let her track us. She will send her forces against us and we will kill them.

Etowah rolled to his feet, his stone hatchet in his hand.

"I dreamt I heard a voice," he whispered to Halberd. "She frightened me."

"She should. The Witch was close at hand."

Etowah shivered. It was not cold.

"Etowah," Halberd said fiercely, "do not go to the Dream World so long as your journey with us."

The startled boy said nothing.

"Answer me! Can you control your visits to that world? Can you sleep and not go there?"

Etowah nodded. "But that is one of my newfound shaman's powers. I struggled to gain access. I worked hard. How can you deny me?"

"The Witch holds sway there, even over me. I do not venture forth in my dreams without the sacred knife. Without it I'm at her mercy, as you are."

"Then loan it to me, that I might dream."

Halberd's instant rage surprised him. He grabbed the boy by one arm.

"The knife is mine, only mine," Halberd whispered. "I pulled it from the skeleton of my dead brother and with it I will slay Grettir. If you want to convince me that you are her slave, then ask me again for the knife. If ever you so much as touch it, I'll kill you."

"I am young," Etowah said, in a small miserable voice, "so I speak recklessly. Accept my apologies."

"I can accept only so many. Remember that Mälar, Usuthu, and I have fought and traveled together for months. We can bear new vexations but seldom. You and I are blood brothers and yet may be friends, but it will go better for you if you think always before speaking and speak anyway as little as possible."

Etowah nodded.

"Take the guard then, and wake me at daybreak."

Halberd curled up near the embers and slept. He was careful not to dream.

Halberd awoke to the sound of snapping branches and Mälar cursing. The sailor and the young shaman sat around a pile of long springy saplings. Mälar studied each one carefully, testing the trueness of the grain and the strength from end to end.

The fire roared. More fresh rabbit dripped fat into the flames. The sun was well across its journey in the morning sky.

Halberd slipped to the river for a long purposeful wash, his first in many days. Usuthu was gone. Birds cawed in the dawn and fish splashed, but no other life showed. Halberd filled his drinking skin.

"Where is Usuthu?"

Neither the boy nor the shipbuilder looked up.

"Gone hunting," Mälar muttered. "Why don't you join him?"

Halberd considered his aching legs.

"I'd rather rest my legs and observe your skill."

"Do so, then, if watching does not involve asking questions. By the way, you needn't draw the Skræling canoes for me—young Etowah has taken care of that. Further, he has an interesting tactical suggestion."

Halberd raised his eyebrows—the two were getting along better than he had expected.

"He suggests that, as long as Usuthu lacks arrows, we travel the river at night. He can fly ahead to warn us of rapids or falls and we would not be detected."

Halberd nodded, impressed. The idea was sound.

"How long to build the canoe?"

"No more than today, tonight, and a bit of tomorrow night."

"When do we sail?"

Mälar looked up from his pile as if seeing Halberd for the first time.

"I just told you. Tomorrow night. Go and get us meat. We need hides for drinking skins and rations."

Halberd pulled on his armor and stepped into the deep woods. Game ran plentifully here. Halberd watched for Skrælings as one nagging question worked at him. Why had all the Eerhahkwoi and Alkonkin hunting parties not noticed them? Earlier flight from those warriors had taught them that they were trackers extraordinaire, better than even Usuthu. Yet they had hidden like children under a clump of leaves and remained undetected. Was it purposeful? Did the Skrælings not want to find them? Or had Grettir promised them some greater reward than vengeance against the man gods?

A flicker in the bushes drew Halberd's eye. When hunting one must never look to see a whole deer, but seek instead to see only the smallest part of one. The flicker came again. It was an ear, moving back and forth. Halberd froze.

The deer drew nearer. It stepped into Halberd's tiny clearing. He dared not reach for a weapon. The deer was right in front of him. A loud whistle sounded.

The deer reared onto its hind legs, turning, but the whistle ended with a *thunk*, and the deer fell dead.

Under it gleamed one of Usuthu's golden shields.

His huge black head appeared between two clumps of bushes.

"I slung it at the beast sideways," he said. "Without arrows I cannot work my will at any distance."

The game in the Unknown World seemed tame and unafraid of man. His scent did not spook the animals and his tread did not frighten them. From just after noonday until dusk the hunters worked the game trails. The deer, antelope, and smaller, fur-bearing animals practically walked onto the points of their swords. It was hardly sport, but hungry men with a long journey ahead do not desire sport.

They desire food.

The stars shone when Halberd and Usuthu dropped their load of skinned carcasses by the fire.

A small drying rack had been assembled by the fire. Halberd draped it with strips of venison while Usuthu pushed large flanks onto sticks and braced the sticks over the blaze. The day of hunting had restored their spirits. Mälar called them and they went to the river's edge.

The skeleton of the canoe was finished. The frame was as long as two men and gently rose to a point at each end. The bow and stern were upswept, not flat like the canoes of the Skrælings on Vinland. The bottom had a slight keel but remained broad and almost flat. Struts lined the deck and, reaching from just below each gunwale, were four seats of wide board.

Mälar looked very pleased and more relaxed than Halberd had seen in months.

"The Skrælings rest upon one knee," he said, "or sit on the bottom of their craft, but I think we need a higher vantage from which to shoot our arrows."

"What arrows are those?" asked Usuthu.

"The boy tells me that we will journey on this river, known to the Skrælings as the Alluwe, for only a short while. When we join the second, larger river, the Attyo, we will encounter a great burial mound, shaped like a snake. In that mound, he affirms, are the graves of many warriors. These once-mighty Skrælings, he says, were buried with all of their arms, and these arms we may steal to replenish ourselves."

By tone of voice it was impossible to tell if Mälar believed the boy or was mocking him. It was Mälar's normal way of relating the advice of another. Halberd was shocked to feel how grateful he was to hear Mälar speaking in that tone. Mälar had not shown such spirit since the two Giants fought to the death. However, none of them had ever seen a burial mound shaped like a snake. Etowah's youthful exuberance made it natural to disbelieve whatever he said.

"You feel well, helmsman?"

"To build any craft raises my hopes," Mälar answered, "but to build a craft of such delicacy and usefulness cheers me no end."

"Apparently," said Usuthu, in a dark tone, "if you wish me to arm myself with the arrows of dead men."

"You robbed them as they fell at your feet in the village," Mälar retorted.

"The arms of men I slay are my booty, earned in battle and by the risk of my life. The arms of ghosts are exactly that. How will they defend themselves in the afterlife if I steal from them?"

"How will I," Mälar said, "defend myself in this life if you do not? I haven't your range with a bow. No living mortal does. Have you found stones for arrowheads here?"

"Mälar," Halberd said with great weariness, "don't play at being dense. We have no time to chip stone arrowheads. Our Grandfather's Grandfathers had forgotten how, so long have Northmen employed arrowheads of metal. Do you expect us now to remember?"

"Don't blame me," Mälar shot back, "if you were too shortsighted to bring a blacksmith along this journey. If you want to live, then swallow your principles—we cannot survive without arrows and we cannot make them. Therefore we will steal."

"As usual, old man," Usuthu said, "you are right and wrong at the same time. I am practical. I will steal from the dead. I will rob graves. I will bust dusty old bones into splinters so I can snatch the weapons upon which those old bones lie. But bury my principles? I think not."

"Fine." Mälar turned back to the frame. "Now pick up those sheets of bark and lay them on the frame. Halberd, you sew them together." He handed the shaman a large bone needle. Running through its eye was a coarse string of brown rootlike twists.

"What is this, Mälar?"

"Root twisted into thick thread. Etowah showed me the root and made the twists. It is apparently the Skræling way."

The mottled gray and white bark lay curled up all around them. Each sheet was a foot or two in length and each as delicate as thick paper.

"This stuff won't tear when we hit rocks or roots?"

"Etowah assures me," Mälar replied in that inscrutable mocking tone, "that though durable, the bark of this tree is also flexible."

"Will it," asked Halberd, "hold when we take the canoe through rapids?"

"We shall never know. We shall never take it through any."

Halberd sighed. When Mälar was happy, he made himself even happier by endless roundabout conversations. It could be very aggravating. On his long journeys shipmates often threatened to throw him over the side, but none ever had. None could.

"All right, Mälar," Halberd said as if talking to a child, "why won't we?"

"Because our young guide will scout the river for us in the form of an eagle. If he spies water too rough for us to cross, we will lift our canoe out of the river and walk around the zone of danger."

"A craft so light can bear us all safely?" Usuthu was shocked.

"I have never seen its like either, Usuthu," Mälar said kindly.

"Old man," Halberd said with some aggravation, "clearly you asked the boy these same questions. You are never so kind to ignorance unless recently cured of it yourself. Why can't you just give us a simple answer to a simple question?"

"Like Usuthu," Mälar answered, "I cannot bury my principles."

Halberd shook his head and returned to his labor. Usuthu spread the thin sheets with his enormous hands, and held them against the wooden frame. Halberd punctured the bark. He wound the needle round and round its edge, lashing the bark sheet to the wooden frame. When one sheet reached its end, Halberd overlapped it with another. The work was painstaking and slow. Sweat rolled into his eyes, which were already stung by the smoke from the torch that Etowah held over the slowly forming canoe.

The parchmentlike bark unrolled with a loud crackling. Some sheets split in his hands and some refused to curl along the contours of the frame. It was frustrating.

"I am not a craftsman," Halberd said, smiling. "I never liked tools or working with my hands. Mälar likes to see me suffer at this work."

"When you commanded a dragon ship, you had a full crew of willing shipwrights," Usuthu said. "Now you must not only captain your ship but build it."

Halberd carefully sewed the bark onto the center of the prow on the curving bow and stern. These sheets he attached along the exact frame line. He left the other end of the sheet hanging. Mälar would want to adjust them as he saw fit.

Twilight had long passed into full night when Halberd noticed that Mälar was nowhere to be seen. Halberd leaned back on his haunches and stretched his aching back. His fingers were full of punctures from the bone needle. His eyes blurred from the unending close-up work.

The river was deathly silent. Etowah lay curled by the fire, sated with venison and fast asleep. Usuthu, as ever, showed no signs of fatigue, boredom, or discomfort. He had held one torch after another unwavering for hours. He gazed off over the river, studying the stars. No night birds sang. The river moved by quietly, lapping at its banks.

"I feel no enemies nearby. This place is safe, I think."

Usuthu jumped at the sound of Halberd's voice.

"I was far from here," Usuthu said, "visiting the spirit of my father. He reminds me that there is no safe place, not for us. Are you finished?"

"I've done all I can."

The canoe was almost covered with bark, sewn in two layers onto the frame, one skin of bark inside and one out. It was a beautiful craft, long and slender, yet sturdy and seaworthy.

Mälar appeared by the fire, bearing in his hands a giant pale ball, which glowed in the firelight.

"Tree sap," he said, grinning idiotically. "If we can scrape it off my hands, we can watertight his bark-covered angel."

That Mälar might praise Halberd or Usuthu for their labors was inconceivable. He expected none for his work. Mälar came from the old tradition of the sea; praise was reserved either to encourage fools or for some extraordinary event.

He could not free his hands to pry off the sticky sap, so Halberd worked a large chunk free. Using a branch as a paddle, Halberd spread the pitch onto each roughly sewn seam. The stickiness of the sap made it almost impossible to work with. A crooked line of thick pitch ran down each seam, giving the canoe a comical glued-together appearance. Usuthu took one look at the sap and refused to touch it. He preferred to hold the torch.

"Usuthu," commanded Mälar, "you are strong. Tear this ball of my flesh so that I might correct the work of my apprentice here."

Usuthu jammed the end of the torch into the ground and yanked the pitch ball free. Several pieces of flesh came with it.

Mälar knelt by the canoe and worked each pitch

seam with his thumb, carefully flattening and spreading the sap until no water could penetrate. He worked like a smith honing a razor-sharp blade. His diligence required hours. When the sky purpled and then finally glowed pink with dawn, the old sea dog sat back with a smile on his face.

"She is done and she should endure. But if we don't sleep, we will not. Come."

They awoke in the late afternoon. Mälar, up first as always, stood waist deep in the river following a stroking motion he was learning from Etowah. He wielded a paddle made from a thick branch with a short channel chopped perpendicular to the length of the shaft. Into that line had been inserted a broad flat piece of wood skimmed from a tree trunk. Wooden pins held the blade onto the handle.

Their meager provisions filled the middle of the craft: two drinking skins, a large pile of dried deer, a few cooked deer flanks, and three Eerhahkwoi hatchets.

"Get your sleeping furs," Mälar called. "Night falls and we must go."

Halberd and Usuthu draped their newly slain and newly scraped deerskins into the boat. Halberd would make the command decisions as captain, but Mälar ruled all matters pertaining to actual sailing.

"Etowah will take the bow seat," the old helmsman said, "from there he can survey the river."

Mälar paused. He and Halberd exchanged glances. From the bow Etowah could never attack anyone else in the boat. Etowah was given the seat of suspicion, as had Halberd's treacherous brother, Labrans.

"Usuthu sits behind him, where there is no seat, then our gear, then Halberd, then myself. I will steer the craft from the rear and only Usuthu will not paddle. We must save him to wield the bow."

"I have no arrows, I will wield no bow."

"Then we will save ourselves from your clumsiness and lack of experience and allow you to serve as our watchman. Come."

Climbing in was not easy. The canoe tipped back and forth as Usuthu tried to get aboard. Finally, Usuthu stood in the water and held the craft steady. The other three clambered in. They held their paddles across their laps.

"Jump up and drop your seat into the boat," Mälar commanded.

Usuthu took a great backward jump out of the water and crashed into the canoe. It rocked dangerously to one side, but held upright.

"If our bottom can endure that blow"—Mälar laughed—"then we need not fear the river."

The canoe drifted lazily out into the current. The bow pointed to the south and west, downstream.

They were off.

Mälar handled his paddle as if born to it. Halberd struggled a bit, but Etowah had the most trouble.

"Etowah," said Halberd, "you guided us in the construction of this boat. How is it that you lack the skill to paddle?"

"I have observed many of these crafts, but I have never ridden in one."

"How is that possible?"

"I have never lived in a village. I am the son of animals, not man."

"Before Etowah tells his tale, which I wish to hear as much as any," Mälar interrupted, "he must fly forth and scout this stretch of the Alluwe."

"How far will we travel in this craft, on this river?" Halberd asked.

"I think we can make twenty leagues a day, with ease. At that rate, barring any delays for battle, we will join our second river in six or seven nights. Once we achieve the Attyo, as Etowah has named it, we have one week's paddling before the serpent mound and another three weeks to the Mesipi."

They slid silently down the river under the slowly appearing stars. The great journey ahead loomed like a bleak winter. No Giants would bear them swiftly across these waters.

But the three of them were, by nature, adventurers. They had lived as nomads, happily homeless, happily rootless. None had traveled for booty to bring home to impress the village of their birth, but for the lure of battle, wild adventures, and unknown lands. Now they had that adventure, and then some.

"I will fly ahead the distance of several nights' worth of travel," Etowah said, his first words to Halberd since he had asked for the loan of Hrungnir. "I will return shortly."

Etowah's slack body fell forward as if he were dead. His face thumped off the upraised prow of the canoe and his right hand trailed into the water. His chest barely moved, as if his breathing had slowed.

Wings flapped overhead. Halberd looked up, but saw nothing. Air *whooshed* down toward him as if a huge bird were overhead in the night sky, but none was visible.

"The savages sleep," he said. "Let us travel."

He dug his unfamiliar paddle into the river and the canoe moved on. Halberd and Mälar achieved an easy rhythm. They were well adjusted to the night time schedule. The eerie night woods were filled with sound. Predators growled and night birds called. Big fish broke the water with their leaps and splashes. Usuthu watched the banks with care, his silver mallet in his hand, waiting for the supernatural to appear. Night was its territory, as day belonged to mortals.

When the moon had faded and only the stars held sway, when hours had passed since a word had been spoken, the air was again filled with the beating of wings. Etowah sat upright with a start. Usuthu, startled out of a daze, straightened up with his mallet in his hand. The canoe swung back and forth on its broad keel.

"Quiet, Usuthu," Mälar snapped, "it is only the return of our scout."

"This riverbank hosts scattered villages for a hundred leagues at least," the boy said. There are trading clearings between them, where tribal cousins may gather, but at night no one goes near. No sentries are out, no one is prepared for our passage. All the villages sleep. There are only four large enough to have war-canoes and these are several days away."

Halberd and Mälar nodded in satisfaction. If Etowah told the truth, then all was well.

"How large," asked the ever-practical Mälar, "are the war-canoes?"

"They would hold twenty men, at least."

"Can a canoe that large catch our small craft?"

"Easily."

"What about rapids," Mälar pressed, "falls, or whirlpools?"

"The Alluwe is open, sluggish, and filled with broad, wide turns. Sometimes forests line its banks and sometimes open fields. There are no dangerous waters, no narrow cliffs, no gorges where one might be surprised."

"You flew as an eagle, then?" Halberd said.

The Skræling nodded.

"Tell us your tale, boy," said Usuthu, with gruff kindness, "that we may appreciate your gifts." He cut his paddle into the river. Halberd followed suit. The boy faced backward in his seat as he told his tale. Though Usuthu sat on the bottom of the canoe, his head was as high as the boy's. Usuthu's long legs extended forward under Etowah's seat.

"I was born," Etowah began as the river burbled beneath them and the stars rotated in the sky, "in the longhouse of a great warrior, an odd man, who was much admired in my village and destined to be chief. He had a glorious and contradictory past.

"When my father was a young man, he refused to go to battle and would stay in the villages when the men fought. He left food out for the wolves and waited by the lodges to see when they came to pick it up. He preferred animals to weapons. He preferred life in the camp to the warpath. For this behavior he was named Stays at Home.

"When finally he went forth and won great triumphs, partly through his magical understanding of the ways of the wolves, the Chief of his village offered his own wife to Stays at Home in gratitude. This Chief believed that his wife and Stays at Home had been lovers. It was both an act of generosity and humiliation. The Chief implied for all to hear that Stays at Home could not gain his own woman.

"But Stays at Home spurned the Chief's wife and took his own, my mother, Sees the Eagles. Sees the Eagles loved the birds of the sky and learned the spells needed to speak with them. For this she was an object of suspicion in my village. Many called her a Witch, but she was not.

"One day, Stays at Home led an advance party against the Arharaks."

"Wait!" barked Halberd. His voice echoed back to them off the deserted, tree-lined riverbanks. A burst of night-bird calls answered his shout. Halberd looked around, chastened. "Who was this person?" he whispered.

"Not a person," answered Etowah, "but a tribe, a fierce tribe who eat the flesh of humans. They live south on the Mesipi. They tattoo their own skin with demonic designs. They eat a mushroom which causes them to see vile visions. We will take this boat through the heart of their territory."

"The demon who attacked us in the Dream World," Halberd said, "he said the word Arharak. I took it for his name, but in truth he was too badly injured to speak his tribal name properly."

"The Witch conspires with this tribe," Usuthu said darkly.

"Let the boy tell his tale," said Mälar.

"The Arharak, unknown to all, had moved farther upriver than ever before. They surprised my father's party and slew them. They dined upon my father's flesh."

"How do you know this?"

"The wolves and the moles saw it happen. The wolves told me." His simple answer offered no opportunity for reply.

"I was but a newborn," he continued, "when the party did not return. The Chief ordered my mother from the village. He feared her knowledge and the respect with which other women listened to her.

"He banished her as a caster of evil spells. He cursed Stays at Home to her face. Sees the Eagles returned to her longhouse and gathered her belongings. Her last act before she left was to bash out the Chief's brains with my father's mace. She fled with me into the forest.

"There the Arharak war party, making their way toward my village, found us. They seized my mother, who flung me into the bushes.

"Her dying words were, 'Wolves and eagles, beasts of the air and of the ground, take this boy and serve him as Stays at Home and Sees the Eagles served you. Sees the Eagles is dead now and cannot help him. When I have been eaten, my spirit cannot return to give him guidance. Remember all we have done for you. Fulfill your duty!'

"The Arharaks ate her as well. They tore her tongue from her mouth and boiled it. They cut her liver from her living chest, sprinkled it with her own gall, and ate the steaming organ raw. They washed in her blood and threw her gutted body onto the fire. There she was roasted and later consumed until her picked bones gleamed in the moonlight. That I saw with my own eyes and remember to this day."

"How old were you then?" Mälar asked.

"Less than three months."

"I," Halberd said gently, "remember nothing prior to my third year."

"I," the boy said with pride and sorrow in equal amounts, "see it happen before me every day."

"That is rather hard to believe," Usuthu said.

"Animals remember their lives, from the first day to the last," the boy said defiantly. "Do not tell me what I know and what I do not. The wolves found me in the bushes and by wolves I was suckled. Wolves raised me and brought me food until I was a sturdy infant. The wolves passed me to the bears and I spent my childhood in their caves and company.

When I became an arrogant and foolish young man, in my fourteenth year, the bears found me to be insufferable, which I was. They consigned me to serve the moles, in order that I might learn humility, which I did. The mole is clever and demanding, and his spirit feels little respect for humans.

"When I was old enough to seek the blood of the Arharaks, the moles bade the eagles finally repay their debt to my parents. The eagles taught me of war and honor and showed my spirit many gifts, among them the power of flight.

"From each of these animals I learned. I learned to avoid man always and to obey the will of the pack. I learned about sacrifice for the good of all. I learned to hunt, to track, to use my nose, and to be cunning. I learned that here in this world, all things live—rocks, trees, water, dirt—all things have spirits, even if man cannot perceive them.

"My spirit may travel in air as an eagle or in the ground as a mole. I have the endurance and tracking ability of the wolf. From the bear I gained awesome strength and many, many spells. The spells I may invoke as a man, but the strength is mine only in the World of Spirits. As a man my strength is but average, I fear."

"And what," said Mälar, "do you hope to learn from us?"

"What man knows. I will learn cruelty and deceit. I will learn how to slay my own species for pleasure. I will finally take my revenge on the Arharaks, the tattooed demons.

"I will guide you down the river. In return, you will bear me to their village. I will slay as many as I can. With that blood on my hands I will bridge the gap between man and animal and become the powerful shaman it is my destiny to be."

His proud whisper carried to the back of the canoe. His tale told, he turned his back, picked up his paddle, and cut into the water.

"Many destinies go unfulfilled," Halberd said. "Do not state the future so plainly. It will not occur as you see it. Nothing does."

"Do you see yourself slaying the Witch Grettir?"

"Yes."

"Why should your desires come about and not mine?"

There was no answer. Dawn was breaking up the black sky. They guided the canoe into the trees at the bank, scrambled out, and drew the canoe out of the water behind them. Usuthu stayed by the bank to wipe out their tracks with a leafy branch. None would know they had come this way.

They made a simple camp. The canoe was inverted. They rested their backs against it. No fire, no shelter, and no conversation. They were all exhausted. A few mouthfuls of dried deer and then deep, deep sleep.

In the Eye of the Serpent

Five days and nights slipped by on the silent river. The days passed in sleep. The nights blurred together. Halberd and Mälar grew strong wielding their paddles. They forgot their battle wounds. Their shoulders healed.

Skræling villages and trading clearings burned from the living forest slid by with no sign of alarm. The villages slept at night, their canoes pulled halfway out of the river onto banks muddy from constant traffic.

The Skræling were all around. The occasional fine-woven reed basket floated past, lost from some village. Mälar snagged all he could. "For later," he would say. Tough-looking little dogs raced to the river's edge as they glided by along the opposite bank. Their yaps echoed across the water, but even if aroused, the drowsy sentries could never pierce the dark night beyond the light of their fires.

On the night of the full moon they hugged the southern bank while on the northern Skrælings danced around a soaring fire. They had no guards out and seemed unafraid. Every warrior wore a terrible wooden mask, carved with long curved noses and downturned mouths. Taller and leaner than the Eastern tribe, they wore long thick skins and waved lances and stone-head hatchets.

"They are Hadena," whispered Etowah, "descended from the builders of the mound. Their tribe and its spirits are charged with the mound's protection."

"Protection from what?" asked Halberd.

"Defilement."

At that news Usuthu turned in the canoe to look at Mälar. He shook his head.

"Are they"—Mälar's sarcastic whisper cut through the night—"as fierce in battle as they are in pageant?"

"No one knows," answered the boy. "They will not fight other tribes except to protect the mound and everyone fears them too much to approach the mound. It is *yacalt*."

"What?" Mälar spoke without patience.

"That is a Hadena word. It means haunted prairie."

"Etowah, this is forest, not prairie."

"Now, yes, but the land will change in two days' travel."

And it did. The thick forests receded from the banks and became open fields. Some fields showed signs of cultivation, some held villages. Forests lined the far edge of the fields. Villages came and went more quickly and each village had more canoes. The river in this area was clearly a roadway.

The Skræling dwellings were different. The wooden longhouses of the Eerhahkwoi disappeared. In their place were mud-wattled walls with long curving eaves. Posts leaned inward toward the center, where four upright poles supported them, leaving the center open to the sky.

Winter became full spring as they traveled. The air

grew humid and comforting. Forests exploded with green and the fields with flowers. It was the time of renewal and love, but for the travelers there was neither.

"Northmen dance in village squares to celebrate the end of winter," said Mälar. "But shipboard we celebrate only the survival of another day."

That night, certain that it was spring and time for his own rites of renewal, Usuthu pulled out the tiny hand-carved statue of a Viking warrior he had made months before. It was the totem of his god, Bahaab Dahaabs. He bowed his head before it and sought counsel.

"You are a knowledgeable man," Mälar teased, "and yet you seek the comfort of your pagan spirits."

"Knowledge," answered the Mongol, "does not remove the terror of the gods."

Mälar looked into the forest moving swiftly by.

"True enough," he muttered into his beard, "or of man either."

They had traveled the river through three huge bends to the south, one up again toward the north, and another turn to south and west. After that turn the river increased in speed. They only guided the canoe now. The river was too swift for their paddles to make much difference.

"Tomorrow night," Etowah said in the late afternoon of the fourth day, "we reach the mound."

"I am ready for a fight," said Mälar.

"We are the invaders here," answered Usuthu. "I need arrows to fight real enemies, men whom we have reason to kill. Why must we slay men with whom we have no quarrel?"

Mälar opened his mouth to reply. Halberd gestured sharply with a downthrust hand. It was a gesture of command. Surprised, Mälar closed his mouth without a word. Halberd had barely spoken since they took to the river.

"We do not have to slay anyone," Halberd said. "We will use all our stealth to steal arrows. If they attack us, we will flee."

"If they let us," Mälar said.

That night they glided by small mounds breaking the surface of the tilled fields. The mounds were taller than a man at their center and gently rounded. They covered about as much ground as a Northman great-house. In some places they rose in clusters of six or seven. Other mounds stood alone under the moonlight. They threw pale shadows, soft and round.

"The presence of death is very strong," said Usuthu. "Ghosts rests in these mounds but they do not sleep. This place draws spiritual power."

Etowah grew clearly fearful. When he was not flying ahead, he covered his head and communed with spirits whom the others could not hear. Without a spoken word, Halberd, Mälar, and Usuthu adjusted their daylight sleeping. They remained awake in shifts, to keep an eye on the boy. If he called on demons, they were ready to slay him, blood oath or not.

Halberd did not visit the Dream World, but Ishlanawanda's face appeared before him anyway. When he awoke in the afternoon, he lay in his furs and thought of her soft skin and tight, graceful body. Of her mouth on him and the heat in her voice when she lifted her head to speak his name. Of the slow patterns she traced on his stomach with her sweet tongue.

Usuthu stood over him.

"We are not sailors tonight, but warriors, as it

should be. Cast thoughts of the woman out of your head."

Halberd made no attempt to get up.

"We won't leave tonight until full dark. We must not be seen."

Usuthu nodded and left to tell the others. They returned and circled Halberd, waiting for his plan.

"Is the mound near a village?" he asked.

"The tail is, but the head is not."

"No riddles tonight, boy," said Mälar.

"The mound," said Etowah, "is shaped like a snake. It is not high, but very broad. It is almost one quarter of a league in length."

Halberd drew in his breath. A quarter league! Few tombs of that size existed anywhere. For sheer scale it would rival the Sacred Pyramids of the Land of Sand. "What power such a place must have," he said.

"And what a force of warriors to protect it," Mälar answered.

"And what armies of ghosts to inhabit it," finished Usuthu.

For a moment no one spoke. The difficulty of their task was clear at last.

"Sentries?" Halberd's voice cracked like a whip. The others remembered who they were and how far they had come. They needed arrows. They would have arrows. If ghosts stood in their way, then ghosts would be bested.

The boy shook his head. "The Hadena know the mound. Others fear it. I believe it has never been assaulted."

Halberd set what little strategy he could.

"When we near the mound," he said, "Etowah will swim ashore and scout the site as a mole. When he returns, we will make for the mound, dig as silently as we can, take what we need, and leave."

Etowah nodded, his fear evident on his face.

"Some plan," said Mälar.

"Are your spirits strong enough," Usuthu asked the boy, "to face this mound in the form of a mole? I mean you no disrespect, but we have to know if you are up to the task."

"I think I can. I am not certain."

"A wise answer," said Mälar. "It's dark enough. Let's go."

Halberd looked to the sky. It was still purple red, with no stars showing. He shook his head.

"Mälar, we know you are not afraid. In your heart, you know it, too. We will leave in another hour. Go and rest."

Mälar did not like being admonished. "You are my captain," he said calmly, and left them.

Etowah prepared himself for battle. He pulled his black hair into a long thin ruff running down the middle of his head. He put on a fringed vest covered with colored stones and dyed quills. The quills formed the shape of a standing bear. Using mud from the riverbank mixed with pigments from his hide bag of magical implements, he painted the claw marks of an eagle on one cheek and the paw shape of the wolf on another. Above his mouth he drew whiskers to honor the mole.

He danced in a shuffling circle, raising his lance to the stars and pointing in all directions. He consigned himself to the good graces of Woncan Tonka.

Usuthu watched him in silence, Halberd at his side. When they were younger and learning to be shamen, they had often performed rituals with this much care and intensity. Now they lived what they had learned. They seldom had the time or energy for so much prayer.

When the moon was high, they flipped the canoe into the water and climbed aboard. Usuthu held his sword in one hand and his silver mallet in the other. Mälar paddled with his sword across his lap. Halberd watched the bank.

Larger mounds appeared. Some were giant cones, taller than two or even three great-houses. Usuthu tapped Halberd from behind and nodded at the Jewel of Kyrwyn-Coyne in its nest at the butt of his broadsword in his shoulder scabbard. It glowed a brilliant white. The power of the Spirit World was strong in the mounds.

Halberd scooped a palmful of river water up to his mouth.

"My mouth is as dry as it was the first time I was in a raid," he whispered.

"Stealth is more difficult than attack," said Mälar. "Now you must fear not only death, but also discovery."

"In case of discovery, old man," Halberd said, "you will stand fast in the canoe while we defile the mound."

"I will not!" the helmsman spat. If he could have, he would have shouted at the top of his lungs. A vein bulged up in his forehead. He was enraged.

"We must be ready to flee. We cannot risk the theft of the canoe. We must have one man in reserve to rescue us if need be."

"Leave the boy."

Halberd looked into Mälar's eyes. He did not have to speak. They would keep Etowah by their side at all times, to guard against treachery.

"I will stay unless I judge that the situation requires me," Mälar replied sweetly. "Then I will come."

Halberd turned away. The sea dog would do his duty, no matter how much he complained.

Just past the middle of the night, Etowah raised one hand. Halberd and Mälar lifted their paddles. Etowah pointed to the right-hand bank. Mälar guided the canoe across the current to the bank on their left. He ran the canoe into a muddy cut. The walls of the cut were a bit higher than their heads as they sat in the canoe.

"Swim over," whispered Halberd, "scramble around the mound as a mole, and return. Do not assume human form for any reason. Do not be heroic. You are a scout, not an advance war party.

"What," said Etowah, "of my empty body resting on the riverbank while I explore? If it is captured or slain, then I spend eternity as the ghost of a mole."

"By the Norns!" exploded Mälar in a piercing whisper. "Why did you not speak of this before?"

"I thought you would beach the canoe on the same bank as the mound. I pointed to that bank."

"Mälar," said Halberd, "you go. Swim over with this boy and guard his body. Steal nothing. Attack no one."

Mälar nodded rapidly. Had he heard one word of Halberd's orders?

He stripped off his Skræling leggings and tunic. He put the Skræling bashing hatchet between his teeth and cinched his belt tighter around his sword. He slid out of the canoe and into the water. He made no more noise than a water snake.

He beckoned to the boy.

Halberd stopped him with a hand on his arm. "No weapons."

Etowah looked at him with great dignity.

"I am a scout," he said. "I require none."

"If you are discovered, obey Mälar. Instantly."

Etowah nodded in the same distracted way as Mälar. He stepped from the canoe onto the cut and from the cut into the river. Mälar led the way, his head carried high, the hatchet in his teeth.

Halberd watched them swim across the bright strip of moonlight on the water. Then they were gone.

Halberd and Usuthu climbed to the top of the cut and lay on their stomachs. The mound rose on the opposite bank, as Etowah had described it. Short and broad and without end. It curved away from them and they could not discern its shape. No fires were visible. The village was hidden somewhere behind the mound. Along the riverbank more than twenty canoes were drawn up onto the muddy bank. Two were huge war-canoes.

"This mound feels potent and evil," Halberd whispered.

"*Yacalt*," replied Usuthu. "Our raid cannot succeed."

"Why not?"

"The Hadena live up and down this river. They will hound us like beasts. If we are not caught now, it will be later."

"Then why do it?"

"I need arrows. Mälar needs a fight. The boy needs to become a man. I believe it is our fate to defile this mound, come what may. Of one good thing I am certain."

Halberd inclined his head.

"The Witch Grettir is not part of this place. It is too strong for her. She avoided the Hadena."

Mälar's head broke the water right in front of them. He smiled as they jumped in surprise.

"The boy is exhausted," he said. "Apparently it is harder to be a mole than one might think."

"Are there guards?"

"Come to the other bank and I will give you my report, O my captain." Mälar smiled again and sank below the river without leaving a ripple.

"Hah," snorted the Mongol. "He's outfoxed you again. He will not linger in the canoe."

"One day," Halberd said as they backed the canoe out of the cut, "you must learn to swim."

"Never."

Mälar was waiting at midriver, water streaming off his gray head. He climbed into the canoe as smoothly as a rat. The boat never tipped.

"The boy sleeps just ahead." He put his mouth to Halberd's ear. "Ship your paddles."

The canoe glided into the shore. Halberd beached the canoe in a cleared space between ten others. The mound stopped just before the bank. Etowah lay in the mud, his ruff of hair soaking wet, his ceremonial vest coated with dirt. Mälar woke him and pointed to the canoe. The boy buried his lance into the mud and made the canoe fast to it with a length of deer hide. Mälar pulled his sword from his belt and gestured Halberd forward. They huddled around the boy.

"I gained the shore and said the spell," he said.

Halberd fought with his own impatience. The boy was young and inexperienced. He did not know how to give a report. He remembered things according to their significance to him, not in the order of their importance to others. Halberd shook his fingertips in a gesture of annoyance. The boy hurried and stumbled over his own words.

"My spirit was that of a mole. I climbed up the bank and scampered to its far edge. I could smell the village. No one was producing the scent of anxiety. I heard no footsteps and smelled no one approaching. I heard only snores. I smelled only contentment." Etowah paused.

"Go on," hissed Mälar.

"From the living," he said.

Usuthu nodded, as if he needed no more explanation. He tightened his grip on his silver mallet.

"Yes." Halberd's whisper was no louder than the gentle moonlight breeze.

"Ghosts are everywhere. I could smell them, hear them. They knew I was there, but they took me only for the ghost of a mole. They are not alert, but their numbers are great.

"How does one kill a ghost, Halberd? Can they attack us?"

"Possibly. Whether they can kill us I do not know. Usuthu may strike down the supernatural with his silver mallet, but he uses it with great discretion. All my teachings call upon me to deal with the dead only with great respect."

"As do mine," whispered Etowah.

"Mine do not," said Mälar flatly. "We need weapons. Go get them."

Halberd and Usuthu scrambled up the low sloping wall. From here they could see the length of the mound. It curved away from them in a long spiral. Far across the field they could make out the shape of an open snake's mouth, earthen fangs bared in the moonlight.

Usuthu pointed to the ground beneath their feet. It seemed as good a place as any. Halberd drew his ax from his belt and began to chop at the soft black earth. When he rested, Usuthu pushed the loose dirt aside. The ax fell into the ground without resistance and the hole widened steadily.

Halberd hit wood. The shock of the impact sent him backward. The ringing blow echoed across the mound. Usuthu's sword was in one hand, his silver mallet in the other. His eyes glowed in the penetrating light of the full moon. His breath was even and calm. As ever, Usuthu showed no fear. It seemed as if no alarm had been heard.

They knelt by the hole. The stench of putrefying flesh was horrible. It sank into their clothes and their hair. Halberd could see a splintered log and, below it, a cloth-wrapped corpse. The eerie moonlight barely illuminated the gloom. Halberd wrestled the log out and pushed more dirt away.

There was a carefully ordered array of equipment surrounding the rotting body. Buried with the corpse were inscribed stone tablets, faded and bug-eaten deer-hide armor, an odd stone pipe, and a wooden mask with a fearsome, long-nosed face. Halberd took the small pipe, a stone tube with a tiny stone bowl, all carved from the same rock, and slipped it into his leather armor.

Usuthu reached a long arm into the hole. He jostled the body aside. The clinging smell became even thicker. The body, old and crusty inside its wrap of rags, broke in two. The two pieces slid further down the log-lined hole. It cracked with a sound like old leaves swept up in the wind.

Usuthu ruthlessly shoved his arm into the newly revealed hole. He hung his head into the hole, the better to see in the dim light. Halberd sat back and surveyed the mound. They were undiscovered. The Mongol pulled his arm out of the hole. In it he clutched a rotting deerskin quiver, bristling with arrows. He smiled fiercely.

Perhaps he had not wanted to rob the dead. But his blood cried out for him to have arrows. Thus armed, he was a true warrior, not a useless passenger fearful of water. Usuthu rooted into the hole once more. He plucked forth a Skræling bow and another quiver.

He gestured for Halberd's help. Then he lowered his arm and sat slowly back on his haunches. The Mongol smiled a small, tight smile. Halberd felt the hair on the back of his neck slowly rise. His flesh grew cold. He turned to see what caused the Mongol to smile such a smile.

Before them were the ghosts of Skræling warriors, the ghosts of the Hadena. More than they could count. Amassed in a rank of ten, the procession stretched as far as the end of the mound. Like the ghost of Mahvreeds the Cautious, these spirits were pale, empty tracings of men, yet they wore men's clothes and carried Skræling weapons. Their transparent faces were stern. The moonlight shown through them, casting horrible shadows on the earthen floor of the mound. None spoke.

"Do you," Halberd hissed from the side of his mouth, "know any dead warriors upon whom you might call?"

"Call the spirit of my noble father and ask him to save me, when I know that I am a thief? Is there no one you can call?"

"Only my two poor brothers." Halberd raised his arms above his shoulders, palms forward. He held no weapons.

"Back up," he whispered.

"Flee from a ghost?" Usuthu answered. "How?"

"Maybe they cannot leave the mound."

"Spirits of dead Hadenas," Halberd said, "we are

sorry to have disturbed you, but we must have arrows. You are dead and cannot be slain. We wish to live a bit longer. We are far from home and have no smiths to forge our arrowheads. We two thieves humbly beg your pardon."

Two venerable ghosts emerged from the front row. Both wore long braids down to their waists and carried hatchets with copper blades. They studied Halberd with care and looked to one another in obvious confusion.

"They do not understand you," Usuthu said.

"Get," Halberd said, "the boy."

But Etowah was standing right behind him. He raised his hands to the ghosts and spoke in the grunts and clicks of the Eerhahkwoi. The aggravated-looking ghosts answered him at great length. Where Etowah had whispered, the two Hadenas made no attempt to keep their voices down. The booming speech echoed over the mound.

Where, thought Halberd, are the living Hadena?

"You two," said the boy, "are thieves, grave robbers, defilers, and have no honor. You must be slain and taught a lesson in the afterlife. I am to slay you because I have proved so worthless to my tribe and blood as to follow your advice."

"Have they power in the world of the living?"

Etowah shrugged.

"Tell them we are blood brothers and you cannot slay us."

The ghosts' reply was short and biting.

"Then I should be slain as well, for having joined you."

"Let us try," Usuthu suggested, "leaving."

Halberd nodded. They backed up slowly, edging

toward the slope of the mound. The horde of ghosts moved with them.

"Is Mälar ready?" Halberd asked.

Etowah nodded.

The most venerable of the ghosts barked.

"Hold, he says," said Etowah, his voice quaking.

"Hold indeed." Halberd drew Hrungnir from the pocket on the back of his leather armor. He flipped the stone knife into his left hand and drew forth his dagger with his right. He beckoned the ghosts forward.

"Come and fight!" he called. "Fight me and bring your mortal brothers if you like. I'm sick of hiding."

Etowah looked at Halberd with shock. Even Usuthu seemed surprised. Mälar's fiendish cackle of laughter sounded across the river.

Halberd's blood pounded in his head. He had not known his frustrations were so great. The battle was joined at last. As usual, Halberd did not care about the consequences.

A Hadena ghost glided soundlessly forward. He raised an empty lance over his head. The moon shone through his pale arm. He flicked the shadowy lance at Halberd. Halberd moved sideways by reflex. He thought the ghost's lance could not hurt him.

It stuck in the ground at his feet and quivered back and forth. Halberd reached for it. He could feel the lance, though it remained transparent. The ghost was atop him, a stone mallet in his fist. Halberd drew a circle in the air in front of the ghost with Hrungnir. He stabbed through the circle with his dagger. Red blood showed on the tunic of the white ghost. The empty warrior vanished. Blood, red, thick, and clinging, coated the blade of Halberd's dagger.

Etowah slumped to the ground, unconscious. Halberd wasted not a glance. He drew another circle before the eldest of the ghosts and stabbed him square in the chest. The old chief disappeared into the night air.

Usuthu swung his silver mallet at two ghosts who moved toward him. As his stroke passed through them, they were gone. Halberd raised Hrungnir, ready to strike again. From behind him came a steady chopping sound, like someone busting firewood for the evening fire.

The massed ranks of ghosts all looked to their rear. A horrible struggle sounded from the end of the mound. Growls filled the air and the ghosts cleared a space as they all craned to see. Halberd and Usuthu backed up even farther. Usuthu hung the rotting quivers from his shoulder and stuck the bow into one of them.

"The arrows seem true and well preserved. I have all I need for now."

The massed ghosts all sat down, as if in counsel. Halberd and Usuthu had no words for their surprise. In at the center of their vast circle stood the enormous ghost of a bear, earnestly consulting with the other venerable Chief. Though the bear was as transparent as the Hadena ghosts, bright crimson blood spotted his chest and claws.

"Etowah," said Usuthu.

The ghost of the bear and the ghost of the man parlayed for many minutes. The Chief shook his head again and again. The bear gesticulated like a man, but the forest behind him showed through his shaggy flanks. The bear dropped to all fours and dug into the ground. The Chief clasped one hand to his chest.

All the ghosts melted into the night.

The bear stood alone for an instant. Then he was gone.

Etowah raised his head from the mud.

"The ghosts have agreed not to seize your souls from your bodies without killing you," he said. "They have agreed to leave you for the living. You are the first mortals who had the gall to rob these graves. The ghosts bear you some grudging respect. They are proud of the power of this mound. They assume you must understand the Spirit World or you would not have been drawn by this power. They will let the Hadena decide your fate."

"Is this," asked Halberd, "good news?"

"I do not know," the youth answered. "The elder ghost claimed they would be much harsher with you than the living Hadena."

"All men who abdicate decisions claim they have the harder heart," said Usuthu.

"I would prefer not to deal with either of them," Halberd said. He turned to the riverbank. There was the source of the chopping he had heard before. Mälar stood in the war-canoe, methodically pounding the bottom with his Eerhahkwoi bashing mallet. There was a splintering crash. Mälar looked up and smiled.

"They cannot chase us by water. Come on."

"Hold."

Halberd turned at the sound of Usuthu's voice. Formed along the edge of the mound, not ten feet away, were at least fifty Hadena warriors. They had come in utter silence. Their hair hung in braids, they wore only breechcloths and feathers in their hair. Their faces were painted with diagonal slashes of black. All held lances, hatchets, and hide shields with odd designs. They stared at the invaders with no expression and, oddly, patience and curiosity.

"The bow is not strung," Usuthu whispered.

"We may not need it. These are not savages," said Halberd. "They know of other worlds. They seem unafraid and curious."

"We need it, anyway," said the Mongol.

"Etowah, come here," Halberd said.

The boy struggled to his feet as the largest of the Hadena came forward. The Hadena threw his lance into the ground and lay his shield beside it. He held his hatchet in one hand and a small knife in the other. He jerked his chin at Usuthu. He gestured for the Mongol to come forward and fight.

Usuthu tucked his silver mallet behind the shield he wore on his chest and stepped forward. His curved sword glinted in the moonlight. The Hadena barely reached the middle of the Mongol's chest.

The Hadena shuffled three steps forward and three steps back. He sang. He raised his hands and lowered them as he moved up and back.

"Etowah," called Halberd, "translate."

The Hadena chanted and Etowah spoke over his song, which rose and fell. Their crossing voices filled the night. The Hadena warriors stood watchful and silent.

"Trees live," translated the young Skræling shaman:

"Rocks live, water lives,
The forest will endure,
And the mountains will stand,
But I will die
I will die

And this is a good day to die.
Perhaps the black white-man/god will slay me,
Perhaps I will slay him
But this is a good day to die."

He finished his song. He looked up at Usuthu's face. He smiled, it seemed, with anticipation.

"I cannot fight this man," Usuthu said. "Speak my words for me, Etowah." The Mongol kneeled and opened his arms wide.

"I am the son of warriors," Etowah called out in the grunting language. The chanting warrior showed some small interest. Neither he nor the other Hadena acted as if it was odd to have a translator for the huge black man. The Hadena's arms hung slack at his side.

"I am a warrior also. A warrior must have arrows, yet we had none. And so we stole from the dead of the Hadena. I am not sorry for that—I acted out of need. But I will not kill to defend myself when I am a thief. I throw myself on the wisdom of the Hadena and ask that I might state my reasons for my dishonorable conduct, for often man acts as he would not, if he had a choice."

Etowah chanted out the last line. Usuthu stood.

"If you will not hear me," he said, "then come forward. I'll rub out a lot of you before I am slain. Much blood will be spilled for nothing. But I do not fear death."

As the ghosts had before them, the Hadena formed an inward-facing circle and sat on the dirt. Passionate voices sprang up from place to place on the circle. Some warriors stood to make their cases. They ignored the invaders.

"Usuthu," whispered Mälar from the riverbank, "string the bow. Let us attack them now."

The Mongol shook his head.

Without turning his head, Halberd spoke to the helmsman. "Are you undiscovered?"

"Yes, and all of their canoes are sunk into the mud."

"Then stay there."

The Hadena broke up their meeting. The moon had left the sky. Only the stars lit the mound. No wind stirred. An old Hadena stepped to the front. The daring warrior stood beside him. The old man's braid was gray. He carried a long pipe made of reddish stone. Smoke curled from its bowl. He waved the pipe toward Usuthu so the smoke shrouded the Mongol's face. He gestured with the pipe in all four directions. He set the pipe at Usuthu's feet.

The warrior rushed at Usuthu. The Mongol sidestepped and the Hadena flashed by. Shocked by the Mongol's quickness, the Hadena still had enough quickness of his own to slash sideways with his knife. The blade scraped along Usuthu's chest shield, throwing sparks into the still night. Usuthu took him by the knife arm. Usuthu held the Hadena's wrist in his two huge hands. Usuthu cracked the Skræling's arm like a twig. The Hadena looked at his hand in dismay as it opened and his knife hit the dirt. He shrugged and picked up his lance.

"I will not kill this man for nothing," said Usuthu. The boy translated. The old chief spoke briefly. The warrior stopped, puzzled.

"Who will kill for honor?" Etowah said.

Halberd and Usuthu shook their heads. The Chief spoke again.

"Who will kill to survive this night?"

Halberd spoke and the boy translated over his voice.

"We will not kill. We will not be killed. We will go."

They backed toward the mound edge. The Hadena watched them impassively. Halberd heard Mälar climb into the canoe. Halberd reached the edge of the mound. Behind him came a hissing sound. They turned.

Rising up from the ground, ready to strike, were five snakes, coiled and angry. The weaving serpents were formed from dirt. Halberd and Usuthu froze in their tracks. Etowah took another step forward, as if to touch these curiosities. A flash of understanding held him in his place.

Mälar scrambled out of the canoe. At the edge of the water he was brought up short. Long earthen snakes, their jaws open and their dirt fangs dripping venom, rose out of each canoe, from the hole that Mälar had cut.

The Chief spoke.

"You will stay until we have chosen your fate," Etowah said. "We have heard of you demons for many months. We know you serve the flame-hair temptress. Your coming is long since foretold. The flame of the mound draws many moths. Clever of you to try to show some honor, clever to behave like men. We know who you are. We shall deal with you accordingly."

Usuthu studied the Chief with care. He whispered into Halberd's ear.

"In the Known World the men who run the great walled cities appear stupid, fat, and corrupt. Yet in this world every leader of Skrælings has proved dignified and articulate. They have a nobility long lost in the civilized states."

Halberd could only nod in agreement. The Chief had finished his speech.

"Great Chief," Halberd began. He paused to allow Etowah time to translate his words. The rest of his speech he spoke in short bursts, to permit clear understanding by the Chief.

"We don't serve the flame-hair witch. We are her bitterest enemies. We travel this river only to find her and cut out her heart. Yes, she is of our tribe, but we are mortal men, not demons."

"You would have me believe," replied the Chief, "that the black white-man/god is of your tribe."

"He is my brother under the skin, though our tribes live far, far apart."

"If you are not demons," asked the chief, "how is it that you understand this boy when he speaks to you in the language of the Eerhahkwoi?"

"We are shamen together, great Chief. I cannot explain how it is."

"We heard," said the Chief, "from the Nokoni, that you travel in the Witch's wake, killing those she left behind and trying to learn tribal secrets as you go. The Nokoni told us you were half-man, half-animal, that you were covered with fur. Indeed, you are."

"Nokoni?" asked Usuthu. "What Nokoni?"

Halberd ignored the interruption. It was not translated.

"O wise Chief," he said, "in our land men grow hair on their bodies and their faces. We are only men. If we were demonic, would we need canoes for travel, would we fight you as men, would we place ourselves at your honorable mercy as we do now?"

"Any being would be wise to place himself at the mercy of fifty Hadena warriors."

"With all respect due the Hadena fighting man, we fear you not. We would happily die opposing you with good cause, but we have no such cause. We would rather be your ally."

The younger Hadena shouted at the Chief, their blood lust apparent. There was no need to translate.

The chief snorted. "Our ally! What could you do for us beside dig up our dead?"

Halberd was exasperated. He had not argued so much in months. He preferred action. He ached to charge the warriors. He hated to be thought a coward. Still, he made one last attempt.

"I am a shaman in my world and in the World of Dreams. I have powers, as does my friend. Surely here in your world there is some evil you cannot undo. Let me attack this evil for you."

The Chief's jaw dropped. His eyes widened. All the Hadena warriors shut up their shouting. They looked at Halberd in awe.

"How," began the chief. He fought for a breath. "How do you know that evil lives among us?"

Halberd glanced at Usuthu. The Mongol answered with a barely perceptible shrug. Halberd's offer was a standard greeting used by shamen offering their hosts a service. It was merely a courtesy. No reply was expected.

"I know much," Halberd answered.

"Speak the truth!" the Chief shouted. "A life dear to me is in peril."

"Truthfully, great Chief, I know nothing. Such an offer is only a ritual, though I meant it sincerely."

"Can you travel in the World of Dreams?"

Halberd nodded.

"Come." The Chief led them down the crest of the

mound. They made an odd procession. First the Chief, then Halberd, Usuthu, and Etowah, followed by the horde of Hadena warriors, silent now, and attentive. He stopped where the mound curved to form the head of the serpent. One eye of the snake was formed by a deep hole, lined with logs.

"In this hole, in this grave, somewhere in the World of Dreams," said the Chief, "lies my daughter, Comes into Sight. She is possessed by a demon who tortures her in the Dream World. The demon is powerful. It has killed our shaman. Our village is without spiritual protection." The Chief paused and raised his arms. He spoke the next words in a bellow of command.

"If you can save her life, you will be spared. We will arm you and send you on your way and give you safe passage through the land of the Hadena."

His warriors erupted with angry shouts and the shaking of weapons. They were not happy.

"Go and talk to your friend," said the Chief. "Tell him he has to repair every canoe before you can leave. He seemed able at smashing, let us see if he is able in rebuilding. We will give him such tools as he needs and food. Make your preparations for your journey."

"Why would you use me for such a task when you consider me a demon?" Halberd shouted into Etowah's ear to make himself heard over the Hadena warriors. Etowah leaned close to the Chief and asked the question carefully.

"Perhaps you are a man. Perhaps a demon is required to fight another demon. I know that my daughter cannot get any worse unless she dies. I know one mortal man who perished trying to save her. She and I have nothing to lose."

The Chief gestured and the shouting warriors parted. The adventurers made their way to the canoes and told Mälar the situation.

"It's your hard luck," he said, "that the old boy never came across a polite shaman before. I know you will do well if you do not think too much. When events overtake you, trust in your sword, not your brain. I have a lot to do and I am hungry. Good luck."

Mälar left them to study the canoes he had to repair. As ever he was a practical old dog. His unstated faith in Halberd lifted the shaman's heart. A smile split his face from ear to ear. He knew he was ready.

Etowah turned to Halberd.

"Let me join you and learn from you."

"You may join me, Etowah, but it is I who will learn from you. You will guide me to the dreams of this girl and then you will awaken. Grettir might snatch you at any moment in that world." Halberd saw the look of disappointment cross the boy's face.

"Swear to me," Halberd said. "I will be busy and will not have time to look after you."

"I will do," said Etowah miserably, "as you say."

"Usuthu," said Halberd, "you must give up all sleep and watch our bodies." The Mongol nodded. He had expected no less.

"What," he asked, "if this is all treachery and they slay us while you sleep?"

Halberd shook his head.

"I will not dwell on the worst possibilities. I need all my strength."

Again the Mongol nodded. They rejoined the Chief at the eye of the serpent.

He started down into the hole without a word.

Halberd, Etowah, and Usuthu followed. Three warriors, armed to the teeth, clambered down behind them. Usuthu kept his sword in his hand, ready to turn and strike.

The hole was dug straight down through layers of buried corpses and tools. The stench was magnificent. They used crumbling bodies as handholds and ancient weapons as braces. The mound seemed to have no bottom. As they toiled down the smell grew worse and worse. The bodies nearer the bottom had been there the longest. Thick white worms and swarming maggots were everywhere. They did not differentiate between the dead and the living. Halberd brushed the slimy creatures from his hair. All soon wore a thick gray coating of ash and dust, the dust made up of the long-since dead.

The Chief ducked his head under a shroud-wrapped body resting on a wooden platform. They had gained a low tunnel, cut from rock and lined with torches. The Chief lowered his head and continued. Usuthu was bent almost double. Halberd had to remove his broadsword from his scabbard. The Chief went around a right-angle bend. Halberd and Etowah followed. Usuthu's path was blocked by the upraised hand of the Chief.

"Only those who will go to the Dream World may see her."

"I need the aid of my brother," Halberd said. "Take us back up and kill us, but I will not go on without him."

The Chief lowered his hand. He waved them into a tiny room. Its walls were stone. The only light came from torches. Their flames waved back and forth. Why should they wave, thought Halberd, while we are so far underground?

The air was thick and unbreathable. To the reek of death was added that of sweat. Old sweat, blood, and vomit. When their eyes adjusted to the gloom, they beheld an older Hadena warrior, his face painted red, his eyes bulging in agony. They leaned over him for a better look. He lay on the floor on his back. His hands clutched at his ears, which were hanging half off of his head. Long stripes of blood were clawed in his face and neck. The nails of his hands were broken. He lay in a congealing pool of vomit. His belly was swollen.

"He is at least three days dead," whispered Usuthu.

"He looks as if he tried to pull something off his face."

"No secrets!" The old Skræling's voice lashed them. "Whatever you say, the boy must translate immediately so I know he does not lie."

A stone lance touched Usuthu. The Hadena at the door to the little room leaned on the lance just a bit. He awaited the command to strike with pleasure.

The boy translated.

"Yes," answered the Hadena, "he was our shaman, the son of my father's brother. He served the mound for fifty winters. He died trying to save my daughter."

Comes into Sight lay on a pallet of furs in darkest corner of the foul, dark room. Her long black hair was unbraided and untangled. Her doeskin dress was spotlessly clean. Her smooth brown skin glowed. Her folded hands rested on her chest. She had long tapered fingers, gentle and delicate. In her round cheekbones Halberd saw the same fierceness and dignity that marked his love, Ishlanawanda.

Halberd leaned over her face. She looked untouched, perfect. He held his ear to her mouth. She was barely breathing. He put his head to her breast. Her heart fluttered, hesitated, beat weakly, and fluttered again. Usuthu leaned over his shoulder.

"She looks unharmed," he said.

"The battle is for her spirit. She is possessed. Her body fights to stay alive."

Usuthu nodded. He could not take his eyes from her face.

"She is," he said in a reverential voice, "beautiful."

Halberd whirled his head. Usuthu appeared to be in rapture.

"Are you enchanted, brother?"

"No," answered the Mongol. "This young woman is exquisite. My heart leaps at the sight of her. I believe we have been fated to meet."

Halberd shrugged. Stranger things had happened.

"Why," Halberd asked the Chief, "is this rotting corpse still on the floor of this room? He has been dead for days."

"He is stone dead, I swear it," said the Chief, sounding for all his dignity like a frightened child. "But when we take hold of his body, it fights us off. It refuses to leave the room."

"Then the demon is using his soul elsewhere."

Halberd grabbed the corpse by one hand and started to drag it into the tunnel. The dead man flipped onto his stomach. He seized Halberd around the ankle. His empty eyes rolled up at the shaman, beseeching him.

"Has he a name?"

"Owl Face," said the Chief.

"O, Owl Face, great shaman," chanted Halberd, "know you not that you are dead? Leave your body and this world and be at peace!"

"He cannot understand your spell," protested the Chief.

"If you hear my translator," Halberd said, "so does he."

Halberd stabbed Owl Face at the base of his neck with Hrungnir. The Hadena guards shoved the Northman against the wall and put their lances at his throat.

The Chief held his hand up. The dead man smiled and curled up onto his side. Blood leaked in drops from his ears. His clawlike hands relaxed and a long death rattle escaped his mouth.

Halberd ignored him.

"Get him out," he told the Chief, "and bring us fur to sleep on, food, and water. Bring more torches for light and bring herbs from the forest. Have your guards wipe down these stinking walls with the herbs to kill the smell."

Halberd settled down on the cold stone floor by his friend. They waited without speaking. There was nothing to say. Halberd would enter the Dream World, enter this young woman's dreams, and slay whatever tormented her. Or it would slay him.

After some time the Chief returned. His warriors bore handfuls of sweet herbs from the forest. They wiped down all the walls and carpeted the floor with pine boughs. The sweet smell of the pine almost covered the clinging death stink. The air in the cave was yellow with smoke. Furs were laid on the pine boughs and water and food placed on the furs.

"Leave us in peace," said Halberd, "that we might sleep and dream."

"I will not leave my daughter's side."

"Then swear your men will not harm us as we sleep."

"I will not. What if she cries out for help?"

"She may well. She is enchanted. Often those under a spell do not wish it broken."

"If she struggles or screams, my men will kill you."

"No," said Usuthu, "they will not."

"We have a stalemate," said the Viking. "You may stay."

The Chief reached out a hand and rested it on Halberd's shoulder. It took Halberd a moment to understand the Chief meant to encourage him.

"Though in this world we used snakes to threaten you," the Chief said, "in the Spirit World or Dream World the snake is our friend. Any serpents you see are there to aid you, drawn by the magic of the Hadena."

"Great Chief, I am Halberd, son of Danyeel. This young Eerhahkwoi is Etowah and my blood brother is called Usuthu."

"I am Moquaw, my name means Bear."

Halberd lay on the fur next to Comes into Sight. Etowah lay next him. Etowah took his hand.

"Take the girl's hand," he said. Halberd did. He closed his eyes.

"Say her name," Etowah commanded.

"Comes into Sight," murmured Halberd. He was drowsy.

"Ask her to allow you into her dream."

"Please, Comes into Sight, permit this shaman into the world of your dreams, the better to understand you."

Etowah's voice faded.

Halberd was far more tired than he had supposed. It must have been the tension of the raid, the exertion of digging, the fear. . . . Halberd fell asleep.

* * *

Halberd moves through a ghastly jungle. It looks like the impenetrable forests in the Land Where It Is Always Warm. The air is dripping with moisture. His breath catches in his lungs. His leather armor chafes him. His hair is soaked with sweat. He feels a tug on his arm. Etowah holds his hand tightly, like a small child. Wind moves through the vines and ferns. Warm, slick rain, unpleasant and somehow frightening, coats them. The rain does not break the grip of the heat.

"Where is the girl?" Halberd has to shout to be heard above the wind and the crashing branches overhead.

"We are in the her dream."

"Are you certain?" Halberd grips Etowah above both elbows. The boy nods, his eyes as wide as saucers.

"Why are you so afraid?" Halberd shouts.

"This place is not real. It stinks of evil. The forces opposing this girl are awesome."

"Which way?"

"It does not matter," the boy answers. "We will find what torments her. Or it will find us."

Halberd and Etowah push their way through the snatching thorns and head-high bushes. Something cackles through the wind. A huge form moves close by. Halberd draws Hrungnir.

A Giantess appears. Halberd is confused. He has not seen any Giants or Dwarfs in the Dream World of this continent. In the Waking World the Giants are vulnerable to Hrungnir, yet Halberd feels naked holding only the stone knife.

Halberd reaches for his sword.

"Etowah, are we in the Dream World?"

"I know only that we are in the world in which Comes into Sight dreams. If she has been carried far from her home, we could be anywhere."

Halberd balances his broadsword and studies the approaching Giantess. She is almost appealing. Twice as tall as Halberd, she has shapely powerful legs and large breasts. She wears a short skirt and a white tunic. Her arms are fair and her skin white. Her proportions are pleasing. Her hair hangs in long blond braids. She looks like a farm girl from Northland but for the iron helmet that covers her entire head.

The dark iron has knobs and odd protrusions that stick out here and there. It is thicker than a battle helmet and no straps hold it in place. There are holes cut for her eyes, mouth, nose, and ears, and her braids hang out. She carries no weapons.

"Shaman," she cries, her voice a muffled echo beneath the iron mask, "I bring you protection against Baldir."

"I do not know Baldir."

"Ah, but you will," she says, stomping closer, "and you will know the red-hot balls of stone he fires through the air with his iron glove. You need this helmet to protect yourself."

"Etowah," Halberd whispers, "wake up now. Leave this place before you are involved in the battle. If the spirits here know me, then the danger is great."

Etowah releases Halberd's hand.

"Think of the girl no matter how else you are engaged. This will lead you to her. If you want to keep her by you, take her hand. Do not wake up until you are sure she is safe. Any action begun in the Dream World continues even after one awakes."

"Spare me your lessons in things I already know, you whelp. Begone!"

Etowah simply fades away.

The Giantess towers over Halberd.

"Baldir approaches through this jungle," she intones. Her deep ringing voice seems at odds with her soft feminine appearance. "He wears an iron glove. He heats stone balls on his forge and hurls them with his iron glove. Only this helmet may protect you against him."

"How is it," Halberd asks, backing up as he speaks, "that you know I am a shaman?"

"Who else could come to this world?"

"So the Skræling girl is a shaman also?"

The Giantess stops. "You ask many questions. Do you want the helmet or not?"

"Who will protect you if I take it?"

"I am a guardian. I offer protection to others. This helmet is forged on the magic smith of the Dwarfs. When I remove it, another falls onto my head, spawned from this one."

"O Giantess," says Halberd, nimbly ducking behind a tree and circling quickly to end up behind the Giantess, "I think I will refuse your gift. I remember a Hadena shaman, Owl Face, who died trying to remove something from his head. Was it your helmet?"

The Giantess whirls at the sound of Halberd's voice coming behind her. She is fast and powerful. Halberd circles again, betting that she cannot see clearly through her visor.

The Giantess stoops to pick something up from the base of a tree. Her arms are flushed red, as if with anger. She stands erect and begins to change. Her body vibrates. Groans emerge from the helmet. Her legs lengthen and dark hair covers them. Her arms bulge with muscle. Her white tunic flattens as her breasts recede. Thick cords of sinew jut from her neck. Oddly, her blond braids do not alter.

"You are not a Giantess, but a Giant," calls Halberd from his hiding place. "What is your name?" He darts in a circle around the turning Giant.

The Giant lifts his right hand overhead. He wears an immense iron glove. In it is a white-hot ball of stone, which glows and smokes in the warm, driving rain. He hurls the ball at the sound of Halberd's voice. The ball flashes through the air. It smacks a tree trunk with such force that the ball punches a perfect round hole through the trunk. The tree does not fall. The round hole steams. The ball bounces onto the plant-choked ground with a thump. It hisses as the rain cools it off.

Halberd is awestruck. "You are Baldir the Hermaphrodite," he cries. "I remember you. You're one of the Furies, one of the Nightmares. You led the Giants in their attack on Aesir, where the gods live. How have you come to be here?"

Another white-hot ball snakes through the air in reply. It bounces once near Halberd and shoots into the air, tearing branches as it disappears.

Halberd darts up behind Baldir. He holsters his sword and tucks Hrungnir into the front of his armor. Baldir stoops for another ball of stone. Halberd springs into a tree, scrambles up the branches, and jumps onto the Giant's back.

The Giant reaches back with his ungloved hand. Halberd clings to the helmet as if riding a pony and draws Hrungnir. He reverses the stone knife and bangs on the helmet with the butt end. A vibrating clang rings out. The Giant drops the stone. It burns a hole straight through the jungle and bores into the ground. The Giant clasps his ungloved hand over one ear. Halberd bashes him again, harder. The helmet rings like an alarm bell in a Heathman monastery. The Giant falls to his knees. Blood runs from his nose. Halberd hits him again. Halberd can feel the vibration of the blow in the Giant's body.

Baldir is disoriented. While still on his knees, the Giant swings his iron glove at Halberd as if swatting at flies. Halberd leaps off the Giant's shoulders as Baldir winds up a crushing blow. Halberd hits the soft earth, rolls over in a somersault, and jumps up between Baldir's feet. He stabs the Giant in the toe as the iron glove swings down. The pain makes the Giant flinch. Baldir smashes himself in the back of his head. The iron glove gongs off the helmet. Even Halberd has to cover his ears against the unbearable noise.

Baldir falls onto his face. Blood runs from his ears and his nose. His iron glove slides off his hand lies out before him. Halberd kneels and sticks Hrungnir into one eye hole of the forbidding helmet. The blade barely touches the surface of Baldir's eye.

"I will blind you now, Baldir, if you do not tell me what I need to know."

A choked cry, half-man and half-woman, comes from the helmet.

"If you blind me," Baldir sobs, "all Midgard will know I have been bested."

"Come you from Midgard? I was taught that Giants may not enter the Dream World."

"You know that I am a Nightmare, a Fury. The

Dream World is my home. For the battle at Aesir I was plucked from the Dream World by a spell cast by Loki's daughter, Hel. She hates the gods of Aesir because they are beautiful and she is horrid."

"I don't care about your past. Where in this odious world is Comes into Sight, the Skræling woman?"

"I dare not tell," sobs the pathetic Giant. "She belongs to Grettir, and woe to any who cross that Witch."

Halberd takes a moment to gather his wits. Only with great effort does he keep from sinking the knife into the Giant at the mention of the Witch's name.

"Grettir," he asks softly, "is here, in this jungle?"

"She sends her messenger to seduce the girl." Baldir sobs with pain. He sounds like a small girl who has fallen from a horse. From a being so huge, the sound is repulsive.

"Why does Grettir care about Comes into Sight?"

"She is trothed to the black shaman who travels with her jilted lover, Halberd. Grettir will corrupt the girl before the black man meets her and manipulate their romance for her own ends."

"Trothed? By whom?"

"It is foretold."

"Are you really so stupid? Why did you say you knew who I am?"

Baldir shakes his head piteously. "These woods are full of brigands and fiends. I was only protecting myself by trying to sound powerful."

Halberd leans down over the helmet to gauge the reaction his words will create.

"I am Halberd, Dream Warrior."

A long choking cry spews out of the Giant.

"I am undone. Grettir will torment me for all eternity."

"Is she immortal?"

"Her spells can be."

"Baldir, if you say one word of my being here, then Grettir will take her revenge on you, yes?"

The half-man half-woman nods.

"Likewise I will take my own, wherever you are, yes?"

Again, Baldir nods.

"Then speak not a word of this, and you will be spared."

Baldir shakes his head. "She is too strong, she will get it out of me, somehow."

Halberd picks up the iron glove. He can barely lift it. He slides it along the jungle floor until a glowing stone ball appears in the palm. Halberd turns and drags the laden glove like an ox at a plow.

"Baldir," he commands, "bend the mouth of your helmet to this ball. Heat the iron so that the mouth melts closed. Grettir cannot force you to speak then."

"But I would starve."

Halberd smashes the side of the Giant's helmet with rage. The beast inside it moans.

"Frustrate me no longer," Halberd spits. "Do it or I shall blind you and cut out your tongue. I will be gone in a day and you may remelt the helmet."

Baldir bends tentatively over the glowing ball. When he draws near the heat, he flinches backward.

"Do it!"

The Giant forces himself to rest his helmet on the stone. A long wail of pain from inside the helmet accompanies the smell of melting metal and searing flesh. The smell of burnt hair and skin drifts out of the iron mask. Baldir rolls onto his back in the rain and beats his fists softly on the fern-covered ground. He drums his heels.

"You will heal," says Halberd. He turns to go.

Baldir beats the ground once, sharply. Halberd faces him. Baldir sits up. Tears run down the outside of his mask. Smoke still trickles out of the nose opening from his burned mouth. He points one huge finger at Halberd. The message is unmistakable.

"If you desire vengeance against me," says Halberd, "you have a long wait. There are many ahead of you, smaller, some of them, but all braver and stronger."

The jungle ends abruptly. Ahead lies a volcanic landscape. The ground is black and sandy. Huge smooth rocks crack the black earth and rise far overhead. Steam escapes the ground from long wrinkled fissures. Weird noises sound behind each great stone. Halberd draws his sword again and moves forward.

He speaks her name, over and over, calling to her, asking her to guide him. Small creatures scuttle across the steaming rock, racing over his toes or shooting past his head. What they feed on or where they go he cannot tell. Thick clouds hang just overhead, reflecting the red glow of the exploding mountains that line the horizon. Molten, flaming rock spews out of their distant tops. The liquid pillars reach into the sky and the muffled booms carry slowly over the black and empty plain.

Halberd weaves in between rock and fissure. He hears a muffled chanting behind him. He doubles back on his tracks. The chanting comes from beneath a knife-shaped stone that reaches into the sky. Halberd circles the rock as softly as he can. A doorway has been burned into the rock. Its edges, now frozen, show where the melting stone ran down the sides of the doorway. The rock is hollow inside.

Scurrying around the inside of the rock is a skinny, muscular Skræling. He does not resemble any Halberd has seen. He wears a long breechcloth of deerskin. It is unmarked. On his head is a black fur helmet from which stick two short curved horns. His eyes are hidden behind a thick black band of paint running from ear to ear. In one hand the Skræling holds a bone rattle, in the other several feathers. The Eerhahkwoi and Alkonkins are smooth-skinned, yet this demon is wiry. He is barefoot. His back is a mass of swirling blue patterns made of paint cut into the skin. His arms are covered with upraised scars, also blue. His cheeks are a series of small horizontal scars. His hands are powerful and knobby. He is a frightening sight.

Halberd peeks into the stone doorway as the Skræling bounces to and fro. The Skræling is fussing over a lovely woman who floats in midair on her back. She is Comes into Sight. The Skræling waves the rattles over her and chants. She writhes in midair and holds out one hand to resist the spell. She seems to be unconscious or entranced. She does not open her eyes or sit up. The Skræling runs the feathers down her body. Again she stirs in protest and again raises one hand up, palm out, as if to push the Skræling away.

Halberd does not know if this is an apparition or a man, like himself, who can visit the Dream World. In the former case Hrungnir is the only weapon that works. In the latter a swift sword stroke will be sufficient. The Skræling hunches his shoulder and cackles.

Halberd slides through the doorway. The ground

inside the rock shifts under his feet, as if he walks on ice floes atop a fast-moving river. Halberd looks down. The ground has become lava, flowing and boiling hot. Halberd stands on stones that float on the melted rock. The Skræling's feet do not touch the ground. He hovers just above the lava. The demon gives no sign that he is aware of Halberd.

Halberd does not trust his balance for a big swing. He draws back his sword parallel to the ground at ankle height. The Skræling shifts to his left and then back to his right. In an instant he will move completely around the girl and see Halberd.

The Viking strikes. He stabs straight ahead and up with his broadsword. The wide blade takes the demon in the small of the back, above his breechcloth. Halberd jumps up and pushes on the blade. It rises through the Skræling's ribs, snapping them as it goes, and bursts through the demon's tattooed chest, spewing blood and clots of organs. The Skræling falls to the rock beneath his feet.

He turns over onto his back and looks at Halberd. His eyes are dim, coating over with the gray film of death. He smiles with bloodstained teeth. He shakes one reprimanding finger at the Viking, as if Halberd is a bad child who has stolen a pie made for dinner.

The Skræling lies back on the rock. His head falls forward. Halberd steps carefully over the molten floor to the demon. He turns the Skræling on his back and, with some difficulty, works his sword free. The girl still floats in midair, unseeing and unknowing.

"I will return you to your father," Halberd tells her. "I fight Grettir, I do not serve her. I will bear you to your betrothed."

Comes into Sight does not speak. She seems to be

still entranced. She raises one hand. She points past Halberd, over his shoulder. He swivels his head to follow the line of her finger. There, in the melted doorway, is the Skræling.

Halberd looks down. There, at his feet, unmistakably dead, is the Skræling. Halberd carefully sheathes his sword. Clearly, it is useless. He shifts Hrungnir to his right hand. The Skræling smiles widely. His eyes glow. They are black and impenetrable.

"Come and kill me again," he says. "No one has killed me for years. I enjoyed it." He makes a careless motion with the rattle in his left hand. A searing pain races up Halberd's arm. His fingers start to open. Halberd does not drop Hrungnir. Despite the pain, he tilts the stone knife upward and points it into the demon's eyes. Halberd channels his will down the knife and into the Skræling's head. The Skræling backs up. He shakes the rattle again.

Halberd goes to his knees. He feels a long lance sticking out of his stomach. He cannot understand it—the demon holds no weapons. Blood pours down his belly. He feels his guts spill onto the floor, slithering like snakes. He looks down. He is unmarked. He looks up again. Two versions of the Skræling stand at the door.

"Who are you, demon?" ask the Skrælings. "I have never seen your kind before. How dare you interfere with me in my world?"

"This," Halberd gasps between clenched teeth, "is not your world. You are in interloper. You are the shaman of the Arharak, here to do the bidding of the Witch Grettir. I know all about you, save your name."

The Skrælings measure Halberd with new respect.

"I am Jeebi-Ug," they say. "This girl is mine. I am preparing her to serve the mistress."

"I want her. I will kill you to have her."

Halberd pushes off the floor and whips Hrungnir into the nearest Jeebi-Ug, just below the ear. The demon's head explodes from the force of the blow. Brains burst into Halberd's face. Jeebi-Ug falls into the lava. A puff of blue-white flame leaps up. The body is gone. Halberd drags the back of his arm across his face. The arm comes away slimy. He can smell the demon's brains on his cheeks.

Halberd turns to the girl. Surrounding her are four Jeebi-Ugs, all smiling.

"Understand?" they ask. "Kill one, two return. Kill two, then face four. Kill three, and six will bar your path. What can you do? Poor, poor mortal."

"I must have this girl," Halberd says.

"You cannot. She is strong enough to resist our spells. She has the power of a great Nokoni. Eventually she will serve Grettir and the Arharak. She will not go with you."

"Your spells kill her body. What good will she do you dead?"

"Her power will live long past her mortal flesh. If her body dies, she will only be bound more tightly to us."

"Power of the serpent mound!" Halberd raises Hrungnir and chants in a singsong voice. "Aid Halberd in his quest for your fair daughter, Comes into Sight! Defy these demons!"

A wall of earthen snakes spring up between Halberd and the Jeebi-Ugs. They weave and strike as the demons try to move. The Jeebi-Ugs howl in dismay. Their howl curdles Halberd's blood.

Halberd freezes for an instant in spite of himself. Another howl forces him to action. He hops across the room from one stone to another. Each rock bobbles slightly in the lava. Halberd tries to move the girl, but a spell holds her in midair. He slashes the air above and below her with Hrungnir. She drops like a rock. Halberd goes to his knees to catch her before she strikes the lava. The skin on the back of his hands sears from the heat. Hair on his arm catches fire and crackles down to his skin.

The girl droops in his arm. He throws her across his left shoulder. Her head hangs down behind him. He has only one hand with which to wield Hrungnir. The girl begins to murmur. The snakes dance and weave, forcing the Jeebi-Ug back. One Jeebi-Ug falls, an earthen snake hanging from his neck. His face swells and goes from brown to black. His eyes bulge in his head. They turn black. His tongue hangs out of his mouth, swelling and swelling. In the space of seconds it goes from pink to purple to blue to black.

No new Jeebi-Ugs rise to take his place. Halberd realizes that the power in this place does not lie with the serpents, but with the mound.

"Comes into Sight," he whispers, shoving at last past the melted doorway of the rock, "if you have the strength to fight, fight now. Arise and slay your captors."

Four Jeebi-Ug face him. Four snakes form a wall between Halberd and the Jeebi-Ugs. Halberd looks about in confusion. The world has changed again. Now he is on a broad plain. Towering thunder-clouds form overhead, larger than any he has seen. Snow pelts the plains, blown on a fierce wind. Huge herds of odd beasts cover the plain, ignoring the snow and feeding placidly. The beasts have four legs and shaggy fur. They are humpbacked, with bright, tiny eyes and short upcurved horns. They are over Halberd's height at the shoulder. Their hooves are cloven and they appear stupid, yet somehow noble.

The snakes are gone. Apparently the Jeebi-Ugs moved the battle to a locale to their advantage, where the power of the mound is lessened. Halberd has no idea how to return to the Dream World. The Jeebi-Ug move apart. Halberd knows they are separating, to make it impossible for him to strike at all of them. In a moment he will be surrounded.

Howling sounds to Halberd's right. Now he knows where the Jeebi-Ug have led him: to their own village, where all the tattooed demons howl to freeze the blood. At this new howl Comes into Sight stirs. She turns her head to appraise the situation.

"What is this place," she says softly, "and who are you? You are not one of the Arharak. Are you their executioner?"

Halberd swings his head to and fro. He tries to keep the Jeebi-Ugs in view. They look worried and are grouping back together.

"I am," he tells her while surveying the enemy and constantly moving. "Halberd, blood brother to your future partner, Usuthu."

"I do not know any man of that name." Her voice is regal, dignified, and calm. The howling comes again, closer. Comes into Sight lifts her head and, Halberd is certain twitches her nose like an animal scenting.

"Put me down," she says.

Halberd swings her to her feet. The Jeebi-Ug gasp and point their rattles at her. She goes to her knees in pain. Halberd kneels beside her.

"This Usuthu"—he speaks directly into her ear so that she might hear him over the pain—"is black of skin, head and shoulders taller than any man in your tribe, and brings great power from his people, who live far away in the direction of the rising sun."

A radiant smile splits her pain-racked face.

"It is he," she says. "I have seen him in my trances."

A wolf appears, loping steadily through the herd of the huge horned beasts. The wolf howls. It was he who had made the earlier noise, not the Jeebi-Ug. The Skrælings see the approaching wolf and gather together.

"Halberd," the wolf calls, "come to me."

"Etowah—what are you doing here? You must return to the Waking World."

Beside him the lovely young Skræling is on all fours. She raises her head and howls in answer to Etowah. At that moment she becomes a wolf. The Jeebi-Ugs turn and run. Etowah and Comes into Sight lope after them. The Jeebi-Ug know enough of the Dream World not to attempt awakening as an escape. They stand back to back and raise their rattles and feathers. Etowah bounds toward them. He leaves the ground in a long effortless leap. His jaws seize one Jeebi-Ug by the front of his head. The crack of the skull carries across the prairie to Halberd. Halberd recovers his wits and runs toward the carnage. Comes into Sight has torn the throat from one Jeebi-Ug and has her muzzle buried in the stomach of another. He screams as her fangs rip out his belly. She bites through an artery and blood pumps out over her gray-silver coat. Etowah, distinguished by his white forepaws, has the last Jeebi-Ug by the ear. The demon is dragged on the ground, screaming in pain and fear. Etowah shifts his grip to the Skræling's skull, and holds him so that Comes into Sight can seize him with her jaws between his legs.

Jeebi-Ug shoves at her with one hand, trying to get his legs together. She clamps down her jaws with such force that the click of her teeth coming together carries even over his endless, piercing panting scream.

As Halberd reaches the wolves they are soaked to the shoulders in blood and body parts. Etowah and Comes into Sight devour the Jeebi-Ug. They crack bones with their jaws and gobble them down. They chomp through the soft organs and stringy muscles, chewing and swallowing as fast as they can.

Halberd approaches with some caution. Their appetite frightens him. He does not want to be next.

"Etowah," he calls, "why do you eat the demons? Are you so completely a wolf?"

"We eat them, shaman," the white-pawed wolf answers, a long bone hanging from his mouth, "so that they cannot make more Jeebi-Ug. That is why we hurry so. If we eat them quickly, we own their souls. They are truly dead and we have their power."

Comes into Sight says nothing. She chews on the Jeebi-Ug whom she killed by emasculating with obvious pleasure. Halberd gestures at the half-eaten demon. Bones crunch and splinter in her mouth.

"This one was the real one, not the copy?"

The wolf nods without pausing in her chewing. Halberd leaves them alone until only hair and skulls lie on the snow-swept plain. The wolves sit back on their haunches and lick their chops with contentment. Halberd has a difficult time connecting this ferocious blood lust with the gentle boy who is Etowah.

The wolves lick one another clean. They pad over to Halberd, who sits in the snow with his hands clasping around his knees. They smile at him with their bloody, pointed teeth. Their eyes glow brightly with friendship.

"Who," Halberd asks after a short silence, "are you?"

"You know me as Comes into Sight," one of the wolves answers. "This is my identity in the Dream World. So long as I hold human form in this world I am vulnerable. My soul in this world is that of a wolf. My sorceress name is Moweaqua: Wolf-woman."

Halberd nods.

"Wolf-woman," he says, "do you know where we are? Do you know where your village is?"

The wolf nods her head. She licks the last morsels of Jeebi-Ug from her muzzle.

"May I hold your paw, and that of my apprentice?"

Moweaqua nods once more. Halberd takes her right front paw in his right hand and Etowah's right front paw in his left.

The wolves and the man awake.

Brokk and Bor

They were far down the river. The hills and cultivated fields of the Hadena territory had given way to wide rolling plains. There were fewer evergreens. The river was wider and sluggish. Summer grew nearer and nearer. The sun's journey across the sky took longer each night.

Their days entered a comfortable routine. Each morning Etowah left the war-canoe that Mowqua had given Usuthu and Moweaqua as a wedding gift and flew down the river. He returned to meet the canoe after it had left the campsite of the night before. Mälar still rode in the stern and Halberd in front of him. Etowah had the bow seat.

In the middle of the enormous canoe was an upraised canopy of deerskin, under which Usuthu lived with his bride. Moweaqua had left the mound with her father's blessing. He feared the jealousy of his young warriors if they saw his daughter living in the village with an outsider. In addition to the war-canoe he had given the couple three quivers of arrows made to Usuthu's specifications by the weapon masters of the Hadena. In return, Usuthu buried the stolen quivers beside their original owners.

No one saw the wedding. Usuthu and his bride did not leave her lodge for two days after her return from the Dream World. On the third day, Halberd, Etowah, Mälar, and Mowqua waited outside. Inside, the two lovers performed ceremonies called for by their opposite cultures. Had he survived, Owl Face would have been the Shaman to handle such duties. His death took from the Hadena their only Shaman, so Usuthu and Moweaqua served as their own.

The village at large did not seem enthralled by the new couple. Doubtless the young men had looked upon Moweaqua as a valuable prize to be won at marriage. Everyone else hoped she would be the source of the tribe's spiritual leadership for decades to come.

"Fate is fate," her father decreed at the subdued feast that followed their eventual emergence from the lodge, "and no man can stand in its way."

The Hadena did not seem to be a sentimental people. The morning after the feast only Moweaqua's mother and father stood at the muddy riverbank to tell her good-bye.

Mowqua spoke directly to Mälar, with minimal assistance from Etowah. Mowqua felt most comfortable with Mälar because they were near one another in age. Also, Mowqua was, like Mälar, a cynical and unreligious man.

"This canoe has painted upon it symbols which will grant you safe passage through the territory of the Hadena," Mowqua said. "Likewise these symbols will mark you as a target to the Arharak. When you gain the Mesipi, stay upon the shore on which the sun sets. The Othage live there, and they are nomadic. The Arharak control the near bank and of them you know plenty."

The Hadena were superb farmers. They loaded the war-canoe with vegetables and grain, neither of which the explorers had seen in months. They also filled woven baskets with wide flat brown leaves.

"This is a leaf which we smoke in our pipes. It provides visions, sometimes, but also peace and contentment. It is a sacrament," Mowqua told Mälar, "so commend it to the gods before you smoke it."

"I have no pipe," Mälar replied.

"Use the one Halberd stole from the mound," the chief replied. "It belonged to another shaman and will be useful in your journey."

He embraced his daughter and watched as her mother did the same. Only the mother cried. Moweaqua slipped under the deer canopy with Usuthu and the door flap was dropped. Mälar pushed the canoe off the muddy bank and then hopped in. Etowah and Halberd dug in with their paddles. They did not look back.

Moweaqua's mother ran sobbing to her lodge. Her father, Mowqua, Chief of the Hadena, stood on the bank watching the war-canoe until it disappeared around a wide bend. When the canoe was no longer in sight, he remained on the bank, staring at nothing.

The canoe that Mälar had built was towed behind the war-canoe on a rope of rawhide. Usuthu and his bride used that canoe to make expeditions to the shore or just to escape the closeness of the war-canoe. Usuthu's fear of water had subsided. He leaped from one canoe to the next happily, and even wielded a paddle, however poorly. His wife counseled him and the others about the tribes whose land they passed through and the spirits to whom they prayed.

Usuthu's happiness was matched only by his vigilance. Whenever he left the boat, his bow was slung over his shoulder.

Moweaqua proved good company. Mälar took to her easily. Etowah seemed awed by her beauty and power. He watched her as if from a great distance. Halberd and Mälar teased him about falling in love with Usuthu's wife, but Etowah's reply was dignified.

"When we are wolves together, we communicate without words as if we are brother and sister. Yet when we are humans, she ignores me. I know she thinks of me not at all."

"Boy," said Mälar in a kindly way, "whatever she or Halberd or you may be in the Spirit World has no bearing on her behavior in this one. She is a woman here, with a woman's desires. She is in love with Usuthu. You do not exist."

At night Mälar and Etowah camped by the fire, but Halberd took to sleeping under the small canoe, alone with his thoughts. The first few nights he had camped near the fire, which was also near the war-canoe. The giggles and moans coming from under the canopy had filled his mind with thoughts of Ishlanawanda.

Halberd wished his blood brother only happiness. In the middle of any day on the river Moweaqua might turn to Usuthu and run her hand up his thigh, or gently put her tongue in his ear. They would exchange no words. They would simply move under the canopy and close the flap.

How has he endured my visits with Ishlanawanda all these months? Halberd wondered. Perhaps because he doesn't see her or hear her or smell her when we make love.

On the evening of their fifteenth day from the

mound, the couple joined the others at the fire for the first time.

"Halberd," Moweaqua said, "you are downcast and miserable. Why don't you go to the Dream World and see your lady love?"

"Cares no one here for my misery?" Mälar asked.

"When have you ever truly longed for a woman?" teased Usuthu's wife.

"Every night for the past fourteen, my dear, why do you ask? Do you have one for me?"

"She does not," said Usuthu.

"Don't you two argue," Moweaqua said. "I will hear Halberd's answer."

"I have been forbidden to return by both Ishlanawanda and the Elders of her village."

"Until when?"

"I don't know."

Moweaqua studies Halberd carefully. "Take my advice, shaman, dream of her tonight."

Halberd lay under the inverted canoe, which was propped up by large logs at either end. He held the butt of his sword, which held the Jewel of Kyrwyn-Coyne, and pushed it toward the sacred stone knife. The two objects resisted one another, no matter how hard he pushed. His arms burned from the effort. Then, the jewel and the knife seemed to link. The sword floated out of Halberd's hand and Hrungnir rose in the air beside it.

Together they cast a warm silvery glow. The sword and the knife, bound together though still inches apart, began to revolve slowly over the canoe. Halberd knew he was safe while under that golden light. He closed his eyes.

He runs down the forest path that leads to her village. The scene is the same as ever. The village is peaceful, with plumes of smoke rising from the center of the tapering deer-hide structures. Ishlanawanda stands at the end of the path.

"Moweaqua, the Wolf-woman, bade me come," Halberd calls. "She felt the time is right."

Ishlanawanda does not move to greet him. Feeling uneasy, Halberd stumbles to a stop.

"I know of her. She has not been to our village but I know of her still. She has power," his love says, her voice flat and broken. "But today she is wrong. The time is not right."

"Why?"

"My father is dead." Tears trickle down her cheeks.

"When did he die?"

"He did not die. He was slain, murdered, assassinated by treachery."

Halberd does not speak. He steps to his love. She recedes a step from him. Maddened, he pounds the ground with his fist.

"Break this shield, let me in, come into my arms."

"I doubt this shield will ever be dropped again."

Halberd can only look into her face. He shakes his head.

"Grettir came here this morning," Ishlanawanda says. "She counseled with the Elders. She lured my father beyond the shield, into the forest. I believe he made love with her. When he stepped back inside the magic spell, he became a spider. A bird perching on a nearby tree, a black bird with a long beak, swooped down and scooped him up. The bird flew into the air and became a puff of smoke. So my father is dead and we have no body to bury."

She breaks into sobs.

"My love," says Halberd, "the bird must be either Huggin or Munin, they are Odin's messengers. Loki has corrupted them somehow. He used one of them for this fiendish purpose."

"Do not tell me tales of your world. It is your world and your visits which have brought this day to pass."

"I think not," Halberd says. "I think Grettir has long had designs on this place. I can help you, but only if you permit me."

Three Skræling Elders appear behind Ishlanawanda. One takes her arm.

"You may not help us, murderer. When next you return here, you will be slain."

Ishlanawanda cries even harder. She cannot raise her head to look at Halberd.

Halberd feels the weight of all the ages on his shoulders. His stomach churns with frustration.

"Do not misjudge your only ally in this fight," he cries, breaking into tears himself, "do not tear me from my love."

"You slew her father because he denied you," one Elder says, his voice as sharp as razors. "Do not think you can slay us."

"Grettir enchanted him and Grettir slew him, not I. Besides," Halberd says, with a flash of understanding, "her father may well not be dead, but stolen away by Loki."

Ishlanawanda's face changes slightly at these words. She is sorceress enough to consider it. Her village Elders are not so wise. Their contempt for Halberd is plain.

"Grettir told us," the Elder says, "that you were her lover."

Halberd burns with shame. "I was, once, but only once."

"You say once, she says forever. Our Chief is dead.

His body cannot be found. His soul is lost or enslaved. Do not tarry here. Do not return."

The Elders lead Ishlanawanda away.

Halberd awoke in his furs below the canoe. He threw them off and raced to the war-canoe.

"Awake, lovers," he cried.

Usuthu burst from the flap, wearing only his breechcloth and carrying his bow. An arrow was already nocked. Moweaqua stuck her head out of the opening. She was wrapped in a fur.

"Why," demanded Halberd, "did you send me to the Dream World tonight? Did you know something had happened there?"

Moweaqua looked shocked and sorrowful at the same time.

"No," she said, shaking her head, "I responded only to your loneliness. I thought if you tried to persuade her father, he might grant you a short visit."

Halberd stared at her in wonder. He had understood every word she said. So, his love had not abandoned him. Ishlanawanda had cast the enchantment that enabled him to understand the Skræling languages. He took heart at the strength of her love. She was strong indeed, to overcome her grief and the spell that protected her village. She would not have helped him if she believed he had conspired in the enchantment of her father. She had cast the spell as a sign of faith in Halberd and their love. All was not lost.

Halberd told Usuthu and Moweaqua what he had learned. He did not waste time with explanations. He assumed that Usuthu had told Moweaqua all of Grettir and Halberd's past.

Usuthu sat on the gunwales and splashed his huge

feet in the river. Moweaqua sat on the bottom of the canoe and rested her head on Usuthu's thigh. No one spoke. The river slapped against the hull.

"Grettir seems to be closing off areas of escape to you," said the Mongol. "She threatens Mälar and worries him to death. She steals the ravens from Aesir and uses them to her own ends. She is readying for an attack. We must treat each moment as if we were under siege."

Halberd did not answer. Usuthu was giving voice to Halberd's own thoughts. The Witch would strike soon.

"All of her attacks are intended to damage my heart, my spirit," Halberd said. "She has tried nothing tactical yet."

Usuthu waited before he answered. "First, to attack your spirits *is* a tactic. You must remain strong. Second, if she mistakes Moweaqua for a vulnerable target, she will pay a dear price. But Etowah is nowhere near so tough as he thinks. His vanity is swollen since his wolf attack on Jeebi-Ug. She will come after him."

Moweaqua nodded. Like Ishlanawanda and indeed, like Grettir, she had never shirked the counsel fires of men. Since girlhood she had been a decision maker and a seer. She expected no less of herself in this company.

"Etowah is easy prey in two areas," she said, "his pride in himself as a warrior, where he is unproven, and the other aspect of a man's life in which he is yet untested."

Halberd and Usuthu understood.

"Women," said Halberd.

"Go to him," Moweaqua said, "and tell him not to be seduced in his dreams. If any female form tempts him, he must run away. This is especially true while he is a wolf."

"I already told him not to dream, at all," Halberd said grimly.

"He's young," she said, "tell him again. Halberd, I apologize for suggesting you go there tonight. I am in your debt. Call on me for any aid."

"You are not in my debt, sister," Halberd replied. "You are one of us. There are no favors owed."

"Come on," Moweaqua said, standing and yanking on Usuthu's arm. "Let Etowah take the first watch. Have him wake me and I shall wake Usuthu. Halberd may sleep tonight."

Halberd found the boy rolled into his furs. Etowah was only a few years younger than Halberd, but he seemed a child in experience.

Halberd prodded him with a toe. Etowah rolled awake with his hatchet in his hand.

"Your readiness while awake is commendable," Halberd said. "Match it while you're sleeping."

"Halberd," Etowah said with some annoyance, "I *was* sleeping."

"We fear the Witch will chose you and that her method is seduction. She may come to you in your dreams or, if you should disobey my orders and visit the Spirit World, she may come to you as a she-wolf."

"I have not dreamed and I will not become a wolf."

"Nor," answered Halberd, "an eagle or a mole or a bear."

"If I don't become an eagle, how will I scout the river?"

"You won't. Not for a while anyway. We can make

do with Mälar's navigation, unless he has forgotten how."

"My memory would only be affected by loss of sleep," said the lump of fur that contained the helmsman. "Now, shut up and leave the boy alone."

Halberd returned to his furs. He tossed and turned, but finally dozed off.

A soft voice entered his consciousness. Sweet kisses moved slowly down his neck.

"Ishlanawanda," he muttered, "I knew you would not forsake me."

He rolled onto his back. Gentle hands tugged his sleeping furs from around him. They flipped up his Skræling tunic. It covered his head.

The knowing hands moved up his thighs, stroking him with love. The greedy mouth was on his stomach, tracing patterns on the muscle and hair. The hands on his legs moved up as the mouth moved down, coming together as the hands kneaded him with care. The mouth consumed him. Her tongue encircled him, drove him insane with long smooth licks. Halberd reached out to embrace her.

One hand raised up and guided his hand. He felt sheer garments and then the silken wetness between her legs. She moaned his name. He was inflamed with need. She straddled him and took him in her hands, aiming him inside her. He raised one hand to throw the tunic off his head. She reached out with a gentle wrist to restrain him.

"Wait," she whispered, her voice a groan of pleasure. He was almost inside her.

Halberd laughed and shook his head to throw off his shirt. It fell from his eyes. As it fell she shoved herself down upon him. He jerked to the side. Something was wrong. He opened his eyes.

Straddling him, her mouth open, her breath coming in pants, her eyes ablaze, was the Witch Grettir.

He was a vain fool. The Witch would not attack the boy. She would not attack Mälar. She had attacked him. He was weak for love and love was her weapon. His desire became murderous anger.

"Yes," she purred, "it is I. I'm the one who loves you, I'm the one you need. Come to me. Love me."

Her voice was hypnotic. Halberd's rage wavered. Why not, he thought, I'm lonely, my love has deserted me, why not? No one else need know. Grettir's hand on him became more insistent. At that moment, Halberd understood the danger.

He flipped onto his side, throwing the Witch off. Her head hit the edge of the inverted canoe and it fell on top of Halberd. She laughed from the shoreline as he groped for his knife or the jewel. The canoe was snatched off of him. Grettir gestured with one hand and the canoe sailed into the air. It tumbled in the night sky as it soared over the river. It crunched into a stand of trees at the shoreline.

Halberd stumbled to his feet, his deerskin tunic flapping, the sacred stone knife, Hrungnir, in one hand.

"Are you real," he called, "or are you in spirit form?"

The Witch, by way of answer, drifted out over the river. She hovered a foot or two over the small windblown waves. She had chosen not to be feral tonight, but beautiful. Her blond hair blew free, her white teeth gleamed in the darkness. She wore her thin white Witch's gown, which clung to her like rain.

Halberd still wanted her. His loins hurt with desire. He fought his lust. He knew it was her weapon against him.

Mälar and Usuthu stood shoulder to shoulder behind Halberd. The Witch laughed with delight. She smiled like a sweet young girl.

"Oh, Mälar," she said, her voice full of charm, "you caught me with your young master. I find you both so wonderful I cannot choose between you."

"Come to this bank, Witch, in the flesh, and then we can talk," Mälar said.

"In the flesh, Mälar, the flesh? Is that really how you want me?"

Something flashed in air. Something knocked Grettir sideways. She squawked like a hen. Blood showed on her cheek. Above them came the sound of wings flapping. Grettir ducked and something unseen *whooshed* by her.

"Pup!" she yelled, enraged. She leveled her hand in the direction of the flapping sound. Usuthu hurled his silver mallet. It turned end over end too quickly to be followed. Grettir heard it coming and swung her hand toward it. She was too late. The mallet struck her in the palm. She screamed. A distinct crack carried over the water. The mallet flew back to Usuthu's hand.

Grettir held her wrist tightly. Pain showed in her face. Her mouth twisted.

"Speak again, Witch," said Usuthu, "and I will dash out your teeth." He hefted the mallet.

Grettir raised her uninjured hand. She pointed not at Halberd but Mälar. She stared deeply into his eyes. She began to fade away.

She grew fainter and fainter. The forest was visible through her and then the stars. Her smile lingered in the air after she had departed.

Halberd turned to Mälar. He did not look like a tough navigator and warrior. He looked like an old, old man.

Etowah walked up to the riverbank. The old man grabbed him by one shoulder and shook him like a rat.

"Unhand me, Mälar!" Etowah pushed at the helmsman's iron grip with no effect.

Mälar shook him again.

"Fool!" Mälar spat. "She will have you for supper. On a ship, no matter what the size, crewmen obey their captain. Do you understand? You were given an order and you violated it. At sea you would be flung over the side."

"But," Etowah turned to Halberd and Usuthu, "I did it to aid my captain. You needed my help."

"Boy," said Usuthu, "we survived many dangers before we met you. We will survive many after. But you may not. Discipline makes a warrior."

"So does sleep," Mälar said. He pushed the boy away from him and walked away.

"Mälar," called Halberd.

The old man waved them off. He did not turn around. He made for his furs.

"Moweaqua," Halberd said excitedly, "you were not wrong to send me to the Dream World. I think I know where Ishlanawanda's father is. Loki would not dare let Odin know that he was using Huggin and Munin. He must be hiding them in Midgard. Loki knows the Giants and Dwarfs. He does them dark favors. They owe him."

"Why," Usuthu asked, "would Loki seize an Elder from the Dream World?"

"Loki is the father of Hel. Grettir promised the stone knife to Hel, only I took it before the promise could be kept. Hel hates me for my attack on her. I believe she petitioned her father, Loki, for aid. Grettir is now in league with Loki and together they weave some trap."

"Bah!" said Mälar. He sat up in his furs out by the fire. The lines of fear were etched in his face. Grettir's unstated threat was working. On a face long so brave, the obvious fear was hard to bear. "If Loki wants to torment a mortal, he would swat you like a fly. He wouldn't bother setting a trap with Grettir."

"No," said Halberd, "perhaps you are right. They wouldn't bother just for me. But Loki has been sniffing around the Dream World for some time, according to Ishlanawanda. He wants power there. Perhaps he will hold her father until he gets it."

"So," said Mälar, "you will go to Midgard and defy the gods. You will steal from the Trickster himself?"

"If he doesn't know it's me, I cannot be harmed."

"Where," Usuthu asked, "do you think he might be?"

"Hidden in the cave of the Giantess Flyting. She is one of Loki's allies against Thor and Odin."

"How will you find her?"

"I think the boy, in the spirit of a mole, can lead me there."

Etowah, at their side and silent, started with surprise.

"What about Ragnarok, your Giant friend?"

"He may well be dead. Anyway, I owe him, he does not owe me."

Mälar rolled back into his furs. Usuthu kissed Moweaqua gently and propelled her toward the canopy. She smiled at Halberd and dropped the door flap.

"What of Thund?" Usuthu whispered urgently.

"Urd? Jotunheim? Many in Midgard want you dead. It is the worst place for you to be."

"No, my brother, the worst place for me to be is here, when I would be with Ishlanawanda."

"So be it," Usuthu said. "We will continue downriver. You and the boy will have to find us."

He took Halberd's arm. He released it and ducked under the canopy.

"Etowah," said Halberd, "now you must become a mole. You will be my guide."

"But you told me that Grettir might snatch me."

"After an attack, she is weak. Now is the time. What are the limits to your endurance in the Spirit World?"

"There are none, so long as I can rest my body when I return."

"Good. You are going to lead me far, far below the earth, into Midgard, where dwell the Giants and Dwarfs. You will attend by my side at all times. I will follow you by the glow of Jewel of Kyrywn-Coyne. In the Spirit World you can detect its presence. Keep close to it at all times."

The boy nodded. His face was filled with terror.

"Rest easy," said Halberd. "When this adventure is done, you will truly be a man. Can you hear my voice once you become a mole?"

Etowah found his mouth too dry to speak. He could only nod once more.

"Get ready. Your job is to find a passage through the earth large enough for me to fit through. We have a long way to go."

Halberd strapped on his armor and put all his weapons in place, save his broadsword. He would need to see the glowing jewel at all times to follow the boy. Etowah climbed into the canoe. He took his usual seat at the bow. His body slumped over as if dead. Moweaqua came out of the canopy and draped a sleeping fur over the empty body of Etowah.

She handed Halberd a sweating drinking skin and a tiny woven basket. In it were dark green triangular root pods.

"Give these," she said, "to any Immortal you must bypass. They cause potent visions, even in those who are not human. For yourself eat no more than one, if you have need of visions. For the Immortals give three or more. Once they are consumed, stand aside."

She kissed him sweetly on the cheek. "I know you will return shortly," Moweaqua said. "We will see you down the river."

The jewel glowed brightly at the edge of the river. Halberd readied himself to jump in.

"Shaman." It was a hissed whisper. Halberd turned. Mälar sat up in his furs.

"Do not sacrifice the boy, I charge you. He reminds me too much of myself when I was young and stupid. If you cannot succeed, run away. Do not defy the Immortals and don't waste your strength trying to kill one."

Halberd nodded. The old man lay back and was instantly asleep.

Halberd plunged into the cool river. The mole made a tiny wake, which Halberd followed. On the other side Halberd reversed his sword and carried it butt forward. The jewel lit his way. If the glow faded on one side or another, he adjusted his course. They made rapid progress, though Etowah cared little for the branches or thorns that slapped Halberd in the face.

A fog-filled clearing revealed a low burial mound.

Wisps of fog clung to its bottom. Halberd ran up its side and discovered a hole at the peak. Halberd climbed feet first into the hole. It was pitch black. The jewel provided some light, enough to see that the sides of the hole were lined with skulls. It sloped downward gently. Halberd slipped his way down, headfirst, until the angle changed. It grew steeper.

Halberd clung to the wall, wedging his toes between the skulls. Reluctantly, he sheathed his sword to gain a free hand. The hole tilted again and became utterly vertical. Halberd braced his back on one side and his feet on the other. He walked down by sliding his rump, then moving his feet, then sliding his rump. Occasionally an old or rotting skull would crumbled beneath his weight, pitching him either forward or back.

Halberd was soaked with sweat. His purchase grew more tentative. He felt a draft coming from below. The hole seemed to widen. He reached out with his feet but could not touch the opposite wall below him. As he shifted for balance several skulls behind him broke free. His back slid down the wall in a series of hard bumps. His feet only brushed the other wall. He scrabbled at the rapidly moving wall but found no holds. The hole opened abruptly and he fell into complete darkness.

He awoke on his back. He raised his hand to his face. Small bits of blood on his forehead were still wet. He hadn't been unconscious long enough for the blood to dry. His back ached but no bones seemed to be broken. His sword was tangled beneath him. He moved cautiously. He seemed to be intact. His ax had fallen from his holster. He groped about in the blackness until it came to hand. He restored it to his belt.

Wind blew into his face directly ahead. He drew

his sword, reversed it, and stepped off into the breeze. The spirit of the mole moved quickly ahead. Halberd scurried to keep up. The ceiling lifted overhead and the draft become stronger. Squeakings and rustling began to drown out the wind.

The entire ceiling seemed to shift. Halberd dropped to his knees and threw his hands over his head. Thousands of bats poured from the ceiling, swooping over his head and tearing out the skull-lined hole to the night sky. They moved in a quivering black mass inside a formless black hole. They whistled by him on the hideous beating of leathery wings.

I'm lucky, Halberd thought, that I didn't throw myself onto my face. The floor of the cavern was knee-deep in bat dung. His sandals broke through the thin crust with every step. Pockets of gas exploded in his face and the odor overwhelmed him. He slogged through the dung until he thought his hair would fall out from the stench.

Ahead he could hear rushing of water. The cave floor stopped. Halberd leaned over and felt the empty black space. He lowered his sword. It touched no ground. Cursing, he sat down in the bat dung on the edge of the cliff. He swung his feet. He could feel the moisture just below. He holstered his sword and slid into the water. It was as cold as Niflheim in winter. He gasped as the frigid current hit his groin. The underground river was waist-deep and moving fast.

A tiny, tiny brush on his shoulder, no stronger than a falling leaf, told him that Etowah would not swim this river, but ride. Halberd drew his sword again. He held the jewel in front of him like a beacon. He let the water take him. He raised his legs in front of him and sat back. The current yanked him into the center of the river. He was off.

He flew around sharp bends and wide curves. The river fell through tiny falls and long narrow chutes. It never slackened. Rough water tossed his legs into the air or along the river's walls. Other streams joined and the current grew even faster. No light showed. Halberd rode the frigid river hour after hour. The bend of the river was ancient; it was worn smooth as glass. No rocks jutted up in its midst. Sometimes the ceiling came within inches of Halberd's head, and he had to duck into the water between breaths. Sometimes it rose so high a galelike wind tore through the passage. Halberd knew he was traveling great distances downward, ever downward.

Halberd lost all feeling in his legs, yet he found no place from which to escape the river. It filled its banks and the cliff walls around it were slick, as if the river often reached high enough to wear them down. Halberd unslung his drinking skin from around his back. He sheathed his sword and held the skin in front of him. Using its sling, he lashed himself to it. The skin bobbled on the surface just under his chin. It would keep him afloat. He chewed a few pieces of dried deer. After swearing an oath not to dream, he fell asleep.

His shivering woke him. He lay on a bed of rough gravel, under a sunless but well-lit sky. Huge drooping trees of black bark and black berries towered over him. Melted rocks lined the river, which here was wide as the Attyo and three times as fast. He lay on the bank of a wide sweeping turn, where the current had tossed him. He shifted his frozen legs. Blood rushed into them, bringing first needles and then sharp coursing pain. Halberd rubbed his legs vigorously. He tried to stand. He braced his hand on the gravel. He put his fingers into a small puddle of fallen and ruined black berries. The juice burned his skin. He yanked his hand away. This was the Poison Tree. He was in Midgard already. The river must have run straight down through the earth.

"Etowah, I believe you can hear me. We are on the outskirts of Midgard. We must go farther and down as well."

He held his sword in front of him, butt first. Etowah led him along the riverbank until they came to a large gray rock covered with moss. The glowing jewel faded to pearly white. Etowah must have run under the rock. Halberd sat down to wait.

An ungainly Dwarf ambled by. He was unusually pleasant to look at, for a Dwarf. He came up to Halberd's waist. His legs were bowed and his arms were enormous and layered with muscle. They were the arms of a Giant. His face was relaxed, with easy-going blue eyes and an empty, happy smile.

This, thought Halberd, is a very stupid Dwarf.

"Mortal," the Dwarf said crossly, "what are you doing in Midgard? Get out of here before I snap your back."

The Jewel of Kyrwyn-Coyne glowed brightly, flashed back to white, and glowed brightly again. Etowah was popping out from the rock and darting under, over and over. Obviously, Halberd had to follow the mole beneath the rock.

"I am looking, O mighty Dwarf," Halberd said, "for the strongest Dwarf in all the worlds."

"What for?"

"In my land in the earth, there is a grave emergency. We need a strong Dwarf to rescue thirty lovely maidens. Whosoever does this will win his pick of twenty of them."

"I am a very strong Dwarf." The Dwarf's hopeful tone brought a smile to Halberd's lips.

"How are you called?"

"I am Vidar."

"Oh, yes," said Halberd, "I have heard of your fame and prowess."

The Dwarf preened a bit. "And you, mortal, how are you known?"

"Ah, I am Kvasir," said Halberd, naming a long-dead warrior from his village. "I live in the Land of Sand."

"Well," said Vidar. "Let's go and save the maidens."

"No, no, no," said Halberd. "First you must prove your strength. Can you lift this rock?"

Vidar studied the boulder carefully. Tears came to Halberd's eye from swallowed laughter.

"That," said Vidar, "is a very big rock."

Halberd nodded. Vidar knelt by the stone and wrapped his ghastly arms around it. His huge fingers gripped so tightly that he dug channels into the stone. He braced his feet and gave a disgusting grunt. The rock shifted an inch. Vidar grunted again, as if he were dying. The cords in his neck stood out. His pleasant face turned blood red. His fingers turned white. The rock shifted again. Vidar let out all his breath and the rock came off the ground.

Vidar held the rock at chest height and smiled at Halberd. He lowered his arms.

"Wait," said Halberd, "you must lift the rock straight up over your head. That is the test."

Vidar gave Halberd a look of peevish disbelief. But he grunted yet again and hefted the rock dead over his head. Both his arms were straight up and locked at the elbow. The rock was easily three times the size of the Dwarf. He swayed back and forth, grinning with idiot pride.

The stone had hidden a small hole, no larger than a man's shoulders. A rock staircase, covered with moss and blocked by cobwebs, disappeared down an unlit hole. Halberd slid into the hole, chopping at the cobwebs with his broadsword. He looked back at the Dwarf. Halberd's head was at ground level.

"I tricked you, Vidar, there is no prize. Thank you, and good-bye."

Vidar's face fell. Halberd raced down the circling stairs. A crash from above cut off all light. Vidar, as Halberd had desired, had flung the stone over the opening to the stairs. Halberd did not want pursuers. He knew he could find another way out.

The jewel lit his way down the stairs. They wound round and round a central pillar. The moss made them slick. The crunchy bugs underfoot made them slicker. The scattered moldy bones lying here and there made Halberd wonder if another stone blocked the lower entrance. He spun around the circular steps till he could stand it no longer.

"Etowah," he called, "I must sit and drink and clear my head." He rested on one step. He drank from his bag and chewed more dried deer. He resumed his climb down. Like the river, the climb seemed endless.

Light showed, reflecting up the worn stone stairs. It flickered like firelight. Halberd reversed his broadsword and crept down the stairs. The light grew brighter. Halberd reached the bottom step. The exit from the stairway was tall and narrow. Halberd edged up to it. It was a passage cut into a tree. The stairway was magical. It did not exist from one point to another.

A fire burned just in front of the exit. Halberd stepped out of the tree, sword up. He was deep in Midgard. No sun showed. Around him hissed the furnaces of the Dwarf smiths. These were the most magical smiths in all the worlds. Even the gods of Aesir came here for their weapons, charms, and gold.

Two Dwarfs looked up in shock when Halberd emerged. One was huge, the other about Halberd's size. The larger had one eye on his bald forehead and two fangs that stuck out of his mouth. He wore a blackened smith's leather apron and held a pair of red-hot tongs. The small Dwarf had long greasy black hair and a face marked with boils and pitted scars. He held a smith's hammer in each hand. He wore a fur vest and leggings of leather.

"No mortal may use that staircase. It is for our customers only." The smaller Dwarf was instantly enraged. He stepped up to Halberd with both hammers upraised.

Though Halberd had, in fact, slain an Immortal, it was not easy to do. Killing a being meant to live forever was time-consuming, dangerous, and had earned Halberd a poor reputation in Midgard.

Halberd dropped to his knees.

"But, great smith, I *am* a customer. I came here on business. The great and noble Dwarf Vidar directed me here."

"Vidar?" said the larger smith. "That idiot? It figures. Well, what do you want and how will you pay for it?"

"I want three things," Halberd said, thinking fast, "and I shall pay for two of them."

"Well?" The Dwarfs went back to their forging.

Their hammers made an unearthly din. The coals of their furnace lit up the gloomy smithy.

"First, I want to know the way to the cave of the Giantess Flyting. For that I will not pay. Second, I want a leash that I might attach to a being in the Spirit World, that he might lead me easily, even though I can't see him. Third, I want a golden orb, big enough to hold a spider, that might travel without damage to itself or the spider, from here to the earth and thence to the World of Dreams."

"Hmmm," said the larger Dwarf, who seemed to be in charge of the forge, "would you bear this orb to the Dream World yourself?"

"If I must."

"What's the payment?" the smaller one asked in a surly tone. His hammers hung limply at his side. He resented having his hammering rhythm interrupted.

"These magic plants," Halberd said. He opened the woven basket. The larger Dwarf took the basket in his hands and marveled at its workmanship. He opened the top.

"What's so magic about them?"

"They will give you a day and a night of prophetic visions, visions of pleasure and madness which will show you great insight into your character and your future. Also, I should tell you, when you first eat them, you are likely to spew your most recent meal all over this forge."

The smaller Dwarf tilted his head like a curious dog. His lank, greasy hair fell over his filthy face.

"Why?"

"Because," Halberd said, his patience wearing thin, "they are hard on the stomach. Now, do you want to deal or don't you?"

"When do you," asked the larger Dwarf, "need all this by?"

"I need directions to the Giantess now. I need the leash and the orb when I return, whenever that is."

"This isn't much of an offer for everything you want. I don't care about insight into my character, though I don't mind having a little fun," said the big Dwarf. The smaller one pursed his lips and glared at his master. "I'll take these magic plants. But only on one condition. You will make yourself available to me at the time of my choosing, to do me a service of my choosing."

"What if I am in an emergency of my own when you need me?"

"Too bad. Do we have a deal?"

Halberd nodded. "If your service involves bringing no harm to any mortal or ally I know or love."

"Good," said the Dwarf. "Now Halberd, Dream Warrior, owes me a debt of honor."

Halberd eased Hrungnir out of its sheath. It was the only weapon he had against a Dwarf.

"How," he asked, as still as death, "do you know my name?"

"Oh, everybody knows you down here, slayer of Thund. How many mortals are there, do you think, who have killed Dwarfs and almost gotten Giants killed?"

"Almost?" Halberd said. "Do you mean that Ragnarok still lives?"

"So far as I know, he does."

"Why help me?"

"I never liked Thund. He had a big yap," said the large Dwarf. "My name is Brokk and this is Bor. We obey no one. Except those with payment. How do you intend to get out of here, anyway?"

Halberd shook his head.

"Your little mole will show you the way? Is that why you want the leash?"

Halberd's voice cut like a whip. "We have a bargain, Brokk. I have hired you and sworn my availability. I will answer no more questions."

"I had heard you had an arrogant temper for a mortal. Fortunately for you, I don't care. I'm a gentle smith, without much of a temper, only interested in stirring up a little mischief now and then. Remember your vow."

"Remember our deal," said Halberd. "Where is Flyting?"

"Go out of our cave. Stay hard by the wall in the dark so none may see you. Follow that wall until the cave below is seen. Slide down any pillar and follow the path. It will take you a day and a night. When you hear Svipdag howl, you are in her cave. Then she will find you."

"I'll be back." Halberd spun on his heel to leave.

"Say, mortal," Bor spoke quietly, "what would you take for that stone knife? Would you like a golden sword that cannot be bested and drops seven more gold swords every month? Or perhaps a ring that might take you anywhere in your world and still grant you forty times its weight a week?"

Halberd shook his head. He felt the whisper of Etowah's feet on his shoulder. They set off to follow Brokk's directions.

Halberd kept low by the wall. It was lit by the flaring fires of the Dwarf forges. Apparently he was in the land of the smiths. Furnaces glowed here and there, and Dwarfs of all sizes and shapes wandered about. The many forges threw their shadows on the wall. Halberd walked until he was exhausted. He found a ledge to sleep on. He gripped Hrungnir tightly and snuggled far back into the ledge so that the shadows hid him. He slept.

He awoke and lay in the darkness, listening to the Dwarfs work their bellows and insult one another. He drank the last of his water and nibbled the last of his rations. It would be a hard trip back to the Attyo River. The path ran out, as Brokk had said it would, at the edge of a cliff. Reaching from the ceiling of the cave above were long thin growths of stone, formed by thousands of years of dripping water. These slick pillars stretched all the way from the ceiling, which appeared to be at least a league above Halberd's head, to the rock floor that jutted over the cliff edge. It was a drop of several hundred feet. Halberd clasped one pillar tightly and swung off the cliff.

Even with his arms around the smooth stone, Halberd dropped fast. He slid down the pillar so quickly he thought his arms would catch fire. Nothing he could do slowed him down. He flexed to hit the stone floor. He looked down. The floor raced up to meet him. Off to the side, Halberd saw a tiny pool. At the last instant, he shoved off the pillar and flew into the pool.

Halberd landed on his back and splashed the pool dry. The noise of his crash brought a horrible snarling from just inside the colossal cave entry. Boiling rock, white and smoldering, came pouring out. Halberd sidestepped the lava stream and went inside. Lying by the door, writhing and snarling, his jaws running with the white froth that became lava when it hit the air, was the great wolf Svipdag.

Svipdag was another of Loki's children. The gods of Aesir feared the huge wolf and bound him for all eternity. His constant anger caused him to froth at the mouth. This froth fed every volcano and earthquake in the world. It suited Flyting that her door would be guarded by such a monster. Halberd circled past the bound Immortal and worked his way back into the cave. Bones littered the floor. Bones small enough to be human, bones so large they could only belong to Giants, and bones of odd sizes, which must be those of Dwarfs.

Many small fires lit the inside of the cave. It stank of death. Skeletons lined the walls. Some sat, some hung in chains. Halberd held Hrungnir in one hand and his sword in the other. He stepped around a small hillock to enter the main room of the cave. It was a dingy, ghastly place. A huge straw pallet lay against one wall. Over the cookfire hung an immense caldron. It bubbled and the smell it produced could only be cooking flesh. Hanging on a hook, high on one wall, was a tiny black cage. It hung too far away for Halberd to see inside, but he knew it had to hold Ishlanawanda's father.

"Etowah," he whispered, "scamper up to that cage and see if it holds a black spider. Talk to the spider. Tell him who we are. Then hurry back to me."

"Who whispers in my cave?" The booming voice made Halberd jump. His heart raced. The small hillock behind him moved. It was not earth, but a blond, fat Giantess. She stood five times taller than Halberd. Her hair was fair, but filthy with grease. She wore man's pants held up with a rope and a filthy cape over her shoulders. Her huge blue eyes showed great cunning.

"It is I, Halberd, Dream Warrior, come to Midgard for one purpose."

"What purpose is that?"

"To give the Giantess Flyting a kiss."

To his amazement, the horrible Giantess blushed. She laughed a wicked, low laugh.

"No, mortal," she said, "you have come to rescue the father of your lover, and to humiliate my good friend Loki."

Halberd felt great annoyance. Everyone in this world knew his business better than he did.

"If you know my reasons for being here, Flyting, why ask?"

"Because, little one, I am bored. I am bored with my diet of mortals like you. I'm bored with my loneliness. And I am bored with Loki using my cave as a hiding place in all of his schemes and conspiracies."

"I want the spider."

"Well, you're going to have to work to get it. Do you know why I'm so bored?"

Halberd shook his head.

"No one ever comes to visit me, that's why. No one ever comes because of the cursed Bleeding Head."

Halberd's face showed his confusion.

"This cave is haunted by the Bleeding Head. It launches itself from hidden corners and attacks whoever comes in. It eats half of them and leaves the rest for me. I have been unable to leave this cave since my childhood. The Bleeding Head would kill me if I tried."

Halberd found it hard to work up much sympathy for this fat, lazy cannibal. His face, however, showed great concern and compassion.

"Why," he asked, "didn't it attack me?"

"Oh, it's bored, too," Flyting said pathetically. "It plays games all the time. No doubt it is lurking around here somewhere, ready to tear your head off."

"Can it speak?"

"Of course it can't speak! If it could speak, I wouldn't be so lonely." The Giantess reached out one pale flabby arm and stirred her boiling caldron. The smell in the cave got worse. "Anyway, I want you to kill it. No one else ever could, though they've certainly tried. You're supposed to be so special, the slayer of Thund and all that, maybe you can kill it."

"If you never leave this cave," Halberd said, "how do you know so much about the worlds outside it?" His head was swimming from the stench and the weight of her constant chatter.

"Loki visits me quite often. He's my only company. We're related somehow. I believe my mother is his daughter, Hel, the ruler of Niflheim."

I believe it, thought Halberd. You're repulsive enough to be the daughter of Hel.

"In that case," said Halberd, "you would do well to hand over the spider. That way you can aggravate your mother as well as you father."

"I'm not handing over anything," she said. "You're going to earn it. Now, go kill the Bleeding Head and I'll give you the cage."

Halberd moved to the fire, which was on the highest point in the cave, to survey the scene. He saw a long black river, more stone growths hanging down from the ceiling, and a desolate stone landscape. There was nothing more.

Something *whooshed* out of the shadows in the roof. Halberd ducked and raised up his sword. A disembodied head, twice as large as Halberd was tall, shot by, jaw agape. Blood streamed from its temples and down the back of its head. Its eyes were dark. Its hair was black and close-cropped. Its lips were twisted into a smile. It squinted as if it had stared into many sunny days. It vanished into the shadows and swooped at Halberd again. It missed him by inches. The Bleeding Head was toying with him. It could easily bite him in half.

Halberd raced back to the fire and knelt by the coals. The caldron stank like a hundred tombs. It glowed red-hot at the bottom. The heat of the coals was unbearable. Halberd made himself sit nearer. His eyebrows began to singe and his red beard to smolder.

Halberd reached into the fire with Hrungnir. He levered out a glowing coal and held it to his mouth.

"Yum, yum," he cried, "what a delicious meal. I'm so glad I learned of this food."

Halberd opened his mouth and pretended to eat. He let the coal slide over his shoulder. He flipped another coal up near his mouth. He did this with five more coals, all the while rubbing his stomach. He acted out great enjoyment of the meal.

The *whoosh* sounded right in his ear. The Bleeding Head hovered right next to him. Its bleeding jaws opened. Rows of sharp teeth, sloping backward like a serpent's, stood ready. The Bleeding Heart did not bite. It watched Halberd with care.

Halberd sheathed Hrungnir. He eased his ax off his belt. He laid the blade flat into the fire and slid it along until it was heaped with coals. Halberd raised the ax up to the Bleeding Head and hesitated in front of its mouth.

The Head nodded eagerly.

Halberd shoveled in the coals. He stabbed upward with his left hand and pinned the Head's jaw to the roof of its mouth. The Head yanked free of Halberd's knife and sent him tumbling across the floor of the cave.

The Head raced around the cave. It bounced off

one wall and then another. It crashed into the floor. It shot up to the ceiling. Smoke poured from its ears and nose. Its flight grew more frenzied as the smoke increased. Halberd stood waiting. Whenever the Head neared him, he struck at it with his ax. The Head moved too quickly to be hit.

The Giantess was beside herself with laughter. She fell back against the wall of her cave, pounding her heels into the floor. The rolls of fat at her waist jiggled up and down.

The Head soared to the ceiling until it was directly above the fire. Halberd understood its purpose. He scrambled away from the fire. He ducked between the pounding filth-covered feet of Flyting. He jumped behind a rock.

The Head hit the center of the caldron at full speed. The impact sent bones and half-cooked flesh splashing across the cave, all carried on a spew of filthy boiling broth. The broth coated the cave. Flyting was drenched. She screamed in pain. Her arms, face, and the fat rolls around her belly turned instantly red. She screamed again, a high wail like a baby's. Halberd put his hands over his ears. The caldron rolled on its side, empty. The Head lay next to it. It looked at Halberd with empty sockets. Its eyes were burned from the inside out. Smoke still trickled out of its ears.

Halberd ran to the cave wall. He raised one end of a straw from the Giantess' bed. The straw was as wide as a sapling. Halberd leaned it against the wall. He braced his feet on the straw and bent double. He grabbed the straw with his hands. Bent over, he walked his way up the pole. Halberd grabbed the black cage off the hook.

The spider inside looked ferocious. It had tiny red

eyes. It scuttled to the bars of the cage and struck at Halberd with its legs. No doubt the Chief thought Halberd was committing a theft, not a rescue. Flyting still screamed.

"Etowah, I hope you are here," Halberd said. "Climb onto my arm."

Halberd slid down the pole. He ran right up Flyting's burned legs, over the bouncing fat, over her huge sagging breasts, and up to her open mouth.

"Shut up!" he screamed. "If you are not quiet, I will throw this spider down your throat."

She stopped in midscream.

The sudden silence was deafening. Halberd took a moment to compose himself. He wound a hand into her filthy tunic.

"Rise up and bear me to the forge of Brokk and Bor. If you falter, you will find an enraged spider in your mouth."

"Don't make me," she wailed in response, "go out there. I haven't been out of this cave in seven hundred years. I don't want anyone to see me." Her voice broke off into racking sobs.

"All right, all right," said Halberd, "just shut up. Take me outside the entrance to your cave and lift me to the ledge above. Can you do that?"

Flyting nodded. She sniffled and reached up to wipe her nose.

"Stop!" said Halberd. "Don't reach up here."

Flyting shuffled toward the cave entrance. She walked past Svipdag, who, if she told the truth, was both her uncle and her brother, without even a glance. At the sight of her the wolf trembled more, and the lava ran thick and gooey down the sloping cave floor.

At the gloomy entrance the Giantess became suddenly coy. She peeked out of the cave like a five-year-old. Seeing no one, she hurried on tiptoe to the ledge.

"Take me in your hand," Halberd said, "and remember what happened to Thund."

Flyting flattened her filthy palm. Already it was studded with blisters from the boiling broth. Halberd climbed onto the palm unsteadily. He drew Hrungnir and pressed it against the artery in her wrist. She bore him to the ledge. Holding the spider cage in one hand, Halberd leaped from her palm. He felt it turn over as he pushed off. It was a mild attempt to kill him, only halfhearted. Halberd could not even get angry. He hit the cliff edge at a lope. He ran away from Flyting without a backward glance. Her sobs of frustration and pain followed him down the path.

Halberd ran as fast as he could. He did not use the warrior's trot. There was no time for hunger or thirst. He had to return Ishlanawanda's father to the Dream World before Loki found out he was missing. Halberd dashed along the path, hugging the shadows. As before, no Dwarf noticed him. The vast scale of Midgard made him feel invisible.

He ran endlessly. Finally, he turned up the trail that led to the forge of Brokk and Bor. He raced inside. He bent over at the knees, gasping for breath. Brokk and Bor looked up from their forge. They smiled to see a mortal suffering so.

"Back so soon?" Brokk laughed.

"Are you ready?" Halberd could barely speak.

"Have some water, mortal, and slow down. All is ready."

Brokk produced a thin woven leash of gold. Six feet long, it glimmered in the shadowy light of the smoldering forge. Halberd took it in his hands. He could feel the magic of it. He held it up to his shoulder and Etowah climbed through the collar. Halberd fastened it. The mole spirit was no more visible, but at least now Halberd knew where it was.

Bor held out a clenched fist. Halberd tapped it with a weary hand. Bor shook his head and produced his other fist, which he had held behind his back. He turned it over. Resting inside was a solid gold ball. It showed no opening or holes for air.

Halberd raised an eyebrow to Brokk.

"Behold, mortal," the Dwarf said. "Only one particular spider may enter this ball, which will grow when he reaches the Dream World so he will not be crushed. Remember, he will rapidly regain his true size when he gets home. The globe needs no opening because only he can pass through its walls. This will prevent anyone who should not from opening it and harming the precious cargo. Also, since we understand the beings who inhabit the Dream World have no use for gold, this ball will return to our hands when your spider is safely home."

"That is not in our bargain. I pay for the gold and you keep it."

"We do not want you to feel cheated. This ball does not need to be carried to the Dream World. When you are outside of Midgard, release it and it will transport the spider home."

Halberd grunted.

"And," said Bor, as smoothly as a jeweler in a Bazaar in the Land of Sand, "this leash will guide you directly to your friends. It will bear you through solid rock and earth. Alas, it can work but once. However, you may keep the gold. Once you reach your friends all enchantments will end."

"How do I know," Halberd demanded, "that these charms are not cursed? What is my assurance that the spider will reach his home or that I will not die trapped inside some cold and unyielding stone?"

Brokk reached out gently. He took Halberd by the neck and lifted him off the stony floor. He dangled the Northman over the forge.

"My word is my bond, mortal, as is yours. We bargained for a fair price. Our charms always work. We have never broken our word about anything made on our forge since the earth began. So, do not make me angry."

Brokk lowered Halberd to the ground. Halberd twisted his head around. His neck did not seem to be broken. It certainly felt like it was.

"I beg your pardon, Brokk, master blacksmith of gold. I live in a treacherous world. I mean you no disrespect."

Brokk said nothing.

"How can I," Halberd thought aloud, "convince the spider to enter the ball? He distrusts me."

"Is he not convinced," Brokk said, "of your sincerity? He has heard us speak of the ball's function."

"He cannot understand our language."

"Put the ball in his cage. It will absorb him."

Halberd opened the tiny gate on the black cage. The spider scuttled to the door. Halberd blocked it with the golden ball. The spider studied the ball carefully. He put his body against it and his front legs sank inside. He pulled back warily. He moved forward. He touched the ball with one leg. That leg went in. Then another. The spider scurried inside the ball. Halberd lifted the ball out of the cage and slipped it into his armor.

"Thank you, Brokk, thank you, Bor. I am at your service. Call me when you need me."

"We will," said Brokk.

"We will," said Bor.

They turned back to the forge.

"Lead me to our companions," Halberd said. He wasn't sure if he was speaking to Etowah or the leash.

The golden leash snapped out to its full length. Halberd was yanked straight at the stone wall of the cave. The wall didn't part, exactly, and yet Halberd was carried inside it. He had a brief glimpse of stone until the blackness closed in.

Then a sudden flash of light and an underground waterfall, larger than anything he had seen on earth. Another rock wall approaching and more blackness. Halberd felt he was soaring upward, ever upward. He smelled water, then dirt.

He exploded out of the ground. He raced through a forest. He looked back. The dirt where he had emerged was undisturbed. There was no hole. Halberd shot through the forest, moving through trees. Then he was underwater, bubbles streaming in his wake. He stopped.

He had no air in his lungs. Sunlight wavered on the water's surface, far, far above. Halberd kicked as hard as he could. He pulled with his arms. The sunlight was close. Closer. Halberd broke the surface with a gasp.

He treaded water, breathing in the sweet air in deep draughts. He dug into his armor, found the golden ball, and held it to the sunlight. It floated out of his hand and into the sky. Halberd watched the tiny ball with one hand over his eyes. He lost sight of it in the glare of the sun.

Facing him was only more riverbank and forest. He turned around in the water. He jerked backward in shock. Two feet away was the war-canoe.

Usuthu and Moweaqua gazed at him with bemused concern. Mälar smiled from the stern and extended his paddle. Halberd grasped the blade and they pulled him aboard.

Death on the Mesipi

"No river," Mälar said, "is that big."

They drifted in the war-canoe at the southern and western end of the Attyo River. As Mahvreeds' map had shown, it emptied into the Mesipi. They stared at the great river from no more than two leagues away.

"The Yellow River, deep in the southern mountains of my father's land, is that wide in places," Usuthu said.

Etowah said nothing. Three days after their return from Midgard he was still asleep. The journey had exhausted him.

"I have seen the River of the Sun by the Pyramids in the Land of Sand," said Mälar, "and it wasn't this big."

"Do you think," asked Halberd, "that we will be able to deal with its currents?"

"The size of this canoe will help. I think we would have been lost in our smaller vessel. But the lovers' canopy must come down and both must wield paddles."

It was done. The Mesipi was so wide where the Attyo joined that no rapids occurred. The Mesipi swallowed the Attyo as if it were a brook. The Mesipi was lined with rolling hills and empty plains. The thick forests of the Attyo were far behind. Covering the western plains were vast herds of the hump-shouldered, shaggy-haired, beady-eyed horned beasts that Halberd had seen in the Dream World.

"The Othage called them the god dog, the buflo," Moweaqua said. "It provides all needs to the Othage. They wear and live under its skin, they eat every part of it, and they use the bones for tools."

"How do they hunt them without horses?"

Moweaqua looked confused for a moment. Then she remembered what her husband had told her of those odd beasts that allowed men to sit on their backs.

"They creep upon them wearing the skin of the buflo," she said, "or they herd them off of cliffs."

Halberd and Usuthu studied the endless empty plains.

"I don't see any cliffs," Halberd said.

Moweaqua waved a hand. "Oh," she said, "they're there. Small bluffs and canyons."

Mälar studied the herds with care. It was hard to maneuver the war-canoe across the swells and currents of the Mesipi to the western bank. The river ran stronger than many hard tides. Small eddies turned the canoe back and bizarre swells would emerge in complete contradiction to the flow of the river. Despite Mälar's best efforts, they observed the buflo from some distance.

"It would take a brave man," the navigator said, "to crawl into a herd of those monsters armed only with a bow and a fur."

"The tribes on the western side of the Mesipi, I have heard, are not like the Hadena or Eerhahkwoi.

They move from place to place with the seasons. They plant no crops. They are fierce."

"And the Arharak?"

"Demons," Moweaqua said flatly. "And if we cannot gain the western bank, we cannot avoid them. We are already in their territory."

"Well," Mälar said quietly from the stern. "With this crew in this weather we cannot traverse this current. No offense to your skill as paddlers. I need ten more like you to make this craft obey. We will have to travel the eastern shore. Hold your paddles."

He swung the canoe off its western course. The current whipped the boat around. The bow pointed south. The huge war-canoe leaped forward like a spirited pony.

"Pull."

All dug in.

The sun beat down from a cloudless sky. To the south great thunderheads massed up in a storm. The hazy light made the distant western bank almost invisible. The magnificent river carried many things in its current; huge trees ripped out of the bank, dead swollen deer and buflo, and, at various intervals, other canoes, paddled by Skrælings they could not identify.

On the shore they saw families moving along well-defined trails. Small dogs pulled triangular sleds without wheels. These sleds were made from two poles lashed together by a wide cargo mat made of hide. The ends of the poles dragged on the ground. The sleds were packed impossibly high, yet the dogs did not falter. Dust rose from their travels. The Skrælings, whatever their tribe, conspiciously ignored the canoe.

"Only the Arharak," Moweaqua said, "would acknowledge a Hadena war-canoe and that would only be to attack us. No one will come close enough to see our strange passengers."

"Should we camp by day and paddle by night?" Mälar wondered.

"No," said Halberd. "The Arharak move about by day. They would find us more easily. We can hold off any attack while on the river with Usuthu's bow. I am not worried and I wish to make progress."

"Why are you not asleep and dreaming, Halberd?" asked Moweaqua.

"I want her father to have time to understand what was done for him," Halberd said peevishly. He was also worn out from his ordeal under the earth. "Remember, too, that he was a spider inside the village's magic spell. He may be a spider still. In that case he cannot tell them of my role in his escape. Let them work it out and call for me, then will I go."

"We are out of meat," Usuthu said, changing the subject as he sensed Halberd's discomfort. "We must put ashore for a hunt before tomorrow."

"We will be inside that thunderstorm tonight," Mälar said. "Let us camp this side of it, and tomorrow we can hunt under the cover of its rain."

The next day found Halberd, Mälar, and Etowah slogging through the swampy edges of the Mesipi. A light rain fell. It was warm and soothing, but Mälar predicted a larger storm shortly. Usuthu and Moweaqua lay offshore in the canoe. Usuthu had argued that he should do the hunting, but Halberd had overruled him. Protecting their canoe was paramount, Halberd had said, and only Usuthu had the bow range to guarantee its safety. The game did not require long-distance hunting.

Mälar made a sea anchor out of fur and showed Moweaqua had to use it. Halberd had given them strict commands not to approach the shore. When the hunt was done, Mälar would swim the short distance to the canoe and paddle it in. Neither Usuthu nor Moweaqua had the skill to deal with any emergency. It was not said aloud, but Halberd did not think the lovers would mind a few private hours.

The three stalked a herd of ten deer that gamboled in the fields just inland from the swampy shore. Half a league to the south they could see a large Arharak village. Their houses were low domed mounds, made of hide or bark. Halberd could not tell the material at this distance. Ropes held the curved logs in place and lashed the roof to the poles. Moweaqua had called these small lodges wickiups. There were more than a hundred of them.

Etowah had not spoken much since he finally awakened. Halberd knew he was consumed with fantasies of revenge against those who had eaten his mother and father. Halberd knew that no force would constrain Etowah, just as no force could have restrained Halberd. For the good of his quest, Halberd hoped that Etowah could be patient, and wait for the right moment to take his vengeance. Halberd was aware, though, that he and the others were deeply in Etowah's debt for all his help. When the boy wanted a raid, many Arharak would die.

As they moved, crouched over, through the clinging mud and scratching thorns, Mälar counseled Etowah about the hunt and the Arharak.

"I would not have believed they were truly flesh-eaters unless you had told me so," Mälar said.

"Why not?"

"I have traveled the world, such as it is known," answered Mälar. "Whenever I have asked people reputed to be cannibals if indeed they eat the flesh of their brothers, they all have the same reply. They say, 'Oh, no, I could never do that, but my enemy, who lives over that hill, he is a terrible cannibal.' So I go over the hill and ask that man and he refers me back to his enemy."

"Do you not believe me, then?"

"Etowah, I do believe your tale. I fear the Arharak."

"Well," said the boy, "I do not. When will we go into this village and burn it to the ground?"

"How do you know the murderers of your parents came from this village?"

"Halberd, I am eighteen winters now. Whoever ate my father is long dead. I don't care who it was. I want the Arharak to feel grief as I feel it."

Halberd and Mälar nodded. There was no argument against such feelings.

"That village," said Halberd, "is a bit large for an army as small as ours. Let us start with one about half that size."

"You make jokes," said the boy. "I do not."

"I am not joking," Halberd insisted. "We do not want to die. Restrain yourself."

"I will not." The boy stomped off through the underbrush. He moved onto higher, drier ground, cutting off the herd of deer and placing it between Halberd and Mälar and the river.

"Don't venture so close. . . ." Mälar whispered urgently. His voice trailed off. "What's the use? The boy is as stubborn as I am."

"The rain will keep the demons in their homes today," Halberd said.

"He should have stayed in the canoe." Mälar watched the boy crash through the bushes on a small hill above them. "He has never hunted meat or even eaten it. Why should he want to kill a deer?"

"I think," replied Halberd, "that he feels blood lust and isn't sure how to express it. He wants to kill an animal before he kills a man."

"Perhaps." Mälar stood straight up in the swamp. Without seeming to fit an arrow into his bow or even aim, he nailed a small deer right through the shoulder and heart. The deer stumbled a few feet before falling over.

Halberd had not even seen the deer. He watched in admiration as the old man scrambled off to gut and bleed his prize. Mälar had lost none of his quickness. Halberd slogged up and was peeling the skin of the deer when they heard a shout from the rise.

"Now, flesh-eater, pay the price for your miserable blood!"

"Oh no!" Mälar dropped the deer and crashed through the clinging vines and thorns.

Halberd drew his sword and climbed the hill on a path parallel to Mälar's. They were moving, by instinct, to encircle the boy's position. The rain came down harder. The wind picked up and the clouds moved lower. The wind shifted direction. Now it came from the south, bringing cold, wet air from the gathering thunderstorm.

The thorns held Halberd. The vines underfoot yanked at his ankles. He slashed at the clinging growth with his sword, but he knew he went too slowly. He could hear nothing from the top of the rise. He could hear nothing but the blows of his sword and the grunts of his own breath.

The brush thinned out as Halberd neared the crest of the hill. His thighs burned from the chase. He heard sword clash against stone. Someone coughed blood. There was a loud thump.

Halberd ran onto a wide flat. The knee-high yellow grass whipped about in the gathering wind. Mälar stood downwind a bit, his sword deep in the side of a tattooed Arharak warrior. The old navigator had one foot braced on the demon's chest while he worked back and forth at his stuck sword.

At his feet lay four more Arharak. Only one suffered a sword wound. The other three simply had no heads. What once was skull and brains was now a dull gray paste. It looked as if someone with no experience of the nuances of battle had bashed them with a stone war club.

Halberd drew his ax and rushed forward. Three Arharak sprang out of the grass. Halberd swung left-handed across his body at one, and left his ax in the Skræling's chest. He slashed a two-handed broadsword swing at the other two and drove them back a step. All took a moment to gain their breath. One Arharak poked at Halberd with his lance. Halberd chopped down on the stone point and stepped on it when it hit the ground. The surprised Skræling did not let go of the lance. Halberd jammed the point of his sword under the demon's chin.

The other Arharak looked over his shoulder, trying to see his back. Halberd stepped up and smacked the man in the side of his head with the flat edge of his broadsword. Halberd wanted to question the Arharak. As the Skræling fell, Halberd saw that there was an arrow hanging loosely from his back. The arrowhead had barely penetrated his blue tattoos.

Halberd turned in amazement to the river. Standing in the canoe was Usuthu, another arrow nocked and ready. The Mongol wasn't exactly a speck, but he was barely distinguishable. Halberd shook his head. He had finally seen the outer limits of Usuthu's range. Even though the Mongol had hit his target, the distance was so great the arrow had had no force. Even by Usuthu's standards, to which Halberd believed he was accustomed, it was an astounding shot.

The Arharak chopped at Halberd's leg with a stabbing knife. Halberd broke the demon's head like an apple.

Halberd waved his hands to indicate confusion and Usuthu pointed downriver, toward the Arharak village. Mälar freed his sword. The two ran through the grass. Another Arharak popped up before them. Mälar barely hesitated before splitting the man from his shoulder to his crotch with one blow. Again the sword stuck and again Mälar had to pause to work it free.

"Go on, go!" he called, waving Halberd forward.

Halberd ran to the top of the next rise. From there he could see it all.

There was no misinterpreting the horrible scene. Ten warriors ran down a long slope to the village, whooping and screaming. Over their heads, carried on their outstretched arms, kicking and screaming, was the would-be warrior Etowah.

As those demons ran into the open ground at the center of the village, a war party of thirty or more boiled out, heading for the high ground where Halberd stood. Halberd ran back to Mälar. He passed the helmsman without a word. Mälar retrieved his sword and followed. Halberd paused long enough to pluck his ax from the chest of the dead Skræling. Mälar stooped to pick up two Arharak lances.

The inhuman cries of the war party sounded at the crest of the hill. The Arharak were fast.

Halberd and Mälar plunged down the steep hill

through the vines. Thorns ripped long scratches into Halberd's side, but he did not feel them. He and Mälar splashed into the deep black mud at the riverbank and flung themselves into the strong current. They swam for their lives.

The hard rain pelted them and thunder boomed overhead. It was no time to be on a river. The wind whipped waves up over their heads, blinding them. Whenever Halberd raised his head to draw a breath, a wave smacked him in the face.

No arrows hit the water around them. Halberd was puzzled. When at last he could see the canoe, he had his answer. Usuthu stood upright in the madly rocking canoe, calmly filling the pursuing Arharak with Hadena arrows.

Halberd fought his way through the mounting waves. He gripped the gunwale of the war-canoe and hoisted himself aboard. Moweaqua sat under the canopy, slapping arrows into Usuthu's outstretched hand. Mälar slid up to the canoe, swimming as effortlessly as a weasel. Halberd yanked him into the boat.

The storm was upon them in full fury. They could not see the western bank or even the middle of the Mesipi. The canoe shuddered in the rising swells. The current moved opposite to the driving wind, bringing the waves straight in over their bow. Lightning filled the sky.

They huddled under the canopy. The rain pounded down. It was like being inside a drum.

"We must get to shore," Halberd shouted. He looked to the bank. The Arharak had disappeared. The raindrops fell as big as his thumb.

"What we must do is kill them all," said Mälar.

Halberd and Usuthu looked at one another. There

were many arguments against it. They had to move south. They might not survive the storm if they stayed on the water. Etowah had spurned their advice and had gotten killed. There had to be fifty or a hundred warriors in the village.

There was only one course.

Halberd nodded.

"All," Usuthu said.

"The Skrælings can't believe we were not drowned in this storm," said Halberd. "They will think us long dead."

"We still might be," answered Usuthu.

"They will not eat the boy before night. We still might save him."

Halberd turned to Mälar in disbelief. He had considered the boy as dead from the moment of his capture. Halberd opened his mouth to argue with Mälar.

Mälar made an impatient gesture with his hand. His eyes burned into them. "There is no discussion," he said. "We ride this storm out right here, no matter what. When it is dark, no matter what, we beach this boat and wipe out the village."

Halberd turned to Moweaqua. "Can you," he asked her, "fight?"

She nodded without hesitation. From her tunic she produced a wicked ivory knife. Its side was worked with carvings of animals.

"Take these," Mälar said, passing her the two Arharak lances. "This is all the weaponry we may spare you. More you will have to earn for yourself."

Mälar wrapped his fur around him and turned away. He watched the waves rise and fall. Usuthu packed one quiver with half of the arrows he had been given. He would use his own in the initial attack. Then he would employ those of the Arharak.

By nightfall the storm had not abated. The wind howled across the river.

"We cannot paddle this boat safely," Halberd shouted to Mälar.

"You are right," the navigator answered. "Take off your clothes and tie this rawhide around you."

Halberd and Mälar lowered themselves into the churning river. Each was tied to a rope that led to the bow of the canoe. They swam side by side, barely moving against the current and the wind. Moweaqua steered from the stern. Usuthu crouched in the bow, ready to haul one of them in if they became exhausted.

Waves crashed over their faces. The current pushed them south and the wind blew them north. Mälar had set a course for the nearest point of land, regardless of the location of the village. Pulling the craft was so tiring that Halberd forgot why he was doing it. He functioned only as muscle, as an ox functions. The minutes became hours and only flashes of lightning reminded him where he was.

Halberd did not understand when his feet finally touched mud. He took the mud for just another obstacle and tried to keep swimming. Mälar touched him on the shoulder. Halberd stood.

"Gather your strength," Mälar shouted. "I want blood. I am not tired."

Usuthu carried his wife over the mud and stood her in the thorns. He yanked the craft into the underbrush and turned away from it.

"Do not leave my side," he ordered Moweaqua. "In the battle put your back to mine. Do not initiate anything and chase no foes. No matter how grave you think the danger is for me, do not attempt to protect me at your peril. I will endure, but if you should be slain, then I cannot live."

She smiled. "So be it."

"Bind yourself to me," Usuthu said, "by will or by spell. Worry not for Halberd or Mälar. They are warriors. If we are separated, come here. Do not leave this spot. Do not search for us, do not call our names."

By way of reply Moweaqua pushed the brush aside and led them toward the village. They trotted along in silence. The rain pelted them and the wind made them cold. Halberd's teeth banged together in his jaw. The lightning crashed around them and they stuck to the slopes of hills, avoiding the crests.

The bushes parted ahead. Usuthu reached out and took a Arharak sentry by the shoulder and leg. He broke the Skræling in half and threw him aside. No one slowed down.

Usuthu slid into the lead. There was no need to talk strategy. They inched forward, looking for guards. Usuthu appeared before the Arharak lookouts, one by one. He rose out of the brush, lifted the Arharak off the ground, and snapped their backs. Some died, some he left writhing in the thorns. The nearer the village, the fewer the sentries. This did not fit the normal pattern.

"They are preparing the feast," Mälar said.

He moved to the fore. They passed drying racks filled with meat and a well. The first of the low, domed wickiups appeared. Halberd now understood their construction. Whippy poles were planted in the earth and bent over double. Hides were tossed over the poles and ropes held the hides in place. Every wickiup they passed, Mälar slashed the ropes with his sword. The pole sprang upright, dumping the hides to the ground. In the terrible storm, every belonging in every wickiup was instantly soaked.

"Let them have no cover," the old man said, his mouth a thin hard line. "Nowhere to run."

Chanting carried over the rain and wind and thunder. They slowed. Halberd took the lead. It was his right and his proper role. They move through the village. A few stragglers came toward them and Usuthu killed them without noise. Any who spotted them from afar Usuthu spitted on his arrows.

They hid behind a large wickiup that faced the central clear patch of ground. A great crowd of warriors jammed the square. Inside the horde of warriors Usuthu could see the women and children.

"They let the children have the choicest parts," the Mongol said.

"I see the boy," Mälar said with joy. "He lives."

Mälar pointed over Usuthu's shoulder. The Mongol crouched in front of him, his bow at the ready. Halberd followed Mälar's finger. Etowah rose up above the rows of Arharak backs. He looked at his companions. He smiled from ear to ear. He bobbed his head as if he was nodding at them. Mälar waved one hand at the boy. Etowah kept bobbing and smiling. His eyes did not seem focused.

"Something is wrong," Halberd said. He rested his hand on Mälar's shoulder.

Etowah's head rose even higher above the Arharak. His neck ended an inch below his jaw. His head rested on an Arharak lance. The bobbing motion came from a warrior parading the boy's head around the cookfire. Another lance rose up. On its point was an arm, cooked and seared. Greedy hands reached upward.

Usuthu fired his first arrow. Etowah's head was

swept from the lance. He fired one after another. None missed. His hands moved too fast to be followed. They were a blur. His arrows took the Arharak in the head, in the back, above their belts. Those that turned were skewered from the front, those that did not, from the rear. The Skrælings screamed and ran for their weapons.

Halberd and Mälar, wielding bows taken from the broken sentries, fired upon the crowd as well. Ignoring the women and children, they aimed only at warriors. Neither man was so great an archer as Usuthu, but both were competent. A small knot of demons massed behind a hide torn from a wickiup and charged their position. Usuthu put his first arrow right through the hide. A Skræling came sailing backward out of the group, pierced through the chest.

"I am done," cried Usuthu. He dropped the empty quiver and slung his great bow across his chest. Usuthu drew his curved sword and charged. Halberd kept his sword in his scabbard. He fired one more arrow and lifted his ax over his head. Mälar was already out in front of Usuthu, hacking a path with his sword.

The Arharak split into two groups. One fled down the main path herding the women and children before them. The other, about twenty men strong, formed a loose knot and charged the Northmen. As always, Halberd took up the lead and Mälar and Usuthu formed a V to his left and right. Halberd had no idea where Moweaqua was.

Two large Skrælings, their faces covered with tattoos, raised feathers and rattles in their hands. They pointed the rattles at the onracing three. A lance whipped past Halberd's ear and took the elder of the demons in his left eye. The force of the toss hurled him into the man behind him. Another lance flicked through the air. This one struck the other shaman in his belly. He kneeled as if praying.

"Brave work, wife," said Usuthu. "Now, stay at hand and cover my back."

Halberd barely paused as he struck the head from the kneeling Arharak. He holstered his ax and whipped out his sword. The demons were upon them. One swung a hatchet at Halberd's face. Halberd did not flinch or lean back. He feinted left with one shoulder. The Skræling swung again, aiming where he thought Halberd would be. Halberd stabbed him gently in the throat and leaned back as the blood streamed forth. Another leaped in front of Halberd. He held no weapons. He carried only a tiny leather quirt. He lashed Halberd across the face with his little whip. Enraged, Halberd chopped the demon's legs out from under him. As the group ran by, Moweaqua stabbed the legless man in the back of the neck.

Mälar kicked the Arharak nearest him in the groin and chopped at the one behind him. Halberd cleared a path by sweeping his broadsword in great arcs before him, keeping the blade parallel to the ground. Something hit him in the thigh. He looked down. An Arharak arrow stuck out of his left leg. He shuffled quickly to the nearest wickiup and leaned against it, the better to fight one-legged.

Mälar came to his right and Usuthu his left. Moweaqua rested against her husband. The Arharak force had been reduced to no more than twenty men. Three times that number lay about the fire, dead or moaning as they died. Most bore Usuthu's arrows. Two young, cooked legs, one arm, and a disembodied hand lay by the huge fire. Etowah's head was gone.

Usuthu had a large gash on his neck. Blood flowed down his shields in a stream. Mälar bore numerous smaller cuts, but no wounds that seemed serious. Halberd's leg began to hurt.

"Where are the internal organs of the boy?" shouted Moweaqua, startling every man, Northman, Mongol, and Arharak, in the square.

A muscular little man, his arms and cheeks laced with blue lines, answered her in a guttural bark. Halberd understood him.

"Long since eaten, demons," the Arharak had said. Halberd translated. Mälar's shoulders slumped. They knew the boy's soul was lost forever. Mälar pushed off of the wickiup wall. He walked calmly toward the row of Arharaks.

"Come and kill me," he said, brandishing his sword. "I'm ready to die, but more ready to kill all of you." Mälar beckoned them forward with his fingertips.

Halberd limped up to the old man's side. Usuthu appeared opposite. Each picked their targets and moved forward. For the first time in the battle they split up. Halberd was suddenly aware, once more, of the weather. It was near dawn, but the sky did not lighten. The rain blew into his face as hard as ever. The wind threatened to tear the soil right off the earth.

"This is where I belong," Halberd said aloud. "In the eye of the storm."

Seven Arharak moved up. Two held lances and the rest stone mallets and hatchets. Halberd flipped his ax up into his left hand. He bent at the knees and crouched low. One of the fools hurled his lance at the Northman. Halberd tossed his ax with a flick of the wrist. The weapons crossed in midair. A blast of lightning followed by an immediate crack of thunder drove everyone flat on their stomachs. The acrid smell of the bolt was in the air. In the booming flash that lit the village like noonday, Halberd could see the Arharak on his back, his heels drumming, his hands clawing at the ax.

Halberd lifted the Skræling lance from the ground beside him. He scuttled forward on his knees. The Arharak were slow in rising. They seemed deafened by the blast. Halberd raised the lance and nailed a warrior through the back of the neck. The lance burst through and pinned the Arharak to the ground. His blood spread in a wide, black pool.

Halberd stood up and chopped the nearest warrior like firewood. Halberd's sword took the demon at the base of his neck. It sliced through his ribs and came out by his side.

Broadsword fighting is momentum fighting. The weight of the sword and the force of the blow carried Halberd around in a circle. As he spun someone struck him on the back of his leather armor. His dagger and Hrungnir, safe in their pouches, absorbed the blow. It carried enough strength to knock him off balance. Halberd fell flat on his face.

He flipped over instantly. Halberd sprang to his feet. His left leg collapsed beneath him. As Halberd fell, two Arharak moved in, thinking him dead. Both raised their hatchets. Falling backward, Halberd swung across his body with all his might. He dealt the first demon a glancing blow on the neck. The weight of the sword broke it with a sickening crack. The blade rose up high off the broken neck and only grazed the shoulder of the other warrior. Halberd hit the ground hard. He raised his feet and kicked.

The Arharak atop him flew backward into the remaining two warriors. Halberd painfully stood on one leg. He dragged the other behind him. The wounded Arharak stepped up. Halberd and he swung at the same time. Sword met hatchet. The skinny demon was strong and he had two legs. Halberd staggered back. Another Arharak jumped in beside the first.

They looked at one another for a moment to decide strategy. Again, Halberd lurched forward when they expected him to go back. He raised his head as if seeing something behind them. They froze for an instant. He swung low. He severed one man's leg outright and that crippled warrior fell into his brother. Halberd leaned in and just shoved with both hands. They tumbled down in a tangle of limbs. Halberd slashed their throats and looked up.

The last Arharak ran down the path. His feet thumped in the mud. They made the only sound in the village.

The thunder boomed again, quietly and from a distance. The rain slowed and became drizzle. The wind dropped. Halberd looked around the village.

Usuthu stood by the fire. Behind him, like pearls dropped from a necklace, trailed a line of dead or twitching warriors. Moweaqua moved among them with her ivory knife, a mad glint in her eye. Tears stained her face. A twitch or a moan brought her instantly to the wounded man's side. There she knelt. Raising the blade over her head and gripping with both hands, she plunged her ivory knife into the Arharak's throat. She worked the blade back and forth until the head was severed. When all the moans had ceased, she ranged through the bodies that bore arrows, searching for wounded she might dispatch.

Usuthu met Halberd's gaze and shrugged. He gestured to a small slice taken out of his shoulder. He seemed neither happy nor sad, neither tired nor hurt.

"This occurred," he called, "while she was distracted. She thinks I am disappointed, but I am not. This was her first battle. I believe she momentarily lost her senses."

Halberd nodded. It had happened to him and, probably, to Usuthu and Mälar as well. Moweaqua had proved to be a warrior. She would run aimlessly from corpse to corpse, hacking and slashing until she was spent. It was her baptism in blood.

His leg throbbed terribly. He found himself on the ground. Halberd carefully sheathed his sword. He studied his leg. Usuthu knelt beside him.

"All dead?"

"Aye," said the Mongol. He jerked his chin toward the high ground beyond the village. The women and children huddled there, looking down at their ruined village with horror. Halberd surveyed the mounds of corpses.

"If the women and children weren't nomads before, now they surely are," he said, hiccuping with laughter. "At least they won't go hungry."

Usuthu looked at him with grave concern.

"Such a remark is beneath you. That is not the way of the shaman," he said. "Show some respect for the dead."

"You are right, brother," Halberd said, "but I cannot. I did not respect these demons alive and I don't respect their corpses. I hope their wives and children dine on them and enjoy the meal."

"Where is Mälar?"

Halberd looked around. Mälar had ranged far

afield in his desperation to kill. The helmsman was at the far end of the central open space.

Mälar was on one knee. Surrounding him was an impossibly large pile of dead Skrælings, stacked like cordwood. The dead covered every conceivable age, from youths to graybeards and many strong warriors in between.

Mälar's sword stuck upright from the Arharak at the bottom of the pile. In both hands Mälar held Arharak chopping hatchets. They were coated with blood, brains, and hair. His arms were soaked in gore to his shoulders. His face was washed with blood. Yet he seemed unhurt. He knelt by the dead Arharak. In front of him lay Etowah's legs.

Mälar wept and wept and wept.

"I think he killed every man in the group which first took the women and children away," Halberd said. "I was not even aware that they had returned." He did not speak of Mälar's tears. Nor would he ever. Nor, he knew, would Usuthu.

"Let him be," said Usuthu. "Now, I must tend to you." He pulled gently on the arrow. It was stuck fast. When he moved it even a bit, the pain went through Halberd like a jagged knife.

"These fiends used arrowheads with barbs," Usuthu said. "Do you know what that means?"

Halberd nodded. Usuthu had to push the arrow through his leg, chop off the arrowhead and draw the shaft back through. Moweaqua danced by, her bloody knife held aloft. She sang a tuneless melody.

"Moweaqua," Usuthu said gently, "come to my side."

She walked over warily. Usuthu stared into her eyes.

"Come back to me, wife," he said. "I need you."

She lost her vacant stare.

"I am very, very tired," she said.

"No doubt," said the Mongol. "But before you can sleep you must hold my brother here by the shoulders and not let him go no matter how he twitches."

Moweaqua knelt behind Halberd. She braced a knee in his back and gripped him with all her strength. He could feel her fingers through his leather armor.

Usuthu took the arrow in both hands. With no sign or warning, he shoved the barbed head all the way through Halberd's leg.

Halberd awoke on the canoe. He lay under the canopy. Mälar sat in the bow, his head on his hand, gazing southward. Usuthu sat in the stern, Moweaqua asleep in his lap.

Thunder boomed faintly to the north. The rain had stopped. The great river was calm as a tiny pond. To the south, perhaps one day distant, the black clouds ended and the red edge of morning glowed.

Grettir Keeps Her Word

The afternoon after the battle was slow and calm. They did not paddle. The canoe drifted down the flat water. Mälar would not speak. Halberd could not move. His bandaged leg had swollen and he had usurped the lovers' bed. Usuthu had found the deer and cut it into strips for drying. The canopy had been rolled back and a new roof of deermeat laid on in its place.

Halberd looked past Mälar's immobile head, down the river to the south. In the pale blue sky odd clouds were forming.

"Mälar," said Halberd, "please break your silence. What are those approaching clouds?"

"My destiny," said the helmsman, his voice flat and uninterested. He did not turn around.

The black clouds grew and grew, tumbling over one another and stacking from the river to the top of the sky. The canoe drifted towards an endless black wall.

Moweaqua awoke. She stood in the canoe. It rocked widely. She pointed to the center of the river, where the clouds met. Marching up the river, in a row, were four waterspouts. The water-borne tornadoes towered overhead, their tops hidden by the black clouds.

The wind picked up now and blew directly on their backs. Swells again rose on the river. They picked up speed. They flew downriver toward the clouds.

Usuthu tried to steer from the stern. He was clumsy and inexperienced. The canoe tossed up and down, stern to bow. Water came in over the gunwales. Mälar would still neither move nor turn.

The canopy of deer meat was snatched away by the wind. Halberd looked to the eastern shore. A line of dark funnel-shaped clouds marched down the bank alongside them. The clouds were several leagues away. Halberd could see the funnels snatching up dirt, trees, grass, anything in their path. A roar came from the funnel clouds.

If the cloud overtook them, they would be crushed like kindling. Halberd called for Mälar to pick up a paddle and stroke. Mälar turned around and looked at him with dead eyes.

The helmsman took off his belt and passed his sword to Halberd.

"I will not need this where I am being taken," he said. "You are a worthy captain. I have enjoyed our journey very much." He turned back to face the oncoming storm.

"I am a fool!" Halberd cried as he comprehended the danger at last. "Usuthu, Grettir rides inside the storm."

Halberd slipped Hrungnir from its pouch. Usuthu stood. His forgotten paddle dropped into the rolling water. The waves threw it against the canoe and it shattered.

They were under the clouds now. The blackness lowered until the clouds almost touched the boat. Usuthu stood and raised his silver mallet over his head in defiance. Moweaqua struggled to her feet in the heaving canoe.

A clean bolt of lightning, jagged and clear, with no offshoots, sprang from the clouds. It lanced into Usuthu's mallet. For a moment he was wreathed silver. Tiny bolts raced from his feet to his head and up and down his arms. Bolts shot down Moweaqua's arms to her feet and back. All of Usuthu's teeth showed. His eyes rolled back in his head and he fell to the bark floor. Moweaqua fell across him.

Halberd raised Hrungnir. What could he do? He could not move. The wind howled across the water. The waves grew even higher. Mälar stood, bracing against the tossing river with no effort. He raised both hands to the clouds.

The black mass parted. An enormous hand reached slowly down. Mälar lowered his arms and stood as if paralyzed. The giant hand snatched the navigator out of the canoe. It slid back into the cloud like a snake into its hole.

Grettir's ghostly form floated over the waves.

"Look for your friend," she said, "in the Temple of the Sun, in the land of the God of War."

She laughed as the wind scattered her pale image across the raging river.

Then she was gone.